ALSO BY ELLIOT ACKERMAN

Green on Blue

Dark at the Crossing

ELLIOT ACKERMAN

Alfred A. Knopf New York
2017

THIS IS A BORZOI BOOK
PUBLISHED BY ALFRED A. KNOPF

www.aaknopf.com

Knopf, Borzoi Books, and the colophon are registered trademarks of Penguin Random House LLC.

Library of Congress Control Number: 2016954679
ISBN 9781101947371 (hardcover)
ISBN 9781101947388 (ebook)
ISBN 9781524711030 (open market)

Jacket design by Kelly Blair

Manufactured in the United States of America
First Edition

For Abed,
on his way home

And afterward? What happened afterward? . . . The way that a great experience comes to an end? A melancholy topic, for a revolt is a great experience, an adventure of the heart . . . But there comes a moment when the mood burns out and everything ends. As a matter of reflex, out of custom, we go on repeating the gestures and the words and want everything to be the way it was yesterday, but we know already—and the discovery appalls us—that this yesterday will never again return . . . We look uncomfortably into each other's eyes, we shy away from conversation, we stop being any use to one another.

—RYSZARD KAPUŚCIŃSKI, *Shah of Shahs*

The morning he went off to his second war, Haris Abadi spent twenty minutes in the sauna of the Tuğcan Hotel. Cleaned by his sweat, he swaddled himself in a complimentary bathrobe, went up to his room and took a long shower. Then he went back to sleep, waking naked on his bed an hour later. Downstairs for a late breakfast, he ate three buttered croissants with jam.

The concierge found Haris in the large, empty dining room, its circular tables set with fine crystal as if waiting for a party that would never come. Leaning over Haris, the concierge grasped the lapels of his suit jacket, where he wore a pinned insignia of crossed gold keys. He asked Haris something in Turkish. Haris didn't speak Turkish and shrugged back, his mouth still full of flaky croissant.

The concierge tried Arabic: "How has your stay been?"

"Good, thank you," said Haris.

"Business or pleasure?"

"Business," answered Haris. There was no other reason to come to Antep, an industrial backwater along Turkey's southern border with Syria.

The concierge looked at the stuffed hiking pack propped against the leg of Haris's chair. "Checking out then?"

Haris reached into a deep internal pocket on the pack, fishing around for his cash. He pulled out a mixed roll of Turkish lira, American dollars and Syrian pounds. He held the wad beneath the table, counting it bill by bill. The concierge hovered above him.

"Two hundred a night, yes?" asked Haris, peeling six hundred lira off his roll.

The concierge nodded, eyeing Haris's dollars. "You're American?" he asked.

Haris handed over the money for three nights. "Here, six hundred."

He felt the concierge taking a closer look at him: his pack, his desert-suede combat boots.

"I'd prefer you pay in dollars," said the concierge.

As hard as he'd worked to become an American, Haris hated the way his new clothes and strong currency betrayed him abroad. He paid in dollars, and the concierge tucked the tight fold of twenties into his vest's front pocket.

"Allow me to find you a cab."

Haris nodded, then got up and went to the bathroom, leaving his heavy pack unattended in the opulent dining room. He didn't seem to care if everything was taken from him.

It had rained the night before, and that morning the late autumn sky cleared, turning the air cold, freezing the sidewalks. Outside the Tuğcan, an old man, a Syrian, swept the slush from the hotel's marble front step with a rolled copy of the daily paper, *Milliyet*. His eyes were sheathed in wrinkles and on his head he wore a keffiyeh. It was held in place by an igal, a coiled wreath, which sat on him like the crown of perpetual defeat. Hunched over, the old man worked slowly, positioning himself so someone from the hotel might notice his pains and offer a bit of charity.

The revolving door spun a turn, and the concierge and Haris stepped outside. The old man looked up at them, holding his face toward the sun. He offered a toothy, rotten grin. His eyes shifted from them to his work, clearing the last of the slush from their path. Haris reached into his pocket. His fingers felt for a coin or folded lira note. Before he could find either, the concierge flicked the toe of a polished oxford at the old man, shooing him away. The old man said nothing. He took a few steps from the Tuğcan's marble front and wandered onto the frozen sidewalk, where he stood like a broken piece of furniture set out in the street.

The concierge reached into his vest pocket and blew a small silver whistle. A yellow taxi with the Tuğcan's logo—a setting or rising sun, it was difficult to tell which—pulled in front of the hotel. Unfolding a map of Syria and southern Turkey, Haris walked to the driver's window. The driver rubbed his thickly stubbled cheeks as Haris traced the route from Antep to the border crossing thirty miles south, in a town called Kilis.

The concierge insisted on loading Haris's hiking pack into the taxi. He slammed the trunk closed. "I hope you'll stay with us again."

With no plans to return, Haris felt uncertain what to say. "Yes," he mumbled. Reaching into his pocket, he pulled out the first coin he found—one lira, a meager sum. He palmed it over to the concierge, who took the gratuity with the same composure a gentleman takes an insult.

Haris slammed the taxi's yellow door, happy to be leaving the Tuğcan and Antep. The concierge headed back toward the hotel, crossing the marble step that had been cleared of slush. Appreciating this clean patch, he glanced to where the old man lingered on the frozen sidewalk. Their eyes met, and the old man straightened himself, fixing his keffiyeh, smoothing its tasseled ends over his narrow shoulders.

Haris's taxi pulled into the street. From its window, he saw the old man ambling toward the Tuğcan's revolving door. The concierge stood on the cleared marble step. He handed the old man Haris's one lira for his labor. As the taxi took the last turn toward the highway, Haris glimpsed the old man's contorted, angry expression when he tucked the coin into his pocket, the concierge having passed along Haris's insult.

The cab followed the D850, a highway constructed as sturdily as anything Haris had seen in Michigan, where he'd brought his sister after his first war. Removing his map, Haris traced the D850 with his finger as it ran out of Antep, or Gaziantep as the map read, though Haris had yet to meet anyone who called it such.

It was a city of two names with three meanings.

Haris could recognize that Antep was a corruption of the Arabic *ayn tayyib,* which meant "the good spring." After the democratic revolutions of two springs past, it augured well to return through a city with this name. A hundred years before, the Turkish parliament had appended the "Gazi," or *ghazi,* meaning "hero," after the city's citizens repulsed a French siege during the war of independence. Yet the city's oldest name, spoken in a dead language, and in this way a hidden language, had a slightly different meaning. In Aramaic the word is *ayn debo,* "the spring of the wolf."

Haris found where the D850 ran out of Antep and intersected the D400, which crossed from Turkey into Syria, passing through cities like Ar-Raqqa and Deir ez-Zor, which had become infamous after two years of civil war. But the route remained anonymous, connecting places yet being no place. When the D400 entered Iraq, it became Highway 10. But always it was the same road: black, straight, its name switching with borders while every other part of it remained unchanged. Haris continued to trace the road with his finger until it spilled into a flat brown Iraqi sprawl along the Euphrates River—Nasiriya—his birthplace and, before the war, his home.

Of his family, he had no single memory of them together, his mother having died in childbirth with his sister, Samia, when he was six. His first home had been on the riverbank. The high marsh grass abutting a simple compound of thick, coarse cement, his mother walking him down to the bank through the brushing grass, his father returning from whatever construction job he worked with the same cement hard on his clothes—memory was texture. Soft grass. Hard cement.

Haris leaned his head against the cracked window. The cold glass touched the bald spot, which, only in the last few months, had spread from his crown. His reddish hair was unusually light, an uncommon but not impossible shade for an Arab, evidence of some recessive trait. Past the glass, farmers' fields flanked the road, spanning in all directions. Clods of harvested earth littered the fields. They stank with a wet-dirt smell. In places the dead stalks of the harvest burned in the dawn, which seemed to rise from the land itself, and the farmers cleared the fields, readying them for winter and the next season's planting.

Haris thought how fertile and lush the land seemed. To live here was to be blessed. He'd always believed that was why life in Nasiriya had been violent and poor—but for the river the land was desert, everything scarce, scarcity breeding violence. Just across this border, in Syria, around cities like Aleppo and Azaz, the land was the same as what passed by Haris's window—rich, wet, harvested. These three years, violence had spread there, as surely as if the land were desert, the people failing the land and what had been given them.

The meter on the dash steadily climbed, blinking close to a hundred Turkish lira. Strewn across the soaked and smoky farm fields were the sagging tents of refugee families. Outside the tents, lost-eyed men sat on plastic chairs, watching the highway. Children played in the churned mud. They chased a dog whose ribs sucked at its sides, taunting it with sticks. When the dog got away, they taunted a child who was slower than the dog.

The rows of tents thickened as the D850 ran closer to Kilis. At the town's limit, the refugees disappeared. The streets became clean. Curbs sprung up on the side of the road, checkered yellow and white, the paint fresh. Where many roads met, roundabouts had been built. Their centers were planted with flowers, tulips mostly. Everywhere traffic lights hung between side posts, changing in unison, swaying on their wires in an uneven wind. The war and the border were less than a kilometer away, and Haris felt there was something cruel in how Kilis thrived despite its proximity to suffering.

The cabdriver pulled up to a stoplight, for a final left turn. From the roadside, a pack of children, their clothes oily with filth, rushed the taxi. Their voices chattered wild as morning birds. The cabdriver ignored their pleas until one boy knocked a little fist against the taxi's door. The cabdriver rolled down his window to curse the boy. Before he could, the children reached their arms inside, clamoring for some charity. The cabdriver swatted at them, shouting the only words of Arabic he seemed to know: "Airy fic! Airy fic!" But the children wouldn't "fuck off." They wouldn't move. A pair now stood in front of the taxi, blocking its way.

Unlike the cabdriver, Haris understood the pleading boys. He rolled down his window and pointed to a plastic shopping bag carried by the eldest, who was no more than fourteen, just a child with an Adam's apple, his jet-black hair slicked back with what was likely pomade but could well have been engine grease. This boy offered up the plastic sack to Haris. The others calmed, sensing Haris might buy one of the cheap knickknacks they hawked. Before they could strike a deal, the cabdriver pointed to the pair who had stepped in front of his taxi. The boy with the black hair nodded in their direction. The pair stepped out of the way.

Haris fingered through the plastic bag—a wooden comb, fingernail clippers, a cigarette lighter.

"Five lira for anything," announced the boy with the black hair, his mouth curling into a sly grin around his wide-spaced teeth.

Haris reached through the window, taking the lighter from the bag, which he passed back to them. "How about this?" he asked, digging a few coins from his pants pocket. A younger boy had approached Haris's window. He was skinny, his face grained in dirt, but he had very clear gray eyes, which watched Haris from behind a pair of thick glasses, their right lens missing. Instead of passing his coins to the sly boy with the black hair, Haris reached toward this other, weaker boy.

Before Haris could pay, the light went green. The cabdriver sped through the intersection, pinning Haris to his seat. As he sat up, Haris tossed a handful of change out his window. He then glanced through the cab's rear windshield. The boys scrambled down the road. The boy with the black hair pried their bodies apart as they wrestled for what Haris had left behind, all except for the younger boy, who, very calmly, stood on the curb and cleaned the one lens of his glasses with the dirty hem of his shirt.

The border crossing in Kilis smelled of sharp, acrid smoke. A pair of Turkish flags—a white crescent pinching a white, five-pointed star on a red banner—flanked what to Haris looked like a rest stop on the interstate. Just past the crossing, in the Syrian town of Azaz, explosions came—*CRUMP, CRUMP, CRUMP*—

the noise like soda cans crushed underfoot. The impacts set off a few distant car alarms. Smoke towered upward, running along the horizon like black stitches, fastening earth to sky.

Haris shouldered his heavy hiking pack. He stood in the dust of the gravel parking lot. The cabdriver pulled back onto the road. It had been a few years since Haris had come near such violence. He remained motionless, transfixed by its familiar power, as if he'd just put an old name to a forgotten face.

Refugees from the morning's fighting crowded the roadside. Some sat straddling their cheap, flimsy suitcases. Others squatted in the dirt with nothing. Few spoke. Those who did whispered. The crowd's attention held on Azaz.

Haris checked his phone for an email from Saladin1984, his contact and fixer in the Northern Storm, a supposedly good brigade of the Free Syrian Army. There were no messages. It was Saladin1984 who'd recruited him to the cause, forwarding along a steady stream of treatises, manifestos and videos, each with an array of political demands that at times Haris found dizzying despite his growing commitment to these ideas. Some materials called for the establishment of a free and democratic Syria, others the removal of President Bashar al-Assad, and many a combination of the two. Haris now composed Saladin1984 a message, explaining that he'd arrived and was ready to cross the border. As he finished, another *CRUMP* came, then more smoke, followed by the manic *pop, pop, pop* of rifle fire. A collective sigh went up from those stuck along the border, as if in a crowded airport terminal a final flight's cancellation had just been announced. A few of the refugees lay down on the cold earth, as though they'd chosen to take a nap. Others wandered aimlessly along the road toward Kilis. In the parking lot's corner, some pressed into a small café run out of an abandoned shipping container, where a squat Syrian man with a push-broom mustache served bitter tea in curved glass cups.

You came to fight, Haris told himself, looking at the distant smoke blooming from Azaz. They're fighting right there. You've fought before— No, he reminded himself. You've been around fighting before. There's a big difference. So are you going to do what you came to do?

Haris tightened down the straps on his hiking pack. He plodded toward the Plexiglas guard booth at the border crossing, feeling the refugees' puzzled looks on him—it was absurd for anyone to walk in the direction they'd just come from. These are the ones who abandoned their country, thought Haris. The Syrians on the other side will be different. Then he remembered how his father had abandoned him and Samia to a chorus of aunts and uncles after their mother died, disappearing into his work, then disappearing altogether, only for Haris to mimic his father—or so he feared—by abandoning his own country to resettle in America with his sister.

Inside the guard booth, two Turkish gendarmes watched television. They sat side by side, reclined in their cheap leather office chairs, smoking Gauloises and laughing at some show. Haris knocked gently on the window. They didn't notice him. He knocked harder, pounding the glass. The gendarmes swung around. The pair were nearly indistinguishable. Both were young, but just old enough so a band of fat rimmed their stomachs. Smeared across their cheeks was stubble. It'd likely grown over their two-to-three-day shift. It appeared as though they lived in the booth.

Haris pressed his U.S. passport against the glass.

The pair slowly stood. Each grabbed a blue tunic from a coatrack in the corner, buttoning its front. The first gendarme, who was a head taller than the other, came to the window. He keyed an intercom, speaking quickly in Turkish.

Not understanding, Haris said nothing.

The tall gendarme slumped his shoulders and sighed. "Yok English."

"Arabe?" asked Haris.

The shorter of the two pushed past his friend. "Shwe, shwe," he said, examining Haris. "The border is closed," he added in broken Arabic.

"For how long?"

The shorter gendarme gazed toward Azaz, where a phalanx of smoke still stabbed at the horizon. "Long time."

Haris stepped away from the glass.

Saladin1984 had assured him that crossing the border would be easy, that the Turks were no friends of Bashar al-Assad, that they welcomed foreigners who wanted to fight against the Syrian regime. Haris checked his phone. No new messages.

He tapped on the glass again. The taller gendarme nudged the shorter one, who stood heavily and approached the intercom. "What else?" he asked.

"I'm not just American," said Haris.

"I see that," said the gendarme. "You speak very good Arabic."

"I'm from Iraq," added Haris. "I only recently became an American."

The gendarme smiled.

Haris felt a quick surge of hope in his chest, like a perfect knot cinched tight.

"You managed to leave Iraq and get all the way to America?" asked the gendarme.

Haris nodded.

"Arriving there, you managed to get citizenship for yourself?"

Again Haris nodded.

"And now you want to cross into Syria?"

Haris said nothing. He looked out toward Azaz.

The short gendarme glanced at his partner, who sat in front of the television, entranced by his program. His eyes returned to Haris's. "You've come here to cross the border and die with them," he said. The gendarme's smile from before, the one Haris had thought was sympathy, dissolved. It hadn't been sympathy.

It'd been pity. "You're a damn fool, and I won't help one fool die with other fools. The border is closed."

As the gendarme went back to his seat, his friend, who hadn't been listening, began to laugh violently, slapping his knee and explaining the punch line to some joke on the television. A smile returned to the short gendarme's face, and soon he was laughing too.

A large tent sat in the wet field. It skirted the gravel parking lot where the cabdriver had dropped Haris off. Wired to the tent's center pole was a speaker. A muezzin called the midday prayer. The first notes of his voice started low, mixing with static. Then his voice rose, becoming smooth. Its call gathered the refugees who waited on the roadside or in the café made from the shipping container. They trickled into the tent's cavernous gallery. Women brought their children, dragging sons and daughters by the hand. Men spoke quietly, finishing their conversations as they filed into the makeshift mosque.

Haris shouldered his pack and walked against the crowd, toward the café. He was hungry. Among the empty plastic chairs and tables, he sat alone, taking out his map, pondering it like a crossword, one beyond his abilities. The laughter of the gendarmes had stirred a surge of embarrassment, which now settled warmly in his stomach like a cheap, stiff drink. The sensation reminded Haris of his first days in America and the awkwardness he had felt when asked the simplest of questions, like where he was from. When he would say "Iraq," the asker would always respond with a variation of either "What should we be doing over there?" or "What's brought you here?" Haris interpreted the former response as one of pity and the latter as one of suspicion.

Could he expect more than pity and suspicion from his new countrymen? Could he expect them to say "I've always wanted to see the gold dome of Karbala"? So to integrate into his new nation, he claimed origins from another: he would be Greek. How Samia laughed when she heard him scatter this lie—to a convenience store clerk, to a bus driver, to the salesgirl who sold Samia her college textbooks. With each of her laughs Haris felt a desire to abandon his sister—at the store, on the bus or without tuition at college—so she might feel the vulnerability he shielded her from. Yet he never would. Instead, he'd gently cuff his hand around her wrist and tell her to laugh all she wanted, that if she was happy nothing could bother him. He enrolled Samia in college. He bought her new clothes for the first day. He did all of this though he could afford none of it.

Staving off loneliness at night, he would occasionally go to a bar. Though he had little taste for alcohol, he remembered when he had worked as an interpreter and the stories told to him by American soldiers—raucous nights of romantic heroics triggered by little more than them walking into a bar. This was never his experience, except for once. He had waited until Samia fell asleep in their apartment, a studio in Dearborn donated by a local Christian charity, complete with a foldout couch, and then he walked, for he didn't have a car, half an hour through the darkness to the lobby of a hotel that had a small lounge sandwiched between reception and its revolving doors. With a week's worth of spare change, he ordered a cocktail poured in a plastic cup. He sat for a while, watching the traffic trickle on and off the interstate's nearby ramp. He finished his drink, and as he fingered loose a Maraschino cherry from among the melting ice cubes, the elevator bell rang.

A woman in a velour sweat suit walked through reception, past Haris, and stepped outside for a cigarette. Through the window, Haris felt her eyes on him. When he glanced up, she stubbed out her cigarette and spun back through the revolving door. She asked Haris if he had a piece of gum, which he didn't. Then she sat next to him, ordering drinks for them both and saying very little. Her silence put Haris on edge so he began to speak about himself. The woman played with the zipper on her grape-purple sweat top, her small breasts barely cupping the white T-shirt beneath. Zip up, zip down. Zip up, zip down. Haris lost interest in his story. When at her suggestion they stepped outside to share a cigarette, her lipstick left a heavy red smudge on its filter. She was older, stalled along some bitter plateau. She wore her hair in two tragic pigtails. After inviting Haris to her room for another cocktail, she said nothing in the elevator and undressed just past her door. Naked, she rested her hands proudly on her hips, challenging Haris to undress as well. Soon he stood in a pile of his clothes. Then she glanced down. "I didn't think Greek boys got snipped." The familiar dread in his stomach returned, but before he could concoct some reply, she pressed herself against him. "Baby, I don't care where you're from."

Being from the United States and Iraq had not helped him with the gendarmes, and sitting in the café Haris tried to figure a way past them. From the serving window, a side of the shipping container that had been welded open and hinged to create a counter, the proprietor with the mustache brought him some hot tea. In the cold air, the glass sweated condensation into its saucer.

Haris checked his phone. Nothing from Saladin1984. It began to rain, and the fighting past the border slowed, its noise becoming softer than the rain. Across the parking lot the midday prayer ended, but everyone remained in the tent, staying warm and dry. Haris put on a waterproof shell he'd kept from his days in Iraq—a pixelated pattern of green, brown, black. The Syrian war had attracted a mishmash of fighters, so even American camouflage would draw little attention.

Behind him, Haris heard the shuffling of feet across gravel. A young man walked stooped over, slow as a grandfather with a bad cane. Holding him by the arm, another man paced alongside. He was a bit older, with a full beard and bloodshot eyes. Slung against his body was a satchel, similar to the kind Haris remembered students wearing when they biked on campus in Dearborn. The pair eased across the parking lot as if they walked on broken glass. They found an outdoor hose coiled in the mud. The stooped-over man wore a sunken, hangdog expression that looked like thirst. His friend turned on the hose, handing it to him. He didn't drink, not at first. Instead, he unbuttoned his black parka and lifted up his red T-shirt, silkscreened with a heroic profile of Che Guevara. A hastily dressed wound was revealed beneath. As the man peeled duct tape from his torso, Haris realized he'd bandaged himself using a cutout piece of carpet. With his bare skin exposed to the cool air, the man lapped water from the hose against his stomach. Relief spread across his mealy, pockmarked face. He seemed almost to smile. Haris tried not to stare, but managed to catch a glimpse of the wound.

An enormous scar, swollen and dry, ran from the man's sternum to below his waistband. The pink, riveted holes of recently unthreaded stitches lined the scar, running at perfect intervals, regular as ties down a rail line. The man continued to lap water against his stomach. Then, as if overcome by the sensation, he dropped the hose at his feet.

The hose snaked on the ground, making a puddle. The man with the red, tired eyes bent down, picking it up, taking a drink for himself. With that done, he turned the hose off, chucked it in the mud and helped his friend back across the parking lot. The two tottered slowly toward the café. Choosing to sit outside in the last of the rain would assure them a table once the storm passed and the refugees emerged from the large tent. Haris watched the pair's slow progress. The man with the scar headed toward him.

"May we join you?" he asked in Arabic.

He was doubled over, as if in more pain after treating his wound. His face was so close Haris could smell his breath, which reeked weakly of medicine.

Haris gestured toward his table's empty seats. The man with the bloodshot eyes waved toward the café owner and growled: "Thalatha chai!"

The owner disappeared beneath the counter.

The pair exchanged pleasantries with Haris, who introduced himself, giving the courtesy of his full name. The two men replied haltingly, calling themselves only Athid and Saied. Haris sensed these weren't their real names. Feeling awkward that he wouldn't be trusted, Haris also felt sympathy. What had each been through and seen that even their identities had become liabilities?

The man with the scar, Saied, pulled a pack of Gauloises from the pocket of his black parka. He offered one to Haris, who refused. He'd quit smoking once he left the States, having his last cigarette outside the terminal at Detroit Metro Airport. Haris had smoked in Iraq, an impulse he'd once struggled to control. He now wanted to feel in control. He wanted this war to feel different than that war.

The man with the bloodshot eyes, Athid, rested his satchel by the leg of his chair and then pulled a book of damp cardboard matches from the pocket of his olive-green field jacket. He handed them to Saied, who struggled to light one. Haris noticed the tips on both Saied's index fingers were missing, as if they'd been neatly guillotined. Haris fished through his hiking pack for the lighter he'd bought from the boys, passing it to Saied.

"Are you looking at my hands?" Saied asked, striking the lighter.

Haris glanced away. "I meant nothing by it." Then he slowly turned back toward Saied, who clutched his palms in his lap, the cigarette dangling from his lips.

"You're not from here," added Saied. "I can tell from your accent. Are you a journalist, maybe a researcher?" Coming from Saied the words *journalist* and *researcher* were as loaded with profanity as the word *pimp* or *pedophile*. When confronted with what felt like an accusation, Haris's reflex was to explain himself.

"I'm American," he said. "I've come to fight with the Free Army." He had rehearsed the words before but only in his mind. Played out as fantasy, this statement always seemed like a manly declaration of who he'd become. But when spoken in his voice, the words sounded flat and ridiculous. A declaration of nothing.

"An American come to fight with the Free Army. Then you *should* look at my hands. The Daesh did this," said Saied, pronouncing the Arabic acronym for the Islamic State in Iraq and al-Sham. He held his fingers up, waving them in front of his face as if he wore many jeweled rings. "To pray, they believe one needs fingers to point toward Mecca. If you don't believe, you are lost to them. They will disfigure your body in the same way they think your soul is already disfigured."

The satchel at the foot of Athid's chair toppled over, moving on its own. Athid snatched it into his lap. A furry head, small and round as a baseball, poked from its opening—a pup. Athid grabbed the scruff of its brown-and-white neck, lifting it like a mother dog would. Whimpering, the pup blinked furiously, as if it didn't yet have the strength to hold its eyes open to the day. From the pocket of his field jacket, Athid broke off a small crust of bread. The pup sawed into it with pointed, sharp teeth, licking its lips, then Athid's face.

"What's its name?" asked Haris.

Athid set the pup on the table, and it stretched itself, sliding its paws forward and lifting its hindquarters. "Bashar," he answered.

Haris laughed. "That's a good name."

"When the regime falls," Athid said, suppressing a smile, "I propose the new government mandate all dogs be named

Bashar, so no one will ever forget that dog of a president. I've started with our little friend here."

Athid was smiling now, so was Haris. Saied sat stone-faced, as if he'd heard the joke enough times. Bashar pranced across the table, leaping up so his front paws leaned on Haris's chest. With a pink tongue he lapped at Haris's stubbled cheek. The pup then jumped back onto the table, turning away, his mouth almost puckered, like that of a child taking a first lick of sour candy.

"He has no taste for you," said Saied. Then, turning toward Athid, he added: "If the Daesh win, your plan won't work. Those savages will behead all of the dogs."

Athid grabbed the pup, which yelped, and placed him back in the bag by his scruff. He grumbled about how long their tea was taking. "Excuse me," he said and went toward the café's serving window.

Saied glanced across the parking lot, to where Athid harassed the café owner, who finished brewing their tea.

"Do you plan to cross the border?" Saied asked.

Haris nodded, looking toward Azaz, where the fires burned hot enough to stay alight in the rain.

"The Daesh care nothing about the ideals of our revolution. All that matters is creating their Islamic State. They have nearly routed the Free Army, still you wish to fight?"

Again Haris nodded. That the cause might be lost meant little to him, and if anything it meant more. He had fought in Iraq for personal gain, at first his citizenship and then money for him and his sister. To sacrifice himself for a free Syria, a cause he knew to be right, was the opposite of all he had done before, fighting alongside the Americans in a cause he felt to be wrong.

"Who's your contact there?" asked Saied. "Nadji-X? Abdullah79? Saladin1984?" Haris blinked, an involuntary response to the familiar name. "Of course, Saladin. I would be careful with his name, lest you cause him problems."

“Where were you fighting when you were wounded?” Haris asked, changing the subject.

Saied glanced toward the sky, as if sharing some joke with the heavens. Haris’s assumption of a direct link between wounds and fighting seemed to amuse Saied. Then he leaned forward, wincing against the pain in his stomach, his eyes narrowing to slits. “I wasn’t fighting.”

Soon the rain stopped, then the tent emptied, and the faithful emerged in ones and twos across the parking lot’s washed gravel. Men with thick, neck-length beards gathered around the café counter. They seemed to search out Athid, going to great pains to greet him with reverence.

“It was Athid who brought me here,” explained Saied. “Among religious men, he is known for his piety.”

Haris said nothing, unsure what Saied meant by this.

The sun began to scoop out the clouds, clearing the sky. With the sun, the fighting across the border resumed. Saied and Haris instinctively stared up at the growing tracks of blue, searching for a plane, waiting to see it go belly over, cockpit toward the ground, the pilot checking his target one last time, then diving down.

“There are no planes,” Saied said. “If the regime were involved, there would be planes. It’s just the Free Army fighting the Daesh.”

It had been a long time since planes flew so far north. In this, the third year of the war, the rebels had turned in on themselves, giving the regime a rest. Sitting on the far side of the border, Saied and Haris listened to clashes between the Free Army and Daesh. The Daesh were winning that fight. The spring and summer protests which had begun the revolution were a memory. Poor supplies, corrupt commanders and, sadly, defections had crippled the Free Army, which had grown from those protests. When the last of the Free Army dissolved, the revolution would finally be over. Then the war could begin.

Saied had stopped looking to the sky. He opened his parka and ran a severed index finger over his red Che T-shirt. "A plane did this," he said. "You asked. It was by a plane."

Haris heard the clinking of saucers, and he turned to see Athid crossing the parking lot. Next to him, the café owner balanced a large steel platter against one shoulder, its rim crowded with glasses of tea and açma baked into tight fists. Athid sat down as the café owner unloaded the platter.

"What were you two discussing?" asked Athid.

"I was telling Haris the story of my injuries."

Athid became quiet for a moment, his stare falling heavily on Saied. "A bit of discretion might be wise."

"Why's that?" snapped Saied. "I'm far from the war. Who can harm me now?" He dropped two sugars in his tea. Haris did the same and then offered some to Athid, who refused. "He's a holy man," said Saied. "No cigarettes, no alcohol, not even sugar."

Athid took a sip of his bitter tea and then buried his hands in the pockets of his field jacket. "To abstain is to have a long life."

Saied stirred the sugar from his cup's bottom. "Do you know about the man who asked his doctor for a long life?" Athid and Haris said nothing. "The man said: I wish to grow very old. The doctor asked him if he drank. No, he answered, not a drop. How much do you eat? Very little, said the man, and always in moderation. Do you smoke? He told the doctor never. And women? I don't touch them, said the man. Then the doctor shook his head, confused, considering all he'd been told. Turning to this pious man, he asked a last question: So why is it you want to live?"

Haris laughed, joining in with Saied. Athid quietly finished his tea.

The three continued to sit together, their conversation easing into a more casual rhythm. Saied told Haris how he hoped to gather enough money to travel to Antep. At one of the city's hospitals, he could get his hasty surgery cleaned up. Then perhaps he could find a job. Haris told both men how, over email, he'd been recruited by Saladin1984 to fight for the Free Army's Northern Storm Brigade, based in Azaz. Saied and Athid seemed to approve of this decision, offering their opinions of the Northern Storm and other brigades. They asked how he planned to cross with the border closed. Haris wasn't certain and told them as much.

"I think something can be arranged," said Athid, leaving it at that.

When the café owner came to clear their table, Haris offered him money to settle the bill. "No need," he replied, stacking their tea saucers. "They've already taken care of it."

Across the parking lot, standing at the café counter, were the Turkish gendarmes. The shorter gendarme, the one who spoke Arabic, caught Haris's eye and gave a slanted grin. He sipped some tea, raising his glass, as if to toast Haris and his new friends. Haris glanced back at Saied, who, upon seeing the two gendarmes, had begun to drum his fingers against the table.

Two nights later, Haris Abadi awoke on the ground in the large tent. He sat up from the cheap-carpeted floor and hugged his knees to his chest. It took him a couple of breaths to remember where he was. It took him a few more to remember why he was there. Slowly he recognized his surroundings and reminded himself of his purpose—the border. The tent's gray canvas roof flapped above him, pulling itself taut and loose with a snapping sound, a grubby aurora borealis moving in strange currents of air. The weather had remained bad, overcast and cold, though it hadn't rained again. Sitting in the dark, Haris listened for the rain.

The fighting in Azaz had ended the day before, but Haris hadn't heard anything back from Saladin1984. With the border still closed, Athid had offered to smuggle Haris across. He'd told Haris he felt obligated, as a Syrian, to help anyone who intended to fight against the regime.

The crossing required rain. There was a tunnel system two miles away, some underground culverts the Turkish farmers used to drain their fields into Syria. Haris and Athid could climb through, but the farmers opened the culverts only when it rained.

Haris continued to listen, hoping for weather. Every corner of the tent stirred with sleeping refugees. A few of them had blankets. Most slept packed together, warming each other in a herd. Haris turned on his phone. After checking its charge, he slid it into his shirt pocket and laced up his boots. A full moon filtered its light through the tent's open flap. Saied's cot was next to the entrance because his wounds often forced him up in the night, or so he'd told Haris. Glancing toward the flap, Haris noticed Saied was gone.

Haris walked past the empty cot as he left the tent. Outside, the moonlight cast a jigsaw of shadows against the earth and the clouds hung low. The air was damp and heavy. He crossed the parking lot and sat in the café. He thought he would wait awhile, to see if the rain would come.

Down at the border crossing, Haris could make out the gendarmes who worked the night shift. Their booth was dim except for the television that played inside, flashing impressions against two silhouettes of equal height. Haris wondered about the gendarmes from before, the short one and his taller friend—where did they go when not on shift?

The coiled hose in the corner of the gravel lot caught Haris's eye. He hoped nothing had happened to Saied—his flayed stomach, his missing fingertips. The idea that Saied had been rushed to some hospital while Haris slept formed slowly in his mind. Before Haris's imagination got away from him, Athid's long shadow arced across the ground like a searchlight as he stepped from behind the café.

He sat next to Haris, tilting back his head, raising his face toward the sky as if to feel the rain on his cheeks. "This is the night," Athid said in a whisper.

Haris leaned his head back too. He felt no rain. The wind

died down, bringing quiet. The moon still shone bright and wouldn't set until the early morning.

"Where is Saied?" asked Haris.

"Watching Bashar," answered Athid. "Get your things."

Haris walked quickly back to the tent. He gathered his hiking pack. He put on his old camouflage rain jacket though there was no rain. Rushing to cross the border, he found himself thinking of Saied, and the little dog.

It was a two-mile walk to the crossing. A dirt path wound through a quilt of partitioned fields, each strewn with untilled soil. In some of the fields pistachio orchards grew, but the Turkish farmers had harvested these trees weeks ago. They looked ugly and mean, their low branches sharp and bare. They would remain this way through the winter, until the next crop's yield.

Haris and Athid's boots crunched against the brittle path. The noise of their steps unnerved Haris—they were too loud. The sky cleared and the moon seemed even brighter. The homes of the farmers speckled the fields. Antennae and satellite dishes sprouted from thatched roofs, pointing north, away from the border. In a window or a door, Haris saw an occasional light. He wondered whether they could take a longer route, one that avoided any home with a light, but he didn't ask Athid. Haris's shoulders ached beneath the weight of his pack. He looped his thumbs under the straps, but this made his thumbs ache. He thought he might ask Athid to slow down, but he didn't do this either.

Athid walked at a brisk pace, but casually, his hands buried in the pockets of his olive-green jacket. He didn't carry a heavy hiking pack like Haris's but a book bag that couldn't hold much more than a change of clothes. It swung like a metronome on his back, keeping time. Now and then, Athid looked over his right shoulder, a few hundred meters to the south, where the ground sloped down, leveling out along the border. A pair of chain-link fences paralleled the border's length, topped with coiled razor wire. The space between the fences was a no-man's-land, just wide enough for two cars to pass.

Athid didn't look at the border for long, but instead searched the ground in front of him. The culverts had been dug into the upturned and resting soil, each sealed with a padlocked manhole cover. Athid and Haris passed nearly a dozen. All were shut. Haris grew nervous. The fields weren't flooded, and when the sun rose they'd be discovered trespassing on some farmer's property. Uncomfortable as this made Haris, what frayed his nerves to their ends was Athid's certainty they'd find a way. It edged on recklessness.

An irrigation ditch appeared ahead of them, a boundary running between two farmers' fields. Water and mud pooled in its dark bottom. It stank of decay. Athid took a step back and charged at it, jumping across. He landed heavily on the far bank. Mud sucked at his feet, but he picked them up easily enough.

Haris stood on the near bank. Athid glanced back, offering his hand. Haris waved it away, cinching down his shoulder straps. Athid offered his hand again. Haris ignored it, taking a few steps back. He too charged the bank, jumping with all his strength, throwing his body forward. His bulky hiking pack turned him in the air, spinning him sideways. He flailed his arms once, clutching toward dry ground. It didn't help. He landed right in the middle of the irrigation ditch, his pack pulling him backward into the stagnant water.

Athid lunged after him, hooking Haris beneath his armpits, dragging him out from his shoulder straps and onto the far bank. Haris was soaked from the waist down, and he stank from the water. Athid leaned into the irrigation ditch and fished out Haris's pack. He sat it next to Haris and stood over him, staring down his nose. Haris struggled to his feet. Water trickled along the backs of his legs, pooling in his boots. He reshouldered his pack, heavier now that it was wet, and stumbled forward. Lending a hand, Athid held the pack's bottom so Haris could properly tighten the straps.

"You should've taken my help," said Athid.

"I thought I could make it on my own."

They continued down the dry path. To their right, in the southern sky, the moon dissolved, setting behind the low-slung hills of Aleppo Governorate. Without the moon, darkness fell through the fields while the first stars formed clear, hardened points above. Haris's waterlogged pack slowed him. Out of breath and with aching shoulders, he wasn't certain how much further he could go. All that he carried dripped a long trail of brackish water in the dust behind him.

On the side of the path, Haris sat waiting. The sound of Athid's steps grew faint and then disappeared entirely as he cut across a barren field to check if one of the culverts was unlocked.

Haris looked at his watch. Through the darkness, he couldn't distinguish the hands on its face. He angled his wrist to the sky, hoping to catch some light. Nothing. Dark as it was, he knew enough night remained for the crossing. That wasn't what bothered him. He wanted to know the time so he might imagine what was going on at home. Maybe if he knew it was five p.m. back in Dearborn—when he'd be finishing his job at the university as a custodian, a handyman who fixed small things—he'd know he had made the right choice quitting such work. Or, if it was seven p.m. back there—when he'd be eating alone, a reheated bowl of rice and spiced lamb baked in a dolma by Samia—he'd know all he had lost by giving up his old life was convenience.

He remembered three a.m., too, the hour when he had returned home after his drink at the hotel. That night, he had assumed Samia would be asleep but found her sitting on his sofa bed, her face in her hands. He hadn't even slipped the door shut when she threw a pillow at him, then another, until a barricade of pillows stacked at his feet. Before he could devise a story of where he'd been, his sister demanded to know why he would sneak out, whether he planned to abandon her, whether he had brought her here for his new life instead of both of theirs.

To assuage his guilt about leaving Samia that night, or perhaps to assuage his homesickness, which itself felt like a form of unquenchable guilt, Haris walked his sister to the university every day that week, waiting outside her classroom in the Michigan winter. The faculty soon asked about the man loitering around campus in a thin camouflage rain jacket, and shortly thereafter offered Haris the charity of a job, which came with a discount in Samia's tuition. His hours now began earlier than Samia's and finished later, so they began to walk separately to the university. He noticed how she started to avoid him, how when he saw her, pushing his mop in the navy slacks and the powder blue shirt that were his new uniform, she would speak to him with her eyes downcast and explain that she was late to her next class.

The spring of Samia's second year she began dating an Emirati boy whom Haris had no reason to disapprove of, whose passport came soused with oil money and stamped with a student visa, and who had a car of his own. Samia had told her brother it was a BMW. Haris made a point of often forgetting the Emirati's name, of lecturing his sister about the poverty and indignity some Arabs (Iraqis, Syrians, Yemenis) faced while others (Saudis, Kuwaitis, Emiratis) indulged in luxury. He also made a point of never being around to see the car.

He took another look at his watch. Sitting on the side of the path, waiting for Athid to return across the field, Haris stared to the south, toward the border, and into the perfect blackness. All he could do was listen, and wait.

The air cooled. Haris strained to hear over the wind. Then Athid surprised him, flopping down on the trailside. He brought his face close to Haris's, speaking in a whisper: "It is unlocked."

Sweat beaded on Athid's forehead, running in rivulets over each temple. Haris felt afraid and nodded once.

Running in a crouch, they moved quickly across the broken field. Haris's footing felt uncertain and mud caked to his boots, his feet becoming heavier with each step. He couldn't see a thing, whereas Athid moved with total certainty, never slowing. Then Athid collapsed to his knees. Haris toppled into him in the darkness. After untangling himself, Haris also stood on his knees. Athid bent over the manhole cover that sealed the culvert. With a jerk from his legs and back, he lifted and tossed it aside.

A warm, decomposing smell belched up from the earth. Athid lowered himself underground. When he stood in the culvert's bottom, its mouth came up to his chest. He glanced back, looking for some assurance Haris would follow. Haris took off his heavy pack and stood at the opening's lip. Athid dipped below, and Haris trailed after him, ducking underground.

On their hands and knees, and at times on their stomachs, the two crept toward the border, dragging their packs behind them. The sloshing of stagnant water and the scampering of subterranean creatures were the only sounds. Athid cursed as the sharp smells became unbearable or as a rat or something else brushed by his leg or over his arm. Haris reached up and touched the sides of the culvert. They felt cool and hard, like cement. Beneath his palms it was all mud.

Haris crawled on his left side. Soaked from the waist down, he did his best to protect his right pocket, which carried his fold of cash, passport and map. Miserable as the passage was, he felt glad for it. To cross into a war should be difficult, he thought. To fight in a war should be even more difficult. When he'd been in Ramadi, that most violent of cities, the war had felt easy. The American soldiers he had translated for would tape a half pound of explosives to a door, blow it in, find the person they were looking for, maybe kill that person, maybe capture him and then return to their firebase at Hurricane Point, a peninsula jutting into the Euphrates River. They'd leave after dinner. They'd return before dawn and have breakfast, watching television and lounging on La-Z-Boy recliners flown in from the States, the sweat still on their uniforms. They would kill someone and in the morning they'd eat cornflakes together.

Traveling through filth and darkness, Haris thought he might find what he was looking for on the other side. And he was happy.

Haris tugged his pack by the handle, grunting, becoming short of breath. Every few minutes, he'd tap Athid on the back, needing to rest a bit. Then they'd continue to plow through the water and filth. The culvert was several hundred meters long, and progress became difficult to measure. They moved in a straight line, but Haris wondered if it was possible to get lost on a straight line. Again he glanced at his watch, knowing he wouldn't be able to see its face.

A hoop of light sliced into the culvert from a sealed manhole cover above. Had they been traveling for that long? Haris couldn't believe morning had already broken. Athid stopped, his neck craning toward the light. He gazed back at Haris. Both their faces were layered in sweat and grime. Haris glanced upward. Athid had kept his word, taking him this far. Haris returned his look with clear, wide-open eyes. Athid's eyes had become heavy-lidded with fatigue. Composting earth flecked the growth of his spongy beard, and it seemed as if a liquid filth might be wrung from it. He considered Haris for a moment further, then frowned. Coming to a squat, Athid bounced on his haunches and then exploded upward, lifting the manhole cover.

Light rushed in.

Not looking back, Athid vaulted from the culvert.

Before Haris could follow, a pair of blue-sleeved arms reached beneath the earth and grabbed him under the shoulders. Haris flailed against their grip, lunging belowground. He struggled to free himself and almost broke loose. Then another set of longer arms clutched after him, joining the first. Haris grabbed the drag handle on his pack, hoping its weight might anchor him inside the culvert. It didn't work. As he was lifted up, light washed against his face, blinding him. But it wasn't daytime. The glare didn't come from above but from the side. Headlights.

The blue-sleeved arms pinned him down. Haris glimpsed the two chain-link fences of no-man's-land. He called out for Athid. No reply. Framed in the glare, two silhouettes moved swiftly against him—one short, the other tall. They cursed at him in Turkish. The headlights caught the stubbled faces of the gendarmes.

Haris offered his hands so they might cuff his wrists, but they didn't. The taller gendarme knelt on his chest. Haris now faced the sky and the night above. The short gendarme groped at his pockets, grabbing after his valuables. Haris bucked wildly. "Don't!"

"Stay still, you damn fool!" the gendarme shouted in Arabic.

Haris got an arm free. He struck the taller gendarme across the face. It wasn't enough to knock him from Haris's chest. Instead, the gendarme rolled his jaw and unholstered a strange-looking pistol. Haris glimpsed the plastic barrel. It fired with a click instead of a bang. A fanged bite sunk into Haris's skin, just beneath the ear. He felt the puncture, then his whole body seized, the Taser's ten thousand volts pulsing through him. His eyelids cramped shut. He smelled his burning flesh, felt his skin turning hotter than his blood.

Everything released.

Haris exhaled, his breath tasting like warm ash.

The taller gendarme dismounted him. He ripped the Taser

wire's teeth from Haris's neck. The shorter gendarme finished rifling through Haris's pockets, taking his cash, passport and map. Haris tried to stand, to come after them, but he couldn't. His body refused him, remaining limp on the soft ground.

The headlights shut off. Perfect darkness returned.

Only Haris's eyes would obey him. He looked frantically for Athid, but found him nowhere. Lying on his back, Haris glimpsed the dome of stars above. Mixing with the stars was galaxy dust, the type which could only be seen far from a city. And Haris felt completely alone.

Standing somewhere above Haris, the two gendarmes argued in Turkish, presumably about what to do with him. Slowly Haris felt his senses recovering, but he didn't move. He hoped the gendarmes would leave him. Soon their chatter stopped. Their footsteps fell into the distance. Haris shifted his eyes in that direction, but he couldn't see through the night.

A car door opened where the gendarmes had disappeared. Haris managed to turn his head toward the sound. The overhead light flashed on inside the cab of a truck. Haris saw a black parka, a red Che T-shirt. Saied's head was hunched down as he thumbed through a wad of cash handed to him by the shorter gendarme, and on the seat next to him sat Bashar the dog. Startled by the flash, Saied glanced up, staring into the darkness. Before Haris could read the expression on his face, the taller gendarme turned off the overhead light.

Haris rested his head in the mud, easing into the earth. He watched the galaxy dust and waited for his body to return to him.

He had nothing now, not a map, not money for travel. He lay sprawled on his back in no-man's-land, and weakness sewed his body to the earth. By morning he'd regained the strength to climb back into the culvert. His hiking pack was no longer there. They'd taken it, too. Enough light found its way underground so he could see the filth he'd waded through the night before. As he retraced his path, crawling past the subterranean creatures, they didn't scamper away from him. The rats stared back from their nests, the insects held in their swarms. They stood their ground, refusing him a place in their world.

When Haris climbed up from the culvert's other end, he gasped in the morning air. The sky was clear. Framed against its blue, farmers fanned out in their fields, clearing the broken stalks of last season's harvest. Traveling in the opposite direction, the partitioned farmland sloped upward. Haris rested often to relax and massage his cramped muscles. The Taser's electricity had left him stooped.

Stumbling along the D850, Haris remembered how he'd come this way by taxi only three days before. Soon the curbs appeared along the roadside, painted yellow and white. Kilis was close. Haris didn't know what he'd do once he got there. All he wanted was to cross the border. The humiliation of being robbed hadn't deterred him. If anything it had hardened his resolve. Tucked in his shirt pocket, he still had his phone. If he could get in touch with Saladin1984 and explain what had happened, he felt certain some arrangement could be made.

To cross into a war should be difficult, he remembered thinking the night before. His downturned eyes followed his feet as he went. He also remembered what the gendarmes at the border had called him: *a damn fool.*

The Americans he had worked with in Iraq sometimes called him *a damn fool,* though they had preferred *dumb shit.* He'd been assigned to a Special Forces detachment then, Team 555, the Triple Nickel as they called themselves. Big beef-fed men with beards stained coppery brown around the lips from chewing tobacco. They spoke slushy, mispronounced Arabic. They went out on raids, only at night. And only the best, most trusted interpreters went out with them. Haris held a special status among the other interpreters: he was Iraqi in a war against Iraqis, and American in a war against Americans—he'd earned that citizenship a few years before. He even had a basic security clearance.

For those who collaborated with the Americans, citizenship seemed the only way to escape their imploding homeland. The other interpreters often asked Haris how he'd navigated the impossible bureaucracy. "Do you remember during the invasion," he would explain, "those American soldiers who were captured in Nasiriya?" Typically, whomever Haris told this story to would reply: "Yes, Jessica Lynch!" beaming as they thought of the pretty American soldier, her face all delicate features and distress, her blond hair, her vulnerability. "No, not her," Haris would interrupt. "I helped them find the other girl soldier, Shoshana Johnson." Haris had never met anyone who'd heard of Shoshana Johnson. She was older than Jessica Lynch, not as pretty, a black woman with cornrows instead of blond hair.

By this time in his story, whomever he told it to would say very little. A question hung in their silence: Why would you, an Iraqi, risk your neck to help an American soldier? Nobody ever asked Haris this question, but he began to wonder himself. What they normally asked was "They gave you citizenship after that?" This usually ended his story because the next question was one he didn't want to answer, and whomever he was talking to didn't want to ask: Then what in God's name are you still doing in Iraq, in Ramadi no less, the asshole of assholes? That was simple: he needed to earn enough money to resettle his sister in the States, and the best job he could get—the only job he could get—was as an interpreter in the war. So Haris Abadi became walking proof among the other interpreters that even if they gave true and faithful service to the United States, even if they achieved their dream of becoming citizens, chances were they'd land right back in Iraq—asshole of assholes.

After a few months on the job, Haris stopped talking about Shoshana Johnson. All of the interpreters knew his story. For the most part they avoided him.

The guys from Triple Nickel didn't avoid him. They treated Haris like a mascot. These professional soldiers cursed him lovingly, appreciating his predicament. The six whom Haris worked with had, between them, fought in Somalia, Kosovo, Colombia, Afghanistan—one had even fought against the Marxist Sendero Luminoso in Peru. They all possessed an overdeveloped appreciation of irony, common among those who trade in violence.

A sergeant named Jim paid special attention to Haris, never missing a joke at his expense. Whenever Haris entered a room, Jim attached the speakers to his iPod, flipping on the Allman Brothers song "Jessica," a seven-minute, thirty-two-second lyricless guitar jam. "Sweet riff, huh, bud?" Jim would say. Haris would never answer. He'd go about his business, translating documents from Arabic to English or cleaning up around the team room. Sometimes Jim would quietly let the tune play, but often he'd tell Haris: "Everybody loves 'Jessica.' Too bad no one ever bothered to write a song called 'Shoshana.'" Then Jim would laugh, often cracking up so hard he'd begin snorting through his flat, piggish nose.

Jim had no qualms about laughing at his own jokes. He also knew nobody liked to be the butt of a joke, so when he finished he'd throw his big hairy arm over Haris's shoulder. "You doing all right, Abadi?" Haris would inevitably smile, feeling a bit uncomfortable with the physical contact—Jim looked like a retired circus strongman, his body a twisted knot of sagging, overused muscles, and in the heat he often went shirtless, reeking as bad as livestock. Standing so close to him, Haris couldn't help but glance at Jim's stomach, which was round, hard, and carpeted in a swirl of hair. Inked right on Jim's belly was a tattooed sun, its rays curled and fiery. Jim's navel was the center of the sun, the dark, stinking heart of the universe.

That was all more than five years ago.

As he walked along the D850, thinking of Jim's stomach, a sharp pain stabbed at Haris's own. The sensation came on fiercely. It rushed outward, toward his joints. They shuddered as if the Taser's voltage had been reapplied. With all Haris had suffered in the last day, his mind struggled to recognize this familiar pain. Then suddenly he put a name to it: hunger.

Haris sat on the road's shoulder.

Fear quickly overcame pain. He had no idea how he would find a meal.

Haris didn't search for a tree's shelter, or dig around for a newspaper to blanket himself. He made no effort for his own protection. He lay on his back at the roadside, not sleeping, not moving, traffic passing by. Recalling his emails with Saladin1984, Haris's mind raced over their old exchanges, groping for the reason he'd decided to come fight, each purpose dissolving quickly, like a match struck to the wind.

> *. . . I am disappointed to hear it will be another two months, but I understand your responsibilities to your sister. Progress across the front has slowed. What will change the balance are more men. All our pain is in the time we wait. We're like your friend Jim. If he'd died quickly, his end would not be so difficult to remember. I've seen many who've died quickly. They feel nothing, knowing nothing of their end. Time is what allows pain. Time is the greatest enemy . . .*

For the rest of the day, Haris lay on the highway's shoulder, his body spent. Eventually he slept, waking late in the night. He was cold in the darkness, and he stared at the branching constellations—Orion, Andromeda—their great movements appearing still. Among the stars, a light hung in low orbit. It flickered with unnatural brightness, clouding the southern sky. It seemed to be a planet, but Haris couldn't say which.

Then the light moved.

Suddenly it blinked out, disappearing.

Haris stood on unsteady legs, looking for the planet. He hoped to find it again in the darkness. Searching the sky across the border, he saw nothing. He lowered himself to the ground. With his head on the earth, he found the constellations he knew, picking out the stars in their patterns. He hoped this would help him sleep.

It didn't.

On the backs of his lidded eyes, he could see Samia. She was taller than Haris, as though she'd stolen his height from him, and fair-skinned for an Arab, with hair that shone nearly blond. He remembered how at night he'd rested on the sofa bed in their apartment, lying awake for hours as he watched over her shut bedroom door. How each morning he would ready himself and then sit fully dressed on the edge of his bed, waiting to see her light switch on in the room before he would rush off to work. She had always been beautiful, not to be kept by a brother. So when the Emirati boy asked her to marry him the winter before graduation, it came as no surprise. Haris could forgive that the boy hadn't consulted him, that by birthright the Emirati could provide more for Samia than Haris could in a lifetime, he could even forgive the sight of the boy's car in the campus parking lot, the lot that Haris cleaned daily, but he could not forgive that the boy proposed to return to the Emirates, to Dubai, with his sister.

Samia told Haris on campus, outside of her classroom, so there would be no scene. "This is a better life," she said. "It's why you brought me here."

"I did not bring you here so that he could take you there," Haris answered.

She gently wrapped her hand around his wrist.

Students jostled against Haris in their rush to class.

"What will you do?" she asked.

He twisted his arm away. Freed from her hand, he realized for the first time that he now had to do something.

Across the border Haris heard a low rumble and opened his eyes. A dim orange glow slowly brushed along the horizon. It smoldered like buried embers. There was another rumble. With it came a single flash, illuminating distant smoke. Like weather forming from the land, the smoke bloomed, tumbling through the orange glow. Distant fires burned, slowly dying. Darkness gradually returned.

Hanging in low orbit, the planet reappeared.

By now Haris knew it wasn't a planet.

As the regime plane flew south, he watched its taillight, feeling more certain about its place in the sky than about anything else above him.

Under a blanket of low clouds, the day held its warmth. By late morning, Haris had already walked another two hours down the D850. After watching last night's bombing, he had awoken feeling refreshed. The war was right there, a purpose for him. On the horizon he could see Kilis and the abandoned tenements where many Syrian families squatted. He had sent Saladin1984 another email that morning and, despite his better instincts, Haris felt optimistic he would hear something back.

It was the optimism of having nothing left.

Until he had lost his passport and money, Haris hadn't realized the burden they had been to him. Actions he felt no pride in had earned his American citizenship. After leaving Iraq, menial work he hated had earned his salary in Michigan. Now he had been given a chance to reinvent himself, to make amends—if he could get across the border.

Then he glanced up the road and his shoulders went slack.

At a roundabout planted with yellow tulips, a traffic light hung from two side posts. It swung from a wire in the breeze. Beneath it were the refugee boys from a couple of days ago—the ones Haris had driven past in his taxi.

A few saw him and pointed as he lumbered their way. The boy with the jet-black hair stepped into the road, taking a look. The other boys lounged beneath several plastic tarps lashed between sapling branches along the median. The low clouds had thickened, turning gray. With rain coming, the boys jockeyed for position under their shelter. Haris saw the little boy from before, the one with the clear gray eyes and glasses missing a lens. There seemed no room for him beneath the tarps. He sat just outside them.

The boy with black hair ambled up the road. "Do you remember me?"

Haris nodded.

The boy asked Haris's name, offering his own: Jamil.

Haris felt certain about what would come next. He waited for Jamil to laugh at him, to take joy in all he had lost. He imagined the taunts—Where is your taxi? I don't suppose you'd like to buy some new clothes from us?

Jamil looked up, holding a palm toward the sky. "It's going to rain," he said. "We have some shelter, nothing much to eat, though. You can wait with us." He motioned for Haris to follow.

Haris didn't want to be cared for by boys.

The sky closed in and the rain came. The boys huddled beneath the tarps slung from the saplings. Jamil stood on the wet, dark road, waiting for Haris.

Haris wouldn't make Jamil wait in the rain, so he followed.

They crouched low, ducking their heads beneath the shelter. Inside it was dim. Row on row, boys lay against each other. A few sat up, blankets or jackets wrapped around their shoulders. Their faces wore dirt like a second skin. Cardboard slats lined the ground, the wet earth creeping through them, smelling of rot. Heavy rain pelted the plastic tarps. Its sound mixed with the boys' chatter, blending their voices into that of a single incoherent child.

Jamil passed among the boys like a school-yard bully, everyone making room in case he wanted it. Now and then he smiled or rested a hand on one of the smaller or weaker boys, his authority a blend of benevolence and menace.

The boy with the gray eyes poked his head into the shelter, smiling at Haris, who smiled back. Jamil noticed, telling Haris the boy's name: Hamza.

Hearing his name, Hamza pressed his glasses up the bridge of his nose. Jamil shooed a few other boys into the storm, making space for Hamza. The three of them came to the center of the shelter. They sat atop a large piece of fresh cardboard with some broken bits of furniture, cedar bark, and newspaper piled next to it. Using a wooden chair leg, Hamza stabbed a burn pit into the wet earth. Above the pit a seam in the shelter would allow smoke to escape. The air was cold and dank, but a fire would help.

Hamza piled the junk into a pyramid. Dirt from digging coated his small hands up to the wrists. Rain fell into the pit, and Hamza continued to work swiftly, as if he'd done this many times before.

"You tried to cross?" Jamil asked Haris.

He nodded.

"If I had money for a fixer to smuggle me, I'd cross too," added Jamil. He took a comb from his pocket, running it through his hair. He again glanced at Haris, who said nothing. "You think I'm too young?"

Hamza looked up at Jamil through his one thick lens. Then he buried his head toward the ground, furiously building the fire, as if its warmth might convince everyone to stay.

"I'm sure younger men than you are fighting," said Haris.

Jamil seemed pleased by this. Younger men. He took care of all these boys. That made him a man.

Hamza finished stacking the wood. He thumbed a lighter, striking sparks but no flame. The rain fell on the unlit fire, threatening to ruin it. Frantically he shook the lighter. Nothing.

"Will you try to cross again?" Jamil asked.

Hamza managed to raise a flame among a few dry leaves. Rain fell on them. They went out. Some embers still smoldered. Hamza brought his face level with the ground, blowing at the embers, billowing clouds of smoke.

"I think so," said Haris.

"You'll need a fixer, and that will be expensive."

The fire wouldn't take. Hamza sat up, his eyes tearing from the smoke. He removed his glasses and wiped his face, which was wet and desperate.

Haris crawled over to Hamza. "Here," he said, pulling out the lighter he'd bought from them. Slowly the flame took and the noise of popping wood mixed with those of rain and the boys speaking beneath their shelter. Warmth spread. The boys quieted. There was only the sound of the rain and the fire.

Jamil stopped talking about the war.

Hamza sat next to him.

Everyone looked at the fire, unable to look at anything else.

After a while, Jamil muttered: "Is that the lighter you bought from us?"

Haris nodded.

Jamil glanced back, managing to turn away from the warmth. "You paid too much, we owe you for that."

The fire lasted longer than the rain.

Haris had fallen asleep on the cardboard. When he woke up the following dawn, the shelter was almost empty. Hamza sat by himself, next to the smoldering embers. He poked at the coals with a sapling branch. The leaves on the branch were green and made dirty by the soot.

As Haris sat up, their eyes met.

Out on the road, Haris could hear Jamil's voice. He was having an argument.

Haris stepped from beneath the tarp. The sky was clear, very sharp and blue. The road was wet and it shone in the sun. Along the yellow-and-white curb, a parked Peugeot coupe flashed its hazard lights. Rinsed by the rain, the black car gleamed. The driver's door was open. Beneath the traffic light, a man stood with his hands crossed behind his back, clasping a notebook, his hair black and curly, his clear eyes precisely like brown marbles. Clean-shaven, his face glowed in the cold, and Haris could hear what Jamil called him: Amir.

A pair of boys stood next to him. They had been trying to sell their combs, fingernail clippers, and other knickknacks to the drivers who were stopped at the light. They'd taken a break to speak with Amir, but Jamil interrupted: "You can't have interviews for free."

"We've already discussed this," Amir told Jamil.

"And you said you would pay."

"I said I would buy something." Amir pointed to the plastic shopping bag on the ground.

"Then buy something." Jamil snatched up the bag and held it in front of Amir, who considered its contents. Nothing seemed of interest.

Haris shuffled down the road, his body stiff after sleeping. The soot of the fire had spread across his clothes. Weakened by hunger, he was tired by even a slow walk.

He approached the traffic light, catching Amir's eye.

Amir went back to rifling through the shopping bag, removing a small packet of pumpkin seeds. "I'll take these," he told Jamil.

Haris sat on the curb among the boys. Amir came over. He crouched in front of Haris, and the boys scuttled away. "You don't look well," he said.

Haris stood as if to walk off.

"Come on, sit," said Amir. He pointed at Haris's camouflage rain jacket. "You've come from the front?"

Every part of Haris wanted to say he had. It would be a small lie. Amir would be more likely to help a down-on-his-luck rebel than an incompetent who couldn't manage to make his way across the border. Haris could invent a story about his exploits in Aleppo or Azaz. It wouldn't be hard. But something held him back. He had come here to fight for a cause he thought was honest. Lying would only spoil that.

"No," said Haris. "I'm trying to cross the border."

"Your accent, you're Iraqi?"

Haris didn't answer but glanced back at Amir, taking the measure of him. Amir spoke Arabic with a lisping accent, one common among well-bred Damascene families or posh businessmen from Aleppo. They appeared to be the same age, but Amir's helmet of well-combed hair, his blue sweater knit heavy as chain mail, these held him apart from Haris and the surrounding desperation. The cuffs of Amir's sweater were dirty, his hands were clean, and Haris felt both attracted to and repelled by him.

Amir offered the pumpkin seeds.

"Thank you," said Haris, taking the packet.

"Where in Iraq are you from?"

"Nasiriya." He fed himself a fistful of seeds. "But I'm not Iraqi. I'm American."

Amir became quiet. His eyes canted upward, as if figuring a sum. "What part of America?" he asked, changing to English, which he spoke with a fluid British accent.

"Michigan," Haris said.

He finished the bag of pumpkin seeds and ran his fingertips along its inside, licking the salt from them. He felt Amir staring.

"So you don't consider yourself Iraqi?"

Haris didn't know how to answer. Instead, he told Amir how he'd been robbed crossing the border and his plans to fight with the Free Army. He spoke about the corruption of Assad's regime, the unity of all Arab peoples, about an Arab's duty to participate in the revolution.

Amir listened, not saying a word.

A car stopped at the intersection's red light. The pack of boys charged toward it with their shopping bag. The driver rolled all of his windows up. The boys knocked on the glass, but the driver kept his gaze fixed to the road. Harder and harder the boys knocked, pleading for someone inside to buy something. They began to shake the car. Then, while the light was still red, it sped through the intersection, its side mirror clipping one of the boys. He yelped, running toward the curb, clutching his elbow.

Jamil picked up the shopping bag. He hurled a tin of shoe polish followed by a roll of breath mints at the car. The junk fell harmlessly. Jamil plodded up the road, placing what he'd thrown back in the bag.

Amir stood from the curb, looking down at Haris. "I've never been much of a fighter, though I was an activist in the revolution's early days, during the protests . . ." Amir's voice trailed off. He glanced at Jamil, who crouched on the roadside, examining the hurt boy's elbow. "The research firm I work with does humanitarian assessments for governments and aid organizations. They pay well and could always use an American who speaks Arabic. If you ever need a job, look me up in Antep." Amir jotted his email address on a scrap of paper, handing it to Haris. "Good luck crossing the border."

He walked off to complete his interviews.

Haris took out his phone to save Amir's information. He had a new email:

The following account has been temporarily disabled—
saladin1984@gmail.com

Frantically, he wrote a response. He sent it, waited a few seconds, then it came back the same way. He sent another, then another. They all came back the same.

Haris's stomach twisted, fear mixing with hunger. The pumpkin seeds had only reminded him how starved he was, that he had no idea how to survive on the border, let alone find money for another fixer to take him across.

Amir crouched next to some of the boys, scribbling in his notebook. This must be an easy way to pass the war, Haris thought. Take a few notes, write a few reports—get paid. When the war finished, Amir could say he had been involved, that he had helped. Yes, thought Haris, an easy way to pass the war.

Another low rumble came from the south, near Azaz. Smoke tumbled across the distant horizon. The rumble became a roar. The smoke thickened. A pair of armored police cars, painted blue, sped down the D850. They ran the red light where Amir interviewed the boys. Anticipating more refugees, the Turkish authorities would reinforce the border.

Amir walked briskly toward his black Peugeot. One by one, the boys either sat along the curb or returned to their shelter of plastic tarps. The gendarmes would shut most of the roads until this spate of fighting passed. No cars would travel by the intersection until then. The boys had no choice but to wait it out.

Haris rushed up to Amir. "There's work in Antep?" he asked.

Bent over the steering wheel, Amir locked his notebook in the glove box. He glanced back at Haris, nodding toward the passenger seat.

Haris ran around the car, quickly climbing in. To leave these boys who had no option but to stay shamed him, so he fixed his eyes on the road. Amir dropped the Peugeot into gear, making a three-point turn. Before they could drive back up the D850, Jamil hurried over. Amir rolled down his window.

"There'll be checkpoints that way," said Jamil. "Go around Kilis, then head north."

Amir opened the glove box, taking out his notebook. Jamil sketched a map of their detour on a page, handing it back.

"Give it to him," said Amir. "I've never been good with directions."

Jamil looked at Haris—clothes caked in mud, head hanging like a bullied dog. He handed him the map.

Haris looked it over.

"You know where you're going?" Jamil asked.

Haris didn't say anything.

They pulled away in the Peugeot.

As they passed through the intersection, Haris caught a

glimpse of Hamza who, standing on the roadside, shut one of his eyes as if giving a playful wink. But he was really squinting through the single lens of his glasses, trying to see inside the car, and who had left him behind.

Haris turned away. He looked down at Jamil's sketch, glad once again to have a map.

II

Haris thought of it as a suicide note. He had written it in the bathroom the night before he left for Detroit Metro Airport. Twice his sister had knocked on the door, asking what he was doing in there. It wasn't a long note, but it had taken a long time to write. In a month she would receive her college degree. That summer she would marry. Samia's fiancé had offered to buy Haris's plane ticket to the ceremony. He'd accepted, but instead used the money to buy a ticket to Antep. Samia didn't need him anymore. After losing their mother and being abandoned by their father, Haris had always loved Samia according to her needs. When he'd earned the money to get them both out of Iraq, he was all she had and theirs was a big love. Once they arrived in Michigan and she began her schooling, Samia's need was less, but enough to hold them together. And that night, as he crouched on the bathroom floor, using the toilet lid as a desk, their love seemed just big enough to allow Haris to get the note right even though she barely needed it, or him.

Important as it had seemed then, he couldn't quite remember all he'd written. He hadn't said anything about going to fight with the Free Army, or even where he was going. He remembered that. To begin her new life, Samia would drift away from him, this he understood, having been left by family before. But he didn't mention any of that. He told her he wouldn't be returning, that he'd transferred his bank account to a new one under her soon-to-be married name, that she should stay in their place until graduation, that his choice didn't mean he wasn't her brother. There was one line in the note he remembered clearly: *The key to undoing might be in doing.*

It was the only explanation he left behind. The rest was logistics.

He set the note in the living room, on an accent table stacked with thick fashion magazines, whose styles Samia would be able to afford after marriage. Haris opened his closet in the living room to finish packing. His camouflage rain jacket hung in the back, a gift from Jim. Samia hated when he wore the jacket. With his dark red hair, Haris could've been taken for a westerner, and in the camouflage jacket Samia thought he looked lean and cruel, like a soldier, not like the interpreter he had been. In those days he had considered himself a soldier, though he wasn't. Perhaps that was why he would still occasionally wear the jacket, so she would see in him what he had once seen in himself.

The morning Jim let him keep the jacket it had been raining for hours. Their convoy had just returned to Hurricane Point. As they pulled into the gravel parking lot, engines idled, then cut out one by one. Jim and Haris stepped from their Humvee, unfastening their body armor. Jim's fit like a second skin, Haris's like a tortoise shell. The early sun cast shadows in Haris's sunken cheeks, adding to his sullen expression. The evening before, Jim had lent Haris the waterproof jacket, taking pity when he saw that Haris was unprepared for the storm. Haris now wore it beneath his body armor. Jim wore sopping fatigues, yet he was smiling from behind his thick blond beard, his crooked teeth running like a broken fence through a thicket. Despite Jim having done him a favor with the jacket, Haris wouldn't look at him. At that moment, he'd hated Jim.

The night before, they had been on a raid, a retribution mission. One of Triple Nickel's sister teams had hit a bad IED—one guy killed, another's back snapped like hard candy. An informant had walked onto Hurricane Point with details about the bomb maker. Jim had interrogated him with Haris translating, convincing the informant to finger the bomb maker's home on a map. Usually the team wouldn't go out on a raid unless a couple of sources confirmed their information, but this informant had identified the type of IED down to its triggering mechanism: a baby monitor. The detail seemed enough.

The team had already taken a sledgehammer to the front door while Haris sat parked in the Humvee, his hands pushed deep into the pockets of Jim's jacket, a cigarette dangling from his lips. Haris listened to the rain as he waited to get called inside. A broken wiper stuttered across the windshield. He played with an empty bottle of Motrin he'd found in Jim's pocket, popping the lid off and on, off and on. The team moved through each room, their flashlights sweeping behind sofas and into corners, the light occasionally spilling through a window and into the street. Aside from some muffled voices, a dog barking here and there, it was quiet. Jim stepped into the courtyard. He flashed his light at Haris, who tossed his cigarette into the wet street and then entered the living room, where a woman cried by the doorway, her breath coming in hyperventilated huffs. One of the guys from the team thrust a black-and-white photo of the alleged bomb maker in her face. "Anya howa!" he shouted.

Jim leaned over to Haris, whispering: "She knows, man."

The woman shuffled toward Haris on her knees, grabbing his pant leg. "He's not here," she said in Arabic.

Haris crouched next to her. "You need to tell them," he whispered.

The woman said nothing. Jim and a few others formed a circle around her, rifles slung across their chests, helmets cinched tight, night-vision goggles hiding their eyes like depraved carnival masks.

"Please," she said to Haris.

He took her elbow gently in his hand. "They're not leaving. He killed one of their friends."

The woman's shoulders collapsed, her chin buckling toward her chest. "He's not here," she said softly.

Haris shook his head at Jim.

Jim walked into a corner room, returning with a boy not more than fourteen years old. His tousled black hair pasted itself against his sweaty forehead, and he wore a loose pajama shirt. Etched across his face was a scowl which did not intimidate.

Pushing Haris out of the way, Jim grabbed the boy by his nape. With a single arm, he throttled him to the floor. The boy's chest hit the ground. He let out a gasp, sounding like too much air through too small a hole. His mother watched, her entire body shaking.

"He doesn't know!" she shouted, lunging at Jim.

"Christ's sake, Abadi. Hold on to her!" Jim snapped.

Haris firmly grasped the woman's elbow.

She swiveled around and slapped Haris clean across the jaw.

Jim lifted his arm, as if to strike her back. Haris placed his body between them. "I've got her," he said.

The woman's shouts turned to whimpers.

"Let's try again," said Jim. He leaned over the boy, who lay sprawled on his stomach. Jim stepped on his spine with one boot, grabbing an arm, pulling it up, slowly twisting it by the wrist. The boy breathed heavily. Jim leaned in front of him, holding the faded black-and-white photo close to his face, like a rag of chloroform. "Ask him where his father is."

Haris asked. The boy said nothing.

Jim twisted the arm a little harder.

"Huw maa ya'rif shay," sobbed the boy's mother.

"What'd she say?" Jim muttered.

"She said he doesn't know," answered Haris.

"I'll break his fucking arm," Jim said calmly. "Tell her."

Jim twisted the wrist a little more. The boy's legs flopped against the floor, his bare feet scuffing the ground, wild as a seizure. He cursed in a throaty voice that sounded like a man's. Then it became quiet but for the boy's panting and the scrape of his feet. Jim adjusted himself, planting his right boot between the boy's neck and ear, gaining an extra bit of leverage. He pivoted toward the woman, as if giving her a last chance.

She hung her head.

Jim shifted his body over the boy, lifting the arm—

"He's hiding in the yard," said the woman.

Desperately, Haris translated.

Jim stopped.

He glanced beneath his boot. The boy's face was clamped with a defeated sort of pain, an expression of pure hate.

Jim released the arm. It fell to the ground like a wet towel. He smiled at Haris, as if they'd accomplished something together, but set into Haris's face was the same expression of pure hate.

"Tell them they're free to go," said Jim.

"What?" asked Haris.

"They're free to go."

"Free to go where?"

Jim didn't answer. He went to search the yard.

This is their house, thought Haris. Free to go where?

He wasn't the boy's father but grandfather. Jim had found the old man hiding in the yard. When they returned to Hurricane Point, Jim handed him over to the Military Police by his flex-cuffed wrists. He also handed off the names of everyone in the house, including the boy: Kareem Tamad. Before the MPs dragged off the old man, a few of the guys snapped photos around him, striking triumphant poses with their prisoner in the parking lot. They planned to send them to their sister team, proof of a job well done.

"What's a matter, Abadi?" Jim had asked. The two sat next to each other on a sofa in the team room. Jim shoveled heaping spoonfuls of cornflakes into his mouth while Haris's bowl of cereal sat in front of him, turning soggy.

Haris took off Jim's rain jacket and set it on the sofa between them.

"The kid'll be fine."

Haris pushed his bowl away.

"We probably just saved somebody's life," Jim added, "maybe yours."

"You think so, don't you?"

"I know so." Jim drank down his milk and left the empty bowl on the coffee table in front of them. "Keep the damn jacket," he said and then walked back to his room to sleep.

Haris cleaned up Jim's dishes and his own.

Two days later, Haris received an email from ABB Ltd., the company he contracted for. Jim had filled out the paperwork for a five-thousand-dollar performance bonus for Haris's critical role in detaining the bomb maker. Haris took the money and swore that as soon as he'd saved enough he would leave the war.

A week later another IED went off, also using a baby monitor as a trigger.

A couple of days after that, the MPs found Jim in the mess tent at dinner and told him they'd be releasing the old man. Jim looked over at Haris, but he didn't hum "Jessica," or ask for Haris to return the performance bonus—Jim didn't ask anything.

Outside it had started to rain again.

Jim stood and headed back to the team room. Haris tossed his food away and followed at a run, zipping up the camouflage jacket Jim had given him, the one he had decided to keep. The one that hung in the closet of the home he had made, for a time, with Samia.

Amir's apartment was on the fourth floor, just off Yusuf Bulvari. Its smog-clouded windowpanes looked down on Antep City Park, which ran like a landing strip of greenery through the ramshackle tenements and traffic-clogged streets. Beneath the canopied elms of the park, Syrians panhandled or rummaged through garbage cans emptied by the municipality with cruel efficiency. On the far side of the park, a tram carried commuters to work. Its electric lines hung dangerously low, in need of tightening. Current flowed through them with unequal voltage, sparking at the circuit joints. From the apartment's window, the sparks could be seen in the distance.

"Looks like muzzle flashes," said Amir. He set a bag of gas station snacks he'd bought Haris on top of a dresser by the window and then dug through its drawers. A mirror covered the apartment's back wall, creating the illusion of more space. He watched Haris through its reflection.

Haris had been gazing out the window, lost in thought.

Amir set a pair of khakis and a gray cable-knit sweater, heavy like his blue one, on the armrest of a lumpy sofa bed. The living room was nothing more than the sofa bed and a small flat-screen television perched on a glass console. Flickering across the screen, the BBC ran on mute. It had been on when they'd arrived at the apartment an hour before. It seemed Amir never turned it off, as if he waited for some piece of breaking news. The apartment had no real kitchen, just a counter and sink in the corner with a mini-refrigerator plugged in next to the door. On top of the fridge was a hot plate.

Amir washed his hands and face in the sink. He sprinkled water in his black curls, running his fingers through his hair. "Take those clothes," he said. "You can change and wash up in the bedroom."

"Thank you."

"I also arrived with nothing. With your English, you might be the first person I've met since coming here who I can actually help."

Haris cradled the khakis and sweater beneath his arm, shutting the door. He set the clothes on an ottoman at the foot of the bed and stepped into the small adjoining bathroom with a phone-booth shower. He ran his hand under the water. It came out cold, and Haris returned to the bedroom, waiting for it to warm. On the side of the mussed bed by the window among some lipsticks and a hairbrush, a studio portrait of a little girl sat atop a stool. Through a half-drawn shade, the evening dumped its orange light on the photograph. Haris guessed the girl was about four. Thick braids woven with ribbons hung to her shoulders, the hair very black like Amir's. She had a wide face and strong jaw, one that held a smile's weight well. She was possibly handsome though certainly not beautiful. Her dark skin matched her hair, and her eyes were blue, perfectly so.

Stacked next to the girl's portrait were a dozen or so notebooks—spiral, leather-bound, Moleskine. Haris noticed one wedged partly open. He lifted it, and a few photographs tumbled from between its pages: the girl growing through her first years, faded portraits of uncles and grandparents. Then Haris came to a photo that seemed out of place among the family snapshots: an abandoned lot planted with crumbling headstones, a little huddled mound unmarked in center frame. He stared at the mound. On the Polaroid's tab, written in long, snaking Arabic, was the name of a road intersection: Al Maysar–Al Jalaa. He tucked the photos back inside the notebook, where blue ink crossed its pages, a desperate scrawl in French.

In the living room, Amir turned up the BBC.

Steam from the shower billowed out the bathroom door. Haris gathered his clothes, noticing the other side of the bed. A folded sheet ran across the top of the blanket. An unwrinkled pillow leaned against the headboard. It looked as if no one had slept there in a while. Neatly arranged on a stool by the pillow stood an alarm clock, a rubber-banded stack of business cards, and a single volume: *Responsible Conduct of Research* by Dr. Adil E. Shamoo, the thick text annotated with multicolored Post-its.

Haris finished his shower. Cradling his filthy clothes, he returned to the living room. Amir stood in front of the console, arms folded, gazing down his nose. He watched the BBC like a statue watches visitors in a museum. Clips from a YouTube video played. A man around thirty, no older than Haris, stood on a road that ran through a field of wind-brushed high grass. He wore a camouflage rain jacket similar in pattern to Haris's. Beneath the jacket, a bright red turtleneck crawled up to the man's chin. A ticker ran across the bottom of the television screen: ABU SAKKAR, COMMANDER OF THE FREE ARMY'S INDEPENDENT OMAR AL-FAROUQ BRIGADE.

"The man had videos on his mobile," explained Abu Sakkar. He looked directly into the camera but spoke past it: "It showed him raping a mother and her two daughters. He stripped them naked while they begged him to stop in the name of God. Finally he slaughtered them with a knife—what would you have done?"

The grainy video cut to a montage of propaganda. Abu Sakkar now stood in the field of grass. He knelt on a red-and-white prayer rug, praying Namaz, invoking the name of God. He walked through a town of narrow dirt lanes and rickety hovels roofed with corrugated aluminum. The residents turned out to greet him. A waving grandmother blew him a kiss. He laughed.

Something about the laugh set Amir off. "You know about him?" he asked, turning away from the television. Haris had followed the war closely. He knew about Abu Sakkar, but he didn't say anything. "This idiot commands a brigade," said Amir, switching from Arabic into his formal manner of English. "You know what he did before?"

Haris shook his head.

"A day laborer," answered Amir, again looking down his nose toward the BBC. "The revolution is now commanded by day laborers."

A disclaimer flashed across the screen: THE FOLLOWING CONTENT MAY BE DISTURBING FOR SOME AUDIENCES. Another YouTube video played, this one heavily pixelated, a recording off a cheap cellphone. Abu Sakkar wore the same camouflage jacket but with a white turtleneck beneath. His Kalashnikov hung lazily by his side, as if the rifle had become too heavy for him. At his feet, a man's tangled corpse splayed against the wet earth. Abu Sakkar stepped on the man's chest. He looked at the camera in the same far-off way as before. "We will eat your hearts and your livers, you soldiers of Bashar the dog." He unsheathed a knife from his belt. He worked at the body beneath his foot. Off-camera a raucous voice cheered: "It looks like you're carving him a Valentine's heart!" When Abu Sakkar finished, he gazed at the camera, raising his hand to his mouth. His lips closed around a wet mass, shining with greasy blood.

The BBC report returned to the other YouTube video. Abu Sakkar again stood on the road, surrounded by high grass. The wet asphalt ran into the distance. He spoke in that direction: "Put yourself in my position," he said. "They slaughtered my brothers. They murdered my uncle and aunt. All this happened to me. I didn't want to do this. We have to terrify the enemy, humiliate them, just as they do to us. Now they won't dare be wherever Abu Sakkar is." The wind blew, parting the high grass. Abu Sakkar faced back toward the camera, saying nothing.

Then he raised his hand and made a V sign with his index and middle finger—V for victory, or for peace. The revolution had brought this well-worn gesture back into fashion, though it meant two very different things, or perhaps the same thing. He walked into the road's distance, his Kalashnikov again hanging heavily at his side.

The BBC's report finished. Amir muted the television, tossing the remote on the sofa. "The commander of the Farouq Brigade—a heart-eating day laborer."

Haris thought about his last job in Dearborn, fixing small things at the university, the tables and chairs at which students like his sister studied. He'd been no better than a day laborer and wondered in what other ways he might be like Abu Sakkar.

Then Amir's cellphone rang. He stepped in front of the dresser and picked it up. "Bonne soirée, ma chère."

A woman's muffled voice came from the receiver.

"I'm also bringing a friend," answered Amir, returning to Arabic. He listened for a moment and added: "Yes, I'd heard she finally left. It will be lovely to see her. Meet you both there." He hung up, setting his phone on the dresser. Amir preened in the wall mirror, picking apart his curls. He evened them out with perfectly manicured hands except for a couple of fingers that were smooth, missing their nails. He palmed down one stubborn lick and shrugged his shoulders, happy enough with his work.

Haris caught his own reflection, standing in his new clothes with the filthy old ones tucked beneath his arm. Wide eyes, mouth slightly agape, rutted forehead—Haris appeared tense, like he was about to ask a question, one he couldn't quite remember.

"You seem upset," said Amir.

"I'm not," said Haris. He held up his dirty clothes, as if asking where he might wash them.

"Let's get rid of those," replied Amir, snatching a plastic shopping bag from beneath the sink. Haris placed the bundle inside, and Amir knotted the handles to contain the stench. "Keep the clothes I gave you. You'll find work quickly. Then you can buy another set at the mall."

"The mall?" asked Haris, his voice wavering.

"You are upset. I should've turned that video of Abu Sakkar off. That's what any reasonable person would do, just turn it off."

"It's not that. I didn't know there was a mall here."

"Oh," said Amir. "The Turks opened it just after the war started. It's right on the park, even has an ice rink. We'll meet my wife and her friend at Big Chefs for dinner, my treat."

"I'm imposing on you enough," said Haris. "I can stay here."

"You're the one doing me a favor," answered Amir. "My wife always complains that this place"—and he waved his hand at the cramped corners of the apartment—"doesn't feel like home. The few times people have stayed with us have been the only times she's snapped out of her homesickness. If we have a houseguest, we have a home."

They left the apartment and walked along Yusuf Bulvari toward Amir's Peugeot. At the edge of Antep City Park, elms crowded the roadside, beautiful yet awkwardly planted, like a garden with too many fountains. The early moon silvered their leaves, which had yet to turn in the late autumn, and the wind creaked through their branches. At the trunks of the larger trees refugees bedded down for the night on cardboard slats, their shoulders blanketed with newspapers, their voices traveling thick as a conspiracy through the patches of shadow. As Haris and Amir passed, the sleeping refugees awoke. The sound of their bodies rustling alert beneath the newspapers blended with the sound of leaves rustling in the branches.

Reaching the Peugeot, Amir held up his hand, asking Haris

to wait a moment. With the bag of dirty clothes cradled in his arm, Amir stepped into the dark elm grove. Nearly out of sight, Haris saw him crouch next to an old man who slept beneath a tattered gray blanket. He placed the bag next to him. The old man stirred. Jogging back to Haris, Amir pulled out his keys and unlocked the car.

As they climbed inside, the old man came out of the park, lumbering toward them. His blanket hung over his shoulders, brushing at his ankles. He grasped the bag to his chest. Cursing after Haris and Amir, his voice traveled in the snatches of wind which gusted between the elms.

"Can't you do better than these rags!"

Amir paused for a moment, as if uncertain what to do or say. Then he smiled, flashing the old man a V sign as he slammed his door shut.

Light from the new mall spilled into Antep City Park, scuttling the refugees deeper into the sanctuary of its dim confines. The Anatolian bungalows of the old city skirted the lowest of its five stories. A neon sign, each letter large as a car, proclaimed: SANKO PARK. The sign glowed brightest at the mall's entrance, where a pair of revolving doors sealed in the hermetic freshness of Tommy Hilfiger, Marks & Spencer and the Apple Store.

On the ground floor, Big Chefs' open-air terrace was fenced in glass. Heating lamps burned in every corner, and white-aproned waiters handed out red wool blankets for the patrons to drape over their shoulders. Clustered in booths and around four-top tables, an international clientele of aid workers, entrepreneurs and well-heeled refugees hunched over meals ordered off a menu that was just as varied—everything from plates of pepperoni pizza to bowls of manti, a Kurdish dumpling in yogurt sauce. The dining room felt like the mess tent of some khaki-clad expedition. Though the patrons dressed to a type, Haris could pick out each nationality by their shoes. The eastern Europeans wore leather oxfords or loafers with dust in the creases, and the Syrians wore obscurely branded cross-trainers like LA Gear or British Knights, while the Americans and the western Europeans wore high-tech trekking boots worth one month of a local Turk's salary. Conversations about humanitarian missions, about politics, about the revolution, rose up from the tables, blending into the single noise of a half-dozen languages that when heard as a whole made one undecipherable clamor, like an apathetic groan, a sound conveying nothing. With Haris by his side, Amir stood at the terrace's threshold surveying the restaurant. Although Amir looked for his wife, he seemed in no hurry to find her. His gaze crept over the crowd, as if hoping he might see someone else he knew.

She sat at a corner table by the glass wall. Above her head she waved lazily, a cigarette's smoke tracing the arced motion of her wrist, her friend sitting across from her. Haris noticed them first and touched Amir on the arm, pointing to the pair. Amir glanced in their direction, but for a moment didn't move. He swept his eyes over one last corner of the restaurant. Then he waved back and went to meet his wife.

When they came to her table she stubbed out her cigarette and stood, offering her hand to Haris. He noticed she was just a bit taller than him, like his sister, and taller than Amir. She introduced herself as Daphne, speaking the *e* with a Gallic accent, as though its pronunciation were a cherished ornament. A pair of lipstick-red sunglasses perched on her head, and a matching red blanket was draped across her narrow shoulders. Beneath it, she wore a stylish ice-blue trench coat. Set above high cheekbones, her mascaraed eyes matched the trench coat and burned cold, reminding Haris of the little girl in the photo. She wore a nose ring, a spec of quartz set in a tiny stud, and each of her words came with a certain force, spoken from a square jaw any boxer would've been proud to have. The roots of her hair were brown, the tips faded naturally to blond. On a woman of less interesting heritage they would've looked dyed and grown out, but later Haris would learn her mother had been French, her father a Damascene. With her strong features, Haris imagined she looked like her father.

The young woman across from Daphne also stood, turning to face Amir.

"Latia," he said. "You made it to Antep."

"Daphne met me at the bus station this morning. I needed to give her something."

Amir didn't ask what the something was, and Haris noticed he practically ignored his wife. Instead, he leaned in and kissed this old acquaintance on either cheek, brushing his body against hers. Latia stepped back, sitting down again. Her full, round eyes flitted to the ground and then returned to Amir, their lashes cupping toward her eyebrows. She lacked Daphne's elegance. Her face's unrefined features appeared as if a sculptor with thick thumbs had molded them. Her long hair was cut with bangs, like she had done the job herself, snipping a curtain so she might see.

Amir remained beside her, refusing to turn away, his gaze filled with a sleepy sort of cunning. "You look wonderful," he said, taking the seat next to her.

"Of course she does," answered Daphne. "She's slimmed down. Too much time in Aleppo."

Latia's eyes wandered out the window, absently shifting between the city's lights and the park's dark interior.

As Haris sat next to Daphne, her eyes fixed on his sweater. "This looks familiar," she said to Amir.

"Some gendarmes gave Haris a rough time," he said.

"You're Syrian?" Daphne gestured to Haris's reddish hair.

"He's American," answered Amir.

"I wouldn't have taken you for an American," she said.

"I'm also Iraqi," said Haris.

"Is that the same as being American these days?" Daphne said, and then glanced across the table and explained that Latia was a Syrian, and also a dear friend who had attended the University of Aleppo with Amir and her. They'd all met in an elective on English literature. "What did we read? Oh yes, *Emma*," said Daphne. She turned to Haris and explained: "Amir found it dull, the characters' obsession with manners. I loved it, however." Then Daphne described how Latia, who'd studied nursing, dropped out of the medical institute after the second semester. "They had to do dissections of cadavers. I wouldn't have made it past the first one either." Again she turned to Haris. "Such unpleasant subject matter."

"Unpleasant?" interrupted Amir. "You spend all your time at that damn Delvet Hospital."

Daphne lit another cigarette. "It's the idea of surgery that I find unpleasant, not the patients," she replied, taking a drag. "I translate for the Syrian families there," she added, glancing back at Haris and Latia.

Daphne then explained that Latia was on her way to Payas, a Turkish resort town along the Mediterranean coast where her uncle rented an apartment. Latia had hired a fixer to take her from Aleppo to Kilis, and then she'd taken a bus from Kilis to Antep. In the morning, she would take a final bus from Antep to Payas.

"That's an expensive journey," Haris said.

Latia said nothing. She looked at Amir, who now answered for her: "I imagine it took a while to save up the money." To which Latia nodded.

"Leaving is a difficult decision," said Daphne, flicking the ashes from her cigarette. Then she pointed the cherry end at Amir. "Though more difficult for some than for others."

Latia crossed her hands on the table. She picked at her thumb where a cuticle jutted up like a loose floorboard.

"Nothing's easy about this," said Amir.

Latia's scooping lashes beat furiously as she listened to Amir and Daphne bicker. From her lower lip, she blew up at her bangs, clearing them from her eyes. The waiter interrupted the deteriorating conversation with the day's specials. Everyone passed along their orders to Daphne, who translated them into Turkish.

Amir added a bottle of raki to the meal.

The waiter disappeared toward the kitchen. The table became quiet. "I stayed for my cats," mumbled Latia.

Haris glanced at her.

"For your cats?" asked Daphne, the cold in her blue eyes coming out.

Latia shifted in her seat, fishing something from her pocket.

"How many cats?" asked Haris.

She took out a Polaroid. Haris barely considered the rust-colored creature, its eyes big and weepy. What he noticed was the writing on the Polaroid's white tab, the same long, snaking Arabic he'd seen scrawled across the bottom of the photo tucked in Daphne's notebook, the one of the unmarked grave.

According to the writing, the cat's name was Simi—Simi with a heart at either end. "That's my tabby," said Latia.

Amir suppressed an affectionate laugh. "You're a wonderful girl," he said. Then he glanced at Daphne. "She stayed for her tabby!"

"Why didn't you take the cat with you?" asked Haris.

"Simi became pregnant. I couldn't abandon her and her kittens."

"So where are they?" asked Amir.

The waiter returned, bringing out the first of their orders, placing a bottle of raki in the table's center. Amir leaned toward Latia. He filled her glass, adding an ice cube and some water, which turned the clear liquor a cloudy white. He filled his own glass in the same manner, returning the bottle to the table's center. Daphne gazed at her husband, her eyes seeming to wonder if she'd be offered the same courtesy. Haris grabbed the bottle's neck. He poured out Daphne's glass and then his own, fumbling with the ice cubes, forgetting the water.

"Cheers," he offered weakly.

The four of them clinked glasses.

While the others ate, Latia continued: "Simi had a large litter, eleven kittens. She couldn't nurse all of them. Each day I had to run five blocks to the store, dodging snipers so I might barter what little I had—some jewelry, silverware, a tea set—for fresh cream smuggled in from the few working farms in the countryside. The city had been nearly destroyed, but for those of us who stayed it was a strangely magical time. The rebels hung bedsheets across the major road intersections, screening their movements and ours. A beautiful tactic. The sun would pass through the sheets glowing red, blue or yellow. If there was wind, it was like walking between the sails of an endless tall ship. My whole world was reduced to five city blocks, eleven kittens and their daily ration of cream."

Latia looked directly at Haris. "Does this sound horrible to you? To call it a magical time."

Haris shook his head no. What he wanted to say, he couldn't he admired her. She had reduced her world to a single thing worth fighting for. He drank down the rest of his raki, poured another glass, letting his head swim pleasantly with it.

"I would've sacrificed myself for Simi," said Latia, "but her kittens eventually grew large enough to survive without me. They no longer needed cream. One morning they all left, moved on it seemed. So I've done the same, coming here."

Latia blew her bangs from her face again. Without asking, she reached across the table and took one of Daphne's cigarettes.

"When's your bus?" asked Haris.

"Tomorrow morning."

"I told her she could stay with us," interrupted Daphne.

Haris glanced down at his glass.

Amir, who'd been watching Latia intently, turned to his wife. "Haris is staying with us."

Latia bit at her other thumb's cuticle.

"I can call Marty," said Amir. He hooked his arm on the back of Latia's chair, lowering his head slightly so it became even with hers. "I work with him at the Syria Analysis Group. He's a good guy."

"Do good guys make money off bad wars?" said Daphne. She lit a cigarette and began to tip ash onto the rim of her plate, having lost interest in her meal. "Why doesn't Haris stay with Marty?"

"I wanted to talk with him about a bit of work for Haris. It's probably best he not be sleeping at his place, too."

"Marty's your business partner," she said to Amir. "You talk as if you're his employee. Getting Haris a job should be easy."

Amir took a thick roll of Turkish lira from his pocket. He set it next to his plate as if affirming to his wife the necessity of his relationship with Marty. He waved over the waiter, who brought the bill.

"Excuse my prying," Daphne said to Haris, "but what's brought you to the border?"

Haris spoke about his home in Iraq, about where he'd lived in Michigan. He talked about coming to fight with the Free Army, but gave few details. When Amir began to explain how Haris had been squatting with Jamil and the boys he interviewed for information on refugee conditions around Kilis, Daphne interrupted her husband. She leaned forward and placed both her hands on the table, closely regarding Haris.

"Your plan is to cross?" she asked.

Haris nodded.

Daphne leaned back in her seat. Her regard shifted from Haris to her hands, which had slid into her lap. Before she could ask anything more, Latia interjected: "I have money for a hotel. It's really no trouble."

"Don't be ridiculous," said Amir. He punched out a text message to set things up with Marty. "You walk Haris back to the apartment," he told Daphne. "I'll drive Latia to the office." On their journey back from the border, Amir had told Haris about the office, a nine-bedroom villa situated in Ibrahimli, one of the wealthiest neighborhoods in Antep. The Syria Analysis Group's headquarters had a pool, a deep bathtub built off each bedroom, and a Syrian woman who did all of the cooking and cleaning. Resplendent as it was, nobody referred to it as anything other than the office.

"You're too drunk to drive," said Daphne.

"And you never learned to drive a manual," replied Amir. He held up his near-empty glass to Latia's full one, forcing her to toast with him and drink a little more.

"I hate to be so much trouble," Haris said.

"It's no trouble," said Daphne as she stood, buttoning up her coat and stuffing her sunglasses in its pocket. "We'll have a nice stroll." Then, addressing Haris but speaking toward Amir, she said: "We'll get to know each other a little better."

Haris glanced out the terrace window, toward Antep City Park. Its trees clawed at the night sky. Beneath them the earth looked cold and foreboding. He followed Daphne from the restaurant. As they left, he asked the waiter to point him toward the bathroom. Haris passed through a swinging door and stood in front of the sink. His reflection upset him—hollow cheeks, lips chapped like coils of old clay, thinning hair flattened to his scalp. The image swam a bit from the raki. He turned the tap cold, splashing water on his face. He turned it hot and washed his hands. They were dry and cracked from his long journey. Like Latia's, his cuticles were frayed.

Haris left the bathroom, crossing the restaurant to meet Daphne outside. As he went, he had a view of their table. A waiter had brought coffee. Amir didn't seem in any rush to leave. He and Latia still sat next to each other, his arm wrapped around the back of her chair, his handsome face considering hers. Whispering in her ear, Amir pressed a fold of cash into her palm, which she quickly buried in her pants pocket. Whatever he said lifted a smile across her lips. He spoke more and more quickly, raising that smile as if he were hoisting some triumphant flag.

Although Latia appeared amused, Haris noticed her eyes. They wouldn't look at Amir. Her stare was fixed right in front of her on the table. She concentrated on a small porcelain pitcher next to Amir's coffee. It was filled with perfectly white cream.

Daphne insisted they return home through the park. A dark cobblestone path wound among the trees. She followed it, staying a half step in front of Haris. Her shoes had heels, nothing too high, but enough to cause her strides to fall in an elegant line. As she walked, she led with her chest, her shoulders thrown back like she was forever stepping onstage to accept an award.

At first neither of them spoke. Haris felt this park was Daphne's place, and he should share the silence until she chose to break it. Bundled heaps slept at the bases of the elms. Haris's boots padded silently past them, but Daphne's heels clacked against the path. A little ways into the park, one of the bundles stirred at her approach. Haris strode in front of Daphne, to shield her from whoever might come at them. She placed her palm on his elbow, nudging him back.

A man advanced through the darkness, wearing a blanket over his head like a cloak. Daphne held up her hand. "As-salamu alaikum." The man pulled the blanket to his shoulders. "Wa alaikum salam," he said, placing his palm over his heart. He appeared no older than Daphne, his smile filled with clean, well-cared-for teeth. The man wasn't a pauper, not by birth at least, but he slept in the park. Haris wondered if he had once been a professional—an architect, doctor, teacher—people like him circled nearly every elm.

Daphne walked past the man. His white smile held as he threw the blanket back over his head, returning to his corner of the park. Every few steps someone would wake to the sound of Daphne's approaching heels. Their cautious eyes would dart down the path and Daphne would greet them. Always they'd return her greeting, their expressions softening, becoming familiar. And always Daphne would move on.

Haris remembered the old man who'd chased Amir from the park earlier that evening. But with Daphne the park transformed into a community. After they'd stopped several times, she whispered an explanation to Haris: "I know many of these families from Delvet Hospital."

"How long have you volunteered there?" he asked.

"About a year."

"And before that?"

"Before the war, I was finishing a master's in contemporary literature. Amir had just finished one in anthropology. We were going to be an academic couple. Then the university shut down, and I taught kindergarten in a school I set up with some mothers."

Daphne's hollow heel strikes became the only sound between them. The path began its slow climb out of the park. As they approached the rows of lit apartment buildings along Yusuf Bulvari, Daphne's pace slowed. The two barely moved, rationing their steps so they might continue to walk together.

"How long do you plan to stay?" she asked.

"Not long."

"Until you can pay a fixer?"

Haris planted his stare just in front of his boots and nodded.

"Working for Marty you'll quickly make enough," Daphne said.

Haris glanced at her and then sped up, opening his stride, leaving Daphne behind. He followed a separate path, which seemed to lead out of the park, the lattice of elm branches clearing overhead, revealing a tangled whitewash of constellations faded by the lights of the city. Behind him, Haris heard her voice: "That's the wrong way." He turned and followed the noise of her steps as they led him the last few paces home.

After summiting four flights of stairs, they stood at the apartment's door. Daphne couldn't seem to remember which key unfastened the dead bolt and which the doorknob. As she stabbed keys into locks, Haris noticed her unsteady hands. Seeing her nerves, he felt a growing awareness that they were a couple returning late to an empty apartment.

The latch sprung free. Across the living room, the television still flashed muted images from the BBC. Daphne marched toward the console, searching for the remote. The television's light pulsed through the room, reflecting off the mirrored wall. Drunk from the raki, Haris felt his head begin to spin. Daphne found the remote on the floor. She shut off the television. The apartment became dark.

"The light switch is to the right of the sink," she said.

Haris turned it on. The two of them stood quietly beneath a single bulb.

Daphne disappeared into the bedroom.

She returned with some sheets and a blanket. "Give me a hand," she said, standing at one end of the sofa bed. Haris came to the other side. They lifted and thrust down its spine so it expanded, filling the room. "Good night," said Daphne. She flipped off the light switch by the sink, stepping carefully into the bedroom. She left her door open a bit. A single strip of light escaped. Reflected in the wall mirror, Haris caught glimpses of her.

She sat on the edge of her bed and kicked off her heels. Leaning forward, she rubbed her eyes. The bathroom faucet ran. When she came back out, she wore only her shirt. Her strong legs were very white, and there was a vulnerability to her bare feet. When she stepped past the cracked-open door, she didn't close it.

He continued to watch Daphne's reflection in the mirrored wall. She came to her side of the bed, gazing at the little girl's photo. The square jaw and blue eyes. The black curls and handsome face. She turned the portrait a little closer toward her pillow, making small adjustments in the same way she might fix her daughter's dress or hair before taking her from the house.

Daphne stood from the bed and put on a pair of sweatpants. Then she took off her shirt. As she moved around the room, Haris couldn't see all of her, just slices. The unblemished skin on her stomach, the deep scars running behind her shoulders, raw and pink, like wings someone had clipped. Her assured walk through the park, the way she'd strutted with those shoulders pinned back, this was a measure not of her confidence but of her wounds.

Haris heard a gentle creak in the box spring as Daphne climbed beneath her sheets. She didn't turn off the light in the bedroom. And Haris suspected she had left the door open not as a seduction but because she didn't want to be in a closed, dark room by herself. Haris put his pillow at the foot of the sofa bed, so he now faced her door. This way he could watch over her.

But as his head hit the pillow, the room began to spin again. He regretted he'd let himself get so drunk.

The night he came to Haris's room, Jim had been drinking. It was a couple of days after Haris had received his performance bonus, a week after Jim had nearly broken the boy's arm. When Haris opened his door, Jim stood in a pair of board shorts, flip-flops and a tank top. He clutched an emerald-green bottle by the neck. His other hand was tucked beneath his shirt, as if he were warming his palm on the sun tattoo around his navel.

"Mind if I come in?" asked Jim.

The interpreters lived in a sprawl of trailers known as the terp ghetto. Most had roommates, but Haris lived by himself. He gazed past Jim and noticed that the other interpreters who milled about outside were watching them. Americans never came to the terp ghetto.

Haris waved him through the door.

Jim stepped into the center of the small trailer. Looking for a place to sit, he turned in a circle like a dog readying to lie down. A desk, chair, and bed filled the room. Taking the chair for himself, Jim leaned back heavily, balancing his bottle on his knee. Haris perched on the bed.

"About the boy last week—"

"Kareem Tamad," interrupted Haris.

"What?"

"That's his name, Kareem Tamad."

"Yeah, okay, Tamad, about him, what you need to understand is—" Jim philosophized about how in order to make an omelet you sometimes needed to crack a few eggs. He offered well-trod explanations of ends and means. He mentioned something about fear versus love and Machiavelli's *The Prince*. He layered his justifications one upon another as if building a cell to contain the irrefutable fact that he'd just about broken the boy's arm while making his mother watch.

Haris sat on the foot of his bed, barely listening. This was his room. Jim had come uninvited. He remembered when Jim had told Kareem Tamad and his mother, in their own house, they were "free to go." Haris didn't have to endure Jim's speech in his own room.

"I feel differently about it."

Slowly Jim nodded his head, arriving at silence.

"I wish you hadn't come to talk about that," added Haris.

"So let's not talk about it," Jim replied. He leaned forward in his chair, inspecting the bottle he held. "I came by because my wife sent me this for my birthday. And because we're friends, Abadi."

He offered the emerald-green bottle to Haris.

The wax seal on its top had been broken. It was nearly full, but appeared as if Jim had taken a few good sips before mustering the nerve to pay Haris this visit. The writing on the label was in Spanish, scrawled in an elaborate cursive. Haris recognized the word *rum* but no others. He continued to examine the bottle. In his hands, it felt as exotic as the idea of a friendship with Jim. He wasn't sure what to say, so he returned the rum.

"Happy birthday," answered Haris.

Jim held up the bottle by its neck, toasting himself. He took a swig and handed it to Haris, who did the same though he seldom drank.

It burned. "Where's this from?" Haris asked.

"My wife's Colombian," said Jim, reclining in his chair. "I met her down there in the nineties." He lifted up his shirt, pointing to his tattoo. "That's also where I got this—El Sol Eterno."

"The eternal sun," said Haris.

"You speak Spanish?" Jim passed Haris the bottle.

He took another pull. "About as well as you speak Arabic."

Holding up the hem of his tank top, Jim gazed down at his tattoo with the nostalgia of a life viewed in reverse. With age, Jim's girth had bent the sun. Some of its rays now stretched longer than others, like solar flares, and his body hair obscured the image like smog.

"Colombia in the nineties," said Jim. "That was a great war. Not too violent but interesting enough—weeks spent in the jungle, weekends spent in Bogotá. Lots of girls, lots of booze. And I was young."

"And the tattoo?" asked Haris.

Jim nodded. "The early Christians believed your soul existed in your stomach. That's where you felt right and wrong, in your guts. The Incans believed the sun was eternal. Eternal sun on my eternal soul."

"You found your soul down there," said Haris as he drank from the bottle of Colombian rum, taking communion with Jim.

"I guess you could say that."

"Do you think you'll go back?"

"To Colombia? No. I mean, only if my wife makes me. The war's pretty much over there. There'd be no point."

Haris turned up his eyes, drawing a blank.

Jim canted his head, shaking it sympathetically. "It's not what I found in Colombia, bud. It's what I found in the war. This is where I belong."

"What about home?"

"This is home," answered Jim. He took the bottle from Haris and drank. They had emptied nearly a quarter of it.

"By making your home here," said Haris, "you've destroyed mine."

Jim drank again. "Or maybe we're now from the same home."

For a while they didn't speak, sharing the bottle instead.

"Doesn't it ever bother you?" asked Haris.

"The war? I have dreams sometimes, if that's what you mean."

Haris didn't say anything. He stared at Jim, waiting for him to complete his thought.

"It's always the same one," Jim continued, his voice lowering. "I'm on a raid, middle of the night. The breach blows, knocking the front door clean off its hinges. The whole team's behind me and we begin the clear, moving through the house quick. We're like water, just flowing. It all feels good. We find our target in the second room. We cuff him. Behind me, the guys begin their interrogation. I go deeper into the house, finishing the clear. All I can see is the beam from my rifle's flashlight. I corner through a door, coming up on a man with an AK. He turns, but before he swings his rifle around I've already leveled my sight on him. I squeeze the trigger and there's just a hollow *click*. I reach into a pouch on my vest to do a speed reload, but I don't find a magazine. I find a ham sandwich instead. I reach into another pouch. Another ham sandwich. The whole thing plays out in slow motion. All I've got is ham sandwiches."

Haris laughed, snorting the rum in his mouth up through his nose. He pinched his sinuses as it burned his nostrils.

"Yeah, I know," said Jim, and he looked at his feet. "But I wake up and every time I'm scared shitless."

Haris wiped his nose on the back of his hand. "You're not sorry about the boy, are you?"

"The boy? You mean Kareem Tamad," answered Jim, a bemused grin spreading across his face.

Haris felt desperate as he waited for an answer. Jim had spent years at war, and Haris suspected the limited capacity within Jim's soul for compassion would eventually become his own. "Are you sorry?" he asked again.

"No," said Jim, fixing his eyes on Haris. "I'm not sorry."

Haris wanted to ask why. Kareem's grandfather hadn't been the bomb maker. If Jim didn't care about taking in the wrong man, maybe he didn't care about taking in the right man. For Jim, maybe there wasn't a shred of meaning in any of this. Maybe for Jim, the whole war was just an impulse fulfilled.

"So if I'm like you," said Haris, "I never get to go home again. Even if the war ends, this place won't be home anymore. I'll have to go to another place, another war."

"Sometimes it just goes on so long," said Jim, "that you lose the cause in the thing." He lit a cigarette.

Haris reached for the bottle. Jim handed it over. Instead of taking a slug, Haris corked it. "It's late," he said, "and we're drunk." He passed Jim back his rum.

"You're right," Jim replied. "Tomorrow will be busy. I need to start looking for another lead on that bomb maker." He stood, cradling the half-empty bottle. It sloshed beneath his arm as he made for the door. "If we get him, I don't care about Kareem Tamad, his mom, or his granddad. It makes it all worth it."

Jim tugged on the doorknob to let himself out. It wouldn't budge.

Haris came over, leaned into the jamb, and then yanked.

"Thanks," said Jim. He paused on the threshold for a moment, allowing his eyes to adjust to the night. As he did, Haris asked: "How old are you today?"

"Thirty-three."

Dark moons hung beneath Jim's eyes. Sunburnt pustules dotted the tops of his cheeks. His once strong arms hung limply at his sides, a pair of dead weights wearing out his shoulders.

"Next month, I also turn thirty-three," said Haris.

Jim grinned, and the crow's-feet that pinched the edges of his eyes spread across his temples. In the whole of Jim's expression, Haris couldn't find a single patch of skin that wasn't wrinkled, burnt, or touched by some part of his experience.

Before Haris could say anything else, Jim laughed. "Abadi, my friend, for thirty-two, you really look like shit."

It was morning but still dark out. A chill had set into the apartment during the night, causing the pipes in the walls to heave. Beneath his blanket, Haris huddled into himself for warmth. Light flashed against his lidded eyes. Amir stood at the foot of his bed, his back to Haris. He had changed into a pair of powder-blue pajamas with a button-down shirt. The BBC was on with the volume muted. Images flickered from the screen, edging out Amir's silhouette while he ate a bowl of cornflakes and read a ticker of scrolling headlines. He took his bites sloppily, occasionally using the sleeve of his pajamas to wipe milk from his chin.

Haris sat up on the sofa bed.

"Apologies," whispered Amir. "I didn't think it'd wake you."

"I wasn't sleeping anyhow."

Amir lifted his bowl to his lips, drinking the last of the milk. He again wiped his chin with his sleeve. He didn't appear sober, but he did appear to be sobering up. The cornflakes seemed to help.

"Won't you get some rest?" asked Haris.

Amir's head swiveled over his shoulder, toward the bedroom. A seam of light poured from behind the cracked-open door where Daphne slept. Amir sat on the foot of the sofa bed, next to Haris. "Not in there," he said. "Her light keeps me up."

"Has she always done that?"

Amir turned off the BBC. Without the news, the glare from Daphne's door seemed brighter. Amir drew his eyes to the apartment's window and Antep's blinking skyline. "When we came here she started sleeping with the lights on and the door open. It's been almost a year."

"When you first arrived, how long did you think you'd stay?"

"Who knows? We came from Aleppo for the hospital. Daphne had been badly hurt in the accident where we lost our daughter, Kifa." Amir took his empty bowl to the sink. Water sputtered and coughed out of the faucet. He turned quickly toward the bedroom, concerned the noise might wake Daphne. Then the water came quietly and he washed his bowl. "Delvet Hospital, where Daphne volunteers, that's where I took her."

Across the park the muezzin cried the morning prayer, bringing Amir to silence. Haris gazed out the window. Dawn broke just below the cityscape—satellite dishes on rooftops, a picket of minarets. The birds took off from their perches and flew, very black against the early sun. Amir held his face in his hands, exhausted, as if he wished to sleep but couldn't.

"All I want is to be rid of here," he told Haris. "Daphne has family abroad, we'd have somewhere to go, but she won't leave." Amir lay himself on the sofa bed, throwing his arm over his eyes, blocking out the daylight, which slowly filled the room. "She can't even remember the accident. What she's learned of her loss, she's learned from me."

Haris stared at him for a while. "What'll you do?"

"I'll stay," said Amir. "I'll work with Marty, conduct research, earn a good living." He rolled his head to the side, glancing toward the apartment's front door, as if into the place he'd come from earlier that evening. "I'm sorry I left you tonight. Latia and I go back a long way."

Amir threw his arm back over his eyes. His mouth opened again as if he might say something more. Haris leaned toward him, listening.

Amir began to snore.

Outside, the sun dangled above the horizon, brightening the living room. Haris took his blanket from his shoulders and threw it over Amir. As he did, he heard the light in Daphne's room switch off.

While Amir slept, Haris thought to make himself useful and fix breakfast. In a cabinet above the sink and in the small fridge he found ingredients: flour, sugar, eggs. In his old life, he'd used the same to cook pancakes for Samia on the weekends. He whisked everything in a bowl and plugged in the hot plate. Its coil soon glowed red. He couldn't find any butter or oil to grease the skillet. From the bowl, he poured the batter into disks, which heated to porousness. Then Haris flipped the pancakes. They steamed and spat.

From Daphne's room, Haris heard the shower running. He thought of her last night, her scars and white skin. He wondered how the hot water felt against her scars, if it pained her or if the steam softened them. He looked at the mirrored wall. The angle found Amir, his reflection stirred on the sofa bed, his snores broke into heavy breathing as he edged awake. Amir pulled the blanket over his head, burying himself in it, struggling to remain asleep.

The shower shut off.

Haris turned away from the mirror, glancing directly at Daphne's slightly unclosed door. Her shadow was cast across the bed. Haris wondered what she was doing—holding the portrait of Kifa, writing in her journal, looking at her scars in the mirror?

He smelled the pancakes burning.

Haris snatched a fork, scraping beneath each one. They stuck to the skillet, lightly smoking up from its bottom. Haris turned off the hot plate. A scrambled heap of cooked batter remained for breakfast.

As he scooped it onto a single dish, Daphne ambled into the living room. She wore the same clothes—the blue trench coat, the red sunglasses perched on her head. She made for the door and then stopped, breathed the air, and found Haris bent over the skillet.

"Breakfast?" she said.

Amir stirred again on the sofa bed.

Haris looked at the mess. "I used to make this for my sister."

He handed her a fork, and they stood above the plate, eating the broken pancakes together. The wet blond ends of Daphne's hair were brushed back and cupped upward at the base of her neck. Standing close, Haris breathed in her freshly rinsed smell. Neither spoke. They didn't want to wake Amir. This wasn't out of courtesy to him. The quiet space they shared was something new, something they were trying out.

Daphne looked intently at Haris as she ate. Haris wondered how, with more time, they might come to know each other. The thought frightened him, but he held it in his mind. He felt an instinct to protect her, and this presented the possibility that she could undo him, that he could abandon the border for her. He knew this because he had felt the same instinct with Samia. His sacrifices for her, they had undone him in the same way.

Amir groaned, waking to the full force of his hangover.

Haris understood why Amir didn't want to return and, pragmatic as that decision was, Daphne seemed betrayed by his wish to move on, by his ability to accept all they had lost. Of course Haris couldn't abandon the border for her.

They finished the plate of scrambled pancakes. Daphne glanced over at Amir. Seeing her husband sprawled out and asleep in his powder-blue pajamas, she grabbed Haris by the elbow. "Good morning," she whispered.

Haris moved to the faucet to rinse the plate and skillet. Water again coughed loudly from the pipes. Before Daphne could make her way out the door, Amir grumbled: "What time is it?"

Her hand froze on the dead bolt. "Just after nine."

Amir hacked into the bend of his elbow. His eyes searched the room. "Is he still here?"

"Are you still here?" Daphne asked Haris, her eyes meeting his.

"Good morning," Haris said, directing his words to Amir but also to Daphne.

"Will you take him to Marty's?" Daphne asked.

Amir rose from the sofa bed. He crossed the room, standing in front of the wall's mirror. Taking a set of clippers from the dresser, he began cutting his nails, except on the two fingers which had pink callused pads where the nails should have been. With a comb he tamed down his curls, speaking toward his reflection: "After last night, I don't think anyone at Marty's will be up until the afternoon. We'll have better luck if we try tomorrow."

Daphne turned toward Haris, a question in her gaze. Haris knew he'd eventually have to leave the apartment and, realizing Amir usually slept on the sofa bed, he knew it was time to go. "I can come meet you tomorrow," he said, "if that's better."

"And stay where?" asked Daphne.

Haris looked out of the window, toward the park.

"You're not sleeping out there with Daphne's friends," said Amir. "We've plenty of room. Marty will be glad to know you, so you'll stay until I sort that out."

Haris nodded a silent thank-you. He started the washing-up in the sink.

"Are you headed to the hospital?" Amir asked Daphne.

She stood quietly by the door, finally saying yes.

"Take Haris with you," suggested Amir. He turned to Haris. "You'll be bored here, and I'd like to get a bit more sleep. Plus, you'll keep Daphne company."

Haris turned toward her. Daphne busied herself with buttoning up her coat, betraying none of her preference. Haris didn't move. He wasn't sure what to do until Daphne threw him a sidelong glance.

Haris put on the cable-knit sweater Amir had lent him and tied his boots. As he dressed, Amir sniffed the air. "Smells good in here. What'd you make, Daphne?"

Before Haris could say anything, Daphne spoke deliberately, as if baiting a trap: "I made pancakes."

Amir turned from his reflection to look at his wife. He seemed moved that she'd cook for him. "You wouldn't mind fixing me a plate, would you?"

"There's none left," she said. Her eyes fell on Haris as she spoke to her husband: "You've slept too long."

Their cab pulled around the curved driveway of Delvet Hospital. Daphne took a fold of lira from her coat pocket. Holding it low, between her knees, she counted out the fare. Haris thanked her as she passed the bills to the driver, mentioning how he would pay her back. She said nothing.

Beyond the entrance's sliding glass door, a receptionist sat bunkered behind a tall desk. She wore a clean white hijab and typed at a computer. She glanced up as Daphne passed. The two greeted each other, speaking for a bit in Turkish. As they did, Haris considered the hospital. The buffed linoleum corridors gleamed beneath fluorescent bulbs. Doctors ducked in and out of private patient rooms. Nurses wheeled carts filled with medications down the ward, or they picked up trays of discarded food from the morning's breakfast.

Daphne and the receptionist finished whatever matter they'd been discussing. The receptionist skimmed her eyes over Haris. Before she could say anything, Daphne added some last point in Turkish. The woman laughed, waving them past as she went back to work.

Haris and Daphne continued down the corridor. "What was that about?"

"She wanted to know who you were."

Haris cocked his head.

"I told her not to worry, you weren't another Amir."

"She knows Amir?" he asked.

"Let's just say since we've been here, Amir has gotten to know lots of the nurses. That's why she laughed."

The two stood in front of an elevator bank. Daphne pushed the down button.

"It's a nice hospital," said Haris.

Daphne gazed along the pristine corridor. "I suppose this part is." She pushed the button again. "They treat Syrians in the basement. The receptionist asked me to help with a man there. It's time for him to leave."

They stepped inside the elevator. Just before they reached the basement, a sweet, stale smell like a mix of tainted water and spoiled food, all blanketed by a sharp chemical antiseptic, pricked Haris's nostrils. The doors opened, and a dank heat enveloped them. Within moments sweat beaded along the arch of Haris's back, beneath his sweater.

Along the basement corridor, parallel to the fluorescent bulbs overhead, heating pipes ran, dripping condensation. No one had buffed the floors and, at the places where the pipes dripped, concentric circles of brown water damage cratered the linoleum tiles. A few private rooms dotted the corridor, but there weren't enough of them. Cots spilled into the hall, each partitioned by little more than a rod and curtain, or nothing at all. Food trays littered the way, but unlike upstairs, not a morsel was left on them. Even if patients weren't well enough to eat, their families hoarded the remnants of their meals. Most of the families, as Haris had learned the night before, slept in Antep City Park.

Haris followed Daphne to a door halfway down the hall. She

stopped before entering and turned toward him. "I'm going to need your help in here."

"Of course," said Haris.

"This patient's brother, a man named Jalindar, brought him from Azaz," said Daphne. "He's been comatose for nearly a month. Yesterday the hospital told Jalindar they could no longer treat his brother. But Jalindar won't leave. He's in there with his nephew, the patient's son."

"What do you need me to do?"

"Play with the boy while I talk with Jalindar," she said.

Haris shrugged. The task seemed easy enough.

"The boy is complicated," said Daphne.

"Complicated?"

"Jalindar and his brother are twins," Daphne continued. "Jalindar had spent a few years working in Kilis away from the family. After his brother was hurt, when Jalindar crossed the border into Azaz to get him, the boy thought his father had recovered. Before that, the boy had only seen his uncle once or twice. Jalindar hasn't explained things yet."

"That doesn't seem right," said Haris.

"You think it's better to explain all of this to a little boy?"

Haris didn't have an answer. "What's the boy's name?"

"Daoud."

Daphne opened the door. Haris followed her inside. Tucked into the corner, a quarter-size window circulated cool, fresh air. A rectangle of light fell from the window, landing in a band along the single bed, which filled most of the room. The bandaged carapace spread across the sheets was barely recognizable as a man. A leg and arm were missing. The face covering left only a wandering eye and half-gaping mouth exposed. The IV stands hung around the bed, keeping the man alive through some hydraulic mystery. The only movement Haris saw was the clear liquid which passed through these tubes. A gust of wind slipped in through the window. The man's free eye blinked wildly for a moment, twitching at the breeze. Then the air stilled and the man's vacant look returned.

On a wooden footstool next to the bed sat Jalindar, his wiry torso hunched forward, his elbows balanced on his knees, clutching a newspaper. He'd been reading aloud to his brother, but choked his words off as soon as Haris and Daphne entered.

"A friend of mine's joining us," said Daphne. "I hope you don't mind."

Jalindar shook his head, standing from his footstool and tucking his newspaper beneath his arm. He offered his seat to Daphne, and his hand to Haris, who shook it. She waved his offer away and sat on the floor with her back to the wall. An awkward silence hung in the room. Haris at first assumed that Daphne would ask after Jalindar's brother, or that Jalindar would tell her how his brother was doing. But the situation became evident. Jalindar seemed to know what Daphne had come to tell him, and Daphne wouldn't do him the discourtesy of asking questions about his brother's condition, the answers to which she had no interest in.

Haris broke the silence: "You must be Daoud. What've you got there?"

In the corner of the room nearest the door, the little boy sat cross-legged on the floor. He leaned over a magnetic tic-tac-toe board, playing by himself. He couldn't have been much older than six. "A gift from my baba," he told Haris.

Haris glanced at the inanimate heap of bandages and plaster in the bed beneath the window. Daoud's eyes didn't rest there, though. When he spoke of his father, he spoke of Jalindar.

"I'm glad you like it," said Jalindar. He crouched next to the boy, cupping his cheek in his hand.

Daoud smiled at him and returned to his game.

A young doctor in a threadbare lab coat stood in the threshold, shuffling a ream of patient records. When he saw Daphne, he greeted her in Turkish, ignoring everyone else. He didn't approach the bed. He stayed in the doorway. The doctor's visit wasn't about the patient.

Jalindar came to his twin's bedside. He hovered over the broken body, as if readying himself to defend it. Daphne and the doctor continued in Turkish. The doctor's words accelerated, moving toward exasperation. His gaze fell intently on Jalindar, who now stood with his back to the bed, his arms clutching its frame at either end as if he tended a goal.

The doctor paused. He looked at Daphne, expecting her to translate. Before she did, she turned to Haris. "Why don't you take Daoud out in the hall?"

Haris smiled at the boy, who stared nervously at Jalindar.

"Whatever you have to say, you can say in front . . ." Jalindar's words trailed off, lacking any conviction.

"Come," Haris said to the boy. "We'll have a game outside."

"Baba?" the boy said to Jalindar, his eyes small and black with fear.

"It's okay," assured Haris. He lifted the boy gently beneath the elbow and picked up the game of tic-tac-toe, leading him into the corridor.

Daoud looked back toward Jalindar, confused by their separation, willing his uncle to make some protest. Planted in the doorway, the young doctor stood with his arms folded across his chest. Jalindar said nothing to the boy, but kept his grip fixed to his brother's bedframe as if in that grip he held on to a chance, no matter how remote, that what had been destroyed could be restored.

Haris led Daoud from the room, pushing past the doctor. He shut the door behind him, and it closed with an unexpected slam, startling the boy.

The corridor was quiet. A jumble of cots, filled with patients surrounded by their families, sprawled in every direction. An occasional nurse or doctor circulated among the cots, never finishing with one patient before the next called after them. Just outside the doorway, Haris and the boy sat side by side, their backs to the wall. Between them, Haris spread out the tic-tac-toe game.

They began to play.

Daoud placed a tiled O in the center of the top row. Haris put an X in the upper-right corner. Daoud placed another O in the board's center. Haris blocked him in the bottom center. Daoud moved to the center-right column. Haris blocked him again. Between moves, Haris considered letting Daoud win. He didn't, though, and they played to a draw.

"Again?" asked Daoud, dissatisfied at the result.

Haris cleared the board and let Daoud begin. "Your first move should go in the corners or center."

Daoud didn't say anything, and again they came to a draw.

"I don't want to play anymore," said Daoud.

"That's not right."

"When I play against Baba, I usually win."

"I'm not your father," said Haris, laughing a bit.

This angered Daoud. He cleared the rest of the pieces. They played again and Haris won.

Daoud stared at the board. A row of diagonal Xs ran across it. The little boy anxiously picked his nose, his grubby fingernails edged in dirt. He needed a bath, and his spiteful gaze remained fixed on the board. He seemed unable to set it up for another round. Haris knew he should feel sorry for this child—his dying father, his masquerading uncle—and he wondered if at some subconscious level the little boy knew the truth. A part of Haris felt the boy deserved a small victory. A game of tic-tac-toe.

The boy picked his nose again.

"You shouldn't do that either," said Haris.

"You're not playing fair!" snapped Daoud. He bounded to his feet and bolted toward the hospital room.

Haris lunged after him, catching his wrist. Daoud picked up the tic-tac-toe board and flung it down the corridor. Its edge caught Haris across the temple. Daoud shook free from Haris's grasp and pushed through the door to where his father was. Haris followed.

In the room, Jalindar sat on the stool. He had pulled it up to his brother's bedside. Across the foot of the bed, the doctor had spread forms, which Jalindar signed as Daphne explained them one by one.

"I'm sorry," said Haris. "He got away from me."

Daoud clutched his uncle's leg. He cried, burying his face in Jalindar's lap, his breath coming in little huffs. Haris froze in the threshold. Jalindar was silent. He gently rested his hand against the side of Daoud's head. The boy kept crying as Jalindar signed the last few forms. Once he was done, the Turkish doctor gathered the papers, returning them to the ream he carried. He spoke some last point to Daphne, who nodded as he strode out the door.

"If you want to take a few minutes to gather your things, that's fine," she told Jalindar.

He looked into the room's empty corners.

Daphne nodded to Haris, and they both stepped outside.

Standing in the corridor, Haris asked how she'd convinced Jalindar to leave.

"I threatened to tell Daoud about his father if he insisted on staying."

"That seems cruel."

"Look at that boy," said Daphne. "You think he doesn't already know?"

She was right, Haris thought. Daoud knew. As much as the boy needed the lie, he knew. "Where will they go?" he asked.

"If they leave now, I promised to take care of their bus fare back to Kilis. The boy will live with his uncle. He's lucky."

Haris wandered down the corridor. Strewn across it were the small X and O tiles from the tic-tac-toe game. He gathered them up along with the board. Just as he finished, Jalindar stepped from his brother's hospital room, carrying Daoud in his arms.

The boy rested his cheek on his uncle's shoulder, looking backward, toward his father.

Jalindar walked by Daphne. At first he ignored her but, after just a few steps he turned around, patting his front pocket, where he'd put the bus fare she'd given him. "Thank you," he said.

Daphne dipped her eyes to the floor.

Before Jalindar could go farther, Haris ran up to him. "This is his."

He offered Daoud the tic-tac-toe pieces and board. The boy refused them, burying his face in the crook of his uncle's neck. Jalindar took the game instead, cramming it into the same pocket as their bus fare.

"Why did your game upset him?" asked Daphne while she and Haris watched the two head toward the elevator.

"I wouldn't let him cheat," said Haris.

"You wouldn't let him cheat, or you wouldn't let him win?"

"Letting him win is cheating."

All through that morning and into the afternoon, Haris helped. When a surplus of medical supplies arrived from the hospital's upper floors, Haris inventoried and stacked the myriad cardboard boxes in a storage closet. When lunch arrived from the cafeteria, he joined the nurses who passed out the trays. And, in the brief moments when he had nothing to do, he watched Daphne negotiate between the Syrian families and the Turkish medical staff everything from the position of a cot in the hallway to the cocktail of medications a patient received.

Shortly after lunch, as Haris gathered empty food trays along the corridor, the young Turkish doctor with the threadbare lab coat returned. A squat, ancient nurse plodded alongside him, her chin leading her body forward. The two stepped into the room containing Daoud's father. Haris looked up and down the corridor for Daphne, but he couldn't find her. He wondered where she'd gone, and quickly realized she'd known what was coming. She had decided not to watch.

A few moments later the nurse and doctor pushed the bandaged, broken man out of the room on a litter. Disconnected from his trickling IV bags, he'd become wholly inanimate. Until his death, his life would be an issue of storage somewhere in the hospital. No one looked in his direction as he passed by, but all along the corridor the chattering families fell to silence. The stubborn squeak of a loose wheel wobbling against his litter's axle became the only noise.

Haris felt a tingling in the hinge of his jaw, an aftertaste of electricity. The memory and sensation of his paralyzed body splayed in the sodden earth returned. He pressed his fingertips into the sides of his legs. This minor act of dexterity calmed him. He remembered how Athid had betrayed him at the border, abandoning him in no-man's-land. This unfeeling, unknowing man was about to be abandoned in the same way. Haris swallowed. He could do nothing.

The doctor and nurse didn't push the litter toward the elevator. Instead, they unlocked a steel door at the corridor's far end. The doctor kicked a wedge beneath it. Haris caught a glimpse of a ramp, sloping down, to a level beneath the basement. Somewhere deep under the hospital Daoud's father would remain out of sight.

Haris finished his rounds, picking up the last empty lunch trays. A hollow chime came from the elevator. It opened, and a single nurse wheeled a handcart toward the dying man's now vacant room. Stacked atop the handcart were another patient's personal effects. A familiar black parka caught Haris's eye. He looked closer: folded next to it was the red Che T-shirt.

III

Saied was somewhere in the hospital. Outside the door of the vacant room, Haris paced the narrow width of the corridor while his eyes roamed up and down its length. His breath was shallow, nervous, but slowed as he set his mind to what he needed to do. He would confront Saied and demand what had been stolen. With his money back, Haris could at least pay for a taxi to the border. But how would he cross? The border was closed. Then, if he did cross, where would he go? His one contact, Saladin1984, had disappeared. And would Saied still have his money? Likely not.

Within moments, Haris's convictions melted away. Saied had taken all he had and given him an excuse to do nothing, to remain safely in Antep. The Free Army was dissolving. Had he come here to fight *against* the regime, which he could still do alongside the Daesh, or *for* the revolution's democratic ideals, which seemed hopeless? *Against* seemed the sole alternative as a thought returned:

Letting him win is cheating.

In the days before Jim's death, Haris had felt certain he'd been cheated by him. Another IED had clacked off just outside

Hurricane Point's main gate a few mornings after Jim's birthday. Once again, the bomber had used a baby monitor as a trigger. The blast had woken everyone. Haris watched from one of the sentry towers as Jim shuffled out the gate wearing his board shorts and flip-flops, his rifle slung on his shoulder. He climbed into the crater's still-smoking belly and recovered a coral-pink transponder. When he came back, he dropped it in the middle of the team room. Into that afternoon and evening, Jim pored over old target files and intel reports, trying to piece together the bomber's identity. Through a process that seemed more divination than analysis, he assembled a short list of five suspects. One of the five was another member of Kareem Tamad's family, his uncle.

"He's an old man," Haris told Jim, looking at the dog-eared dossier photo.

Their office was empty. The rest of the team had left for dinner. Jim sat shirtless behind his plywood desk, two computer monitors projecting their glow against his face. He peered above them at Haris, who sat in a folding chair by the door.

"Who's an old man?"

"Hassan Tamad," said Haris, holding up the photo. "Kareem's uncle."

"Your point?"

"You know it's not him."

"I don't know it isn't him."

Jim tucked back behind his computer, returning to his work. Haris got up from his chair and left. He would've said more, but Jim didn't know where Hassan Tamad lived or how to find him. There seemed little point in pressing the issue.

Then a couple of days later Kareem Tamad got picked up by the Iraqi Police.

The night of the raid, Jim had logged Kareem and his mother as persons of interest in BATS—Biometric Automated Toolset System—a nationwide law enforcement database. When Kareem got stopped at a checkpoint driving with some friends, the police searched the car and cross-referenced his identity card within BATS. Jim's log entry then earned Kareem a visit to a holding cell on Hurricane Point.

It was evening when Jim knocked on Haris's door. In the crook of Jim's arm Haris looked for a bottle, imagining no other reason for him to visit the terp ghetto again. But when Haris saw Jim wearing his desert camouflage uniform, he knew they wouldn't be drinking.

"The Iraqis brought the boy in."

"The boy?"

"Yeah, the boy—Kareem Tamad."

Haris put on a uniform to match Jim's. He wished Jim had worn his usual board shorts and tank top, at least that might differentiate them. He dreaded the idea of the interrogation to come and didn't want to stand in front of Kareem wearing the same uniform as Jim.

They arrived at the detention facility wedged into Hurricane Point's far corner. Jim swung open the heavy steel gate. Welded to its front was the Ba'ath Party's eight-pointed star. Haris thought how ignorant the Americans were to disband the Iraqi army, civil service, and police as part of de-Ba'athification while leaving these symbols up and erecting their bases in Saddam's old palaces.

Inside the one-story blockhouse, an American soldier from the Military Police sat at a plywood desk. Ragged copies of *Star* and *Us* magazines rested in stacks on its corners, flanking a black phone. Absentmindedly the MP thumbed through the worn pages, each one limp as a wet rag. Tucked into his bottom lip, an enormous chaw blackened his teeth.

He stood when he saw Jim. "All right there, Sarge."

"All right," answered Jim. He fished a folded piece of paper from his cargo pocket. "I've got an interrogation clearance for Kareem Tamad." He spread the form flat on the desk, next to the phone. The MP dialed a long sequence of numbers. Holding on the line, he pulled an envelope of chewing tobacco from his pocket. He offered a plug to Jim, who refused, but none to Haris.

The MP hung up the phone. "No answer," he said. "Here are his personal effects." From the desk drawer, he handed Jim a zip-locked evidence bag. "You can get started. I'll try again in a bit. Tamad's in lucky-number thirteen." The MP folded the interrogation clearance in half and slid it into his copy of *Star.*

The light switch to cell thirteen sat on the wall by its solid steel door. In the outside world, the sun decided night and day. In the cell, that power resided with the jailer.

Jim seemed to understand this. He flicked off the switch. He flicked it back on. Kareem's shadow frantically broke up the sliver of light which leaked from the foot of the cell door. Then Jim flicked the switch off and left it off. Nervous sounds, like pacing footsteps and a chair or desk being moved, came from the darkness inside.

"Let's give him a bit more time like that," said Jim.

Haris fixed his eyes on the ground.

"I just want to know where his uncle lives, okay?"

Haris didn't reply.

"OKAY?"

"Okay," said Haris, staring at the switch.

Jim took a heavy breath, turning the lights back on. "It's his fault if he's afraid of the dark."

You're a liar, thought Haris. A rush of hot blood shot from his stomach to his limbs. Feeling it, he thought of Jim's tattoo, what he had said about the soul residing in your guts. Jim knew Kareem wasn't scared of the dark—he was scared of being helpless. The hot blood in Haris's guts proved to him his soul still felt, even if Jim's didn't.

Jim opened the cell door. Haris followed.

Kareem sat in a metal folding chair. Without saying anything, Jim flex-cuffed Kareem's right wrist to one of its legs. Filling the cell, a plastic table rested just beyond Kareem's reach. Jim emptied the bag with Kareem's personal effects across it: pocket change, cigarettes, a comb, a cellphone. Pulled up to the table was a wheeled and cushioned office chair. Jim sat in the chair, fiddled with the mechanics underneath it, and reclined heavily, having loosened the back support. Haris stood, leaning his shoulder against the cold cinder-block wall, just to the side.

"Remember me?" asked Jim, pointing to Kareem's sprained left arm, the one that hadn't been flex-cuffed and now hung in a sling.

Haris translated, but instead of simply repeating the words as he usually did, he appended a "he says" to each statement, as if this distanced him by some degree from Jim.

"I remember you," said Kareem.

Haris couldn't tell if the *you* he referred to was him or Jim.

From his cargo pocket, Jim removed a satellite map of Ramadi and a photograph of Kareem's uncle. He held up the photograph and pointed to the map. "Where does he live?"

Kareem's expression knotted, as if he didn't understand the satellite image being shown to him. This was expected. Most Iraqis couldn't comprehend the idea of an overhead image. They knew direction from a vantage no higher than the ground.

Jim had once told Haris a story about an informant of his, a man who helped him track an insurgent commander named Abu Yahya. The informant often reported on the aftereffects of drone strikes, hanging out around the rubble to confirm who'd been killed. One day he arrived at Hurricane Point to report on a strike which had just missed Abu Yahya. While the informant chomped peanuts from a tin and drank lukewarm Coke, Jim asked how he'd learned the details of what had happened. The informant told Jim he'd heard Abu Yahya talking in his cousin's grocery store, a locale the commander frequented. Jim became excited, wanting to know where the grocery store was. Perhaps it could be targeted for a similar strike.

When Jim pulled out a satellite map, his informant gave the same blank-eyed look as Kareem. "Pretend," said Jim, "that you are like a hawk." He waved his hands, imitating broad wings. "And you are flying over your home." Still the informant couldn't conceptualize the map laid before him, or how to be a hawk. "Okay," said Jim, "let's pick a place you know and you can walk me to your cousin's shop from there." The informant smiled through his mouthful of peanuts. He could do this. "How about the bus station downtown?" asked Jim, but the informant still looked confused. He slurped his Coke. "Or the central police headquarters? Can you tell me how to get to your cousin's shop from there?" The informant shook his head no. Becoming frustrated, Jim said: "Start from a place everybody knows, anyplace, and tell me how to get to your cousin's shop." The informant set down his peanuts. "A place everybody knows?" he asked, his voice wandering. Then an enlightened smile flashed across his face. "How about I show you how to get to my cousin's shop from Abu Yahya's house!" At this point in the story, Jim folded his arms and leaned back. "So I told him, why don't you just show me where Abu Yahya's house is." Then Jim laughed and muttered to himself: "Ignorant fucks."

Now Jim leaned over the satellite image on the desk, telling Kareem: "We're going to find him with or without you."

"You don't need my help then," Kareem answered.

Jim shrugged. "You're right," he said. Hovering over the table, he sorted through Kareem's things with feigned interest. "I don't need your help." He picked up the comb, teasing out his auburn beard, grinning at Kareem. "But I want it." With his other hand, he played with the cellphone, flipping through the contacts. "Who's this?" Jim asked, holding the screen up to Kareem's face as he scrolled number to number. "Your mother? Brother? We've got their info now." Jim pulled a pad from his pocket and scribbled down phone numbers and names. With his wrist bound to the chair, Kareem sat as straight as he could.

Finally, Jim placed the cellphone back on the table. He crouched next to Kareem. "Translate exactly what I'm saying," he told Haris. "We," said Jim.

Haris paused a second. "We," he repeated in Arabic.

"Can do this the easy way." Jim spat the words in a hot whisper next to Kareem's ear.

Haris repeated them.

"Or the hard way," said Jim. Before Haris could translate, Jim gently squeezed Kareem's left elbow in its sling, applying more and more pressure until the boy bucked in his chair, gritting his teeth.

Jim released his grip. Sweat trickled over Kareem's temples, running through the peach fuzz on his cheeks. "Show me on the map," said Jim.

Kareem didn't reply but began to pant, overcome by the pain in his slung arm. Jim glanced at Haris, who stood by the wall. "Tell him I'll break his other arm if he doesn't tell me."

Before Haris could translate there was a knock at the door. The MP walked in. "Uh, Sarge—" He paused a moment, surveying the scene. "Headquarters doesn't have a copy of your interrogation clearance. You want to hop on the phone and help sort this out?"

Jim stepped away from Kareem, putting the table between them.

"Yeah, all right," said Jim. He walked outside.

The door shut, and Kareem's breath slowed. He levered himself upright in his seat. Jim's cushioned office chair sat empty, but Haris chose to stay leaning against the wall. He felt Kareem's hateful gaze on him but said nothing. Eventually, Haris glanced back. "What he said is true," he told Kareem.

"That my uncle is the bomber?"

"No, that he'll find him with or without your help."

"Then why bother speaking with me?"

"If you tell us," said Haris, "it will take less time."

Kareem laughed. He craned his neck against his shoulder in order to wipe the sweat and tears from his face. "Time? What should I care about your time? You want the Americans to stay as long as possible so you can keep collecting their money."

"That's not why I work with them," said Haris. As he uttered the words, his mind raced to find the reason. After the invasion, the reason was inevitability. Their will was inevitable. Their wealth was inevitable. Any man with reason wanted a job with the Americans. These years later, in this room, Haris felt their reason and his own slipping away.

Whether through mercy or disinterest the boy sat quietly, not asking Haris for answers. Don't look at me with pity, thought Haris. You're the one bound to a chair, your arm in a sling. He was certain the boy could read these words in his expression.

"If you'd let me help you, I would," offered Haris. He stepped toward Kareem, who flinched, jerking back in his chair. Haris knelt, took a knife from his belt, and cut loose the plastic flex-cuff. His hand now free, Kareem made an orbit with his wrist, working the stiffness from it. Haris took the pack of cigarettes from the table. He offered one to Kareem and took one himself.

While they smoked, Haris listened intently outside. He could hear Jim's muffled phone conversation and he prayed Jim wouldn't return at that moment.

"How can you help me?" asked Kareem.

"I don't want your uncle taken in the way your grandfather was."

Kareem shrugged, as if this too was inevitable.

"If you tell me where your uncle lives," said Haris, "I'll warn you when the Americans come for him."

"And why would you do that?"

"Because they're wrong, and I want to be in the right for once," said Haris. "I believe you, your uncle, your grandfather, all of you, have nothing to do with these bombings."

Kareem took a few silent drags, his mind seeming to work over the possibility of what Haris offered. "And if I don't?"

Haris nodded toward the door. "He comes back in this room."

"And you?"

"I translate."

Kareem stubbed out his cigarette on the bottom of his chair. He leaned forward and sat the butt on the table next to the rest of his things.

"You swear this?" he asked.

Haris nodded, and took a piece of paper and pen from his pocket.

With his one good hand, Kareem sketched a map to his uncle's house from Hurricane Point. Haris held the sheet of paper still for him. The two worked together, speaking quietly as Kareem annotated the route in detail, marking each turn with some landmark. Once they had finished, Haris punched Kareem's cellphone number into his own. He tested the number, and Kareem's phone vibrated on the desk.

Jim returned to the room. When he saw Kareem leaning over the table and freed from his seat, his eyes widened, becoming insufficient apertures to contain his anger. Immediately, Haris held up the map. "He told me where his uncle lives."

Jim snatched the sketch from Haris and looked it over. "You sure he's telling the truth?"

Haris nodded, feeling certain about this.

Kareem sat back down, and Jim towered over him, holding the sketch toward his face. "You know what we'll do if you're bullshitting us?"

Kareem nodded as if he knew.

Jim nodded as well, as if he knew.

Jim and Haris left the cell, shutting its door behind them. They stepped into the hall and walked past the MP, who still sat at his desk reading.

"Done already?" he asked. "That was fast."

Jim said nothing, but left his interrogation clearance and Kareem's personal effects on the MP's desk.

The steel gate with its eight-pointed star creaked open as Haris and Jim stepped outside. The evening had turned to night, and with it came a chill. Jim pulled a small flashlight from his pocket and took another glance at the map. "Looks good," he said. "I know just about where this is."

Haris said nothing.

"How the hell did you get him to talk?" asked Jim.

Haris paused, his eyes resting on the orange halo of floodlights that illuminated Hurricane Point. These marked the way back to his trailer in the terp ghetto. "I said if he didn't tell you, he'd be left in a dark cell until we found his uncle and that this would take a very, very long time."

Jim laughed softly. He kicked at the dirt with the toe of his desert-suede combat boot, and then he rested a heavy palm on Haris's shoulder. "See, Abadi, I told you. They're all afraid of the dark. Ignorant fucks."

Haris found Daphne in the cafeteria on the hospital's ground floor. She sat at a table by herself, next to a wide bay window. A block of afternoon sun washed out the room, glinting against the quartz stud she wore. A cup of tea sat in front of her, its saucer resting on a pile of broken sugar packets. Her red sunglasses covered her eyes. Haris sat next to her. She didn't move. He touched her shoulder. She startled awake, pushing her sunglasses up her head. With her fingertips, she wiped the sleep from her eyes.

"You all right?" asked Haris.

She blinked a few times. "I'm fine," she said. "I don't sleep well at home." She looked at him, his expression alive with whatever he'd just seen. "You all right?"

"I've found something," he said, and told her about Saied, the robbery at the border, the red Che T-shirt in the basement. His story poured quickly from him, the sentences blending and pursuing each other, becoming barely intelligible in places, but conveying the essential facts of what had happened. Daphne nodded steadily, taking a few sips of her tea, which had turned cold over the course of her nap.

"I'm not sure I understand," she said.

Haris froze, his mind doubling back over all he'd told her. "What do you mean you don't understand?"

Daphne rested her tea on the saucer. "Why don't you just go down there and get your stuff back?" she asked.

"Without some leverage, Saied won't return what he took."

"You think I'm leverage?"

"He's a thief," said Haris. "He's committed a crime. You could tell the hospital staff to remove him."

"If they removed every Syrian who'd committed a crime, the hospital basement would be empty!" A few tables down, a pair of nurses stared at Daphne. She spoke more softly. "Three years of this has turned honest people into criminals. He is probably, like you, a good man."

"All I want is to cross the border," said Haris. "If you won't help because of what he did to me, help because I'm willing to cross when so many aren't."

"I never said I wouldn't help."

Haris smiled at Daphne. She returned a sharp look, which cooled his enthusiasm. "But I won't help under the assumption that you're a good man punishing a bad one," she added. "I'm exhausted by those ideas. He took something from you. You're going to take it back, nothing more. Agreed?"

Haris nodded, and they stood, leaving the brightly lit cafeteria for the elevator bank. As Daphne threw away her tea, she leaned over to Haris. "I wonder what he did before the war."

"Not sure, why do you ask?"

"Just curious," said Daphne. "I guess none of that matters."

Haris turned the doorknob and pressed the jamb with the toe of his boot. It was unlocked. Daphne stood behind him. Her eyes ran along the corridor, checking that none of the hospital staff saw them creep inside. The other patients watched with a languorous curiosity, interested, but too tired to question what Haris and Daphne wanted with this man.

The door hinges creaked as they entered. A shutter covered the window in the room's top corner. Neither could see a thing. Haris shut the door behind them, pressing the button on the knob's top. It locked with a metallic click. Across the room came a rustling of sheets.

"I'm supposed to rest," spoke a weak, sleepy voice. Haris recognized it immediately, feeling a swell of relief. He then groped for a moment by the near wall, until Daphne's assured hand located the light switch. She flipped it on.

Saied clamped his eyes shut. "I told you, I'm supposed to rest."

He lay on his back, swaddled below the waist in white bed linens. A light blue hospital blanket was draped over his shoulders, keeping him warm. His exposed chest and stomach dried in the open. The old, jagged scar ran the length of his belly from breastbone to groin. Carved parallel to it was a new, clean scar, the result of his most recent surgery. The doctors had left his wounds unbandaged, to heal in the foul air. But as clean as his fresh scar appeared, his old scar had worsened. It had purpled in the week or so since Haris saw him last, and his skin had become jaundiced, sticking nearly translucent to a cavern of ribs that smelled like a bellows with his every breath, concealing the deeper wounds to his organs.

"You're supposed to rest!" snapped Haris. "What am I supposed to do?"

At the sound of Haris's voice, Saied torqued upright in his bed. Before he could speak, he winced against the pain from both his fresh wound and his old one. Saied's arms clutched toward his stomach, but he dared not touch the agony of his scars. His mouth opened, but it took a moment for his breath to form words. Winded, he said: "Of course you'd find me here." Then a weak, amazed laugh escaped him.

He lay back down.

"I want what you took from me," said Haris. Flung across the stool at Saied's bedside were the red Che T-shirt, a pair of worn-out tennis shoes, and the black parka. Haris began rifling through the pockets.

"You won't find your things in there."

From the clothing, Haris pulled a half-empty pack of Gauloises, a cheap Nokia smartphone, and a thin billfold—less than fifty dollars' worth of Turkish lira and Syrian pounds. He tossed the contents on the floor.

"You took nearly three thousand dollars from me!" shouted Haris.

Daphne reached over, gently grabbing his arm at the biceps. She held her index finger to her lips. "Shhh," she said, as if soothing Haris but also telling him to keep his voice down lest the medical staff hear them.

Haris stepped to the edge of Saied's bed, towering over him. "Where's my passport?" he mumbled through a clenched jaw.

"I sold my share of your things," whispered Saied. His eyes didn't meet Haris's but wandered up toward the ceiling and the shuttered window. "How do you think I paid my way to the hospital?"

"I traveled here to help your country, and you robbed me," said Haris. His breath came heavier now. Anger welled up from his stomach, driving him toward tears. It wasn't his passport or money which had tapped this reservoir of emotion but the fact that he'd been duped. From his bed, Saied fixed the black narrows of his eyes on Haris. Pity filled their gaze, a type familiar to Haris. Jim had looked at him the same way after the raid at Kareem Tamad's house: play by the rules of the game you're in, the eyes seemed to mock.

"Where's your partner, Athid?" asked Haris. He slumped onto the stool next to Saied's bed. Resting his face in his hands, he thought of all that had been taken from him—both here and in other places before.

"Why? Do you still wish to cross the border?" asked Saied.

Haris wearily glanced up. "Yes."

Saied turned his head toward the window above him.

"Would you mind letting some more light in?"

Haris propped the stool against the wall and, standing on it, pulled back the shutter. He climbed down and sat again by the bed.

"If you wish to cross safely, it costs quite a bit of money," explained Saied.

"You took all my money."

"Yes, but you'll need some, a few thousand dollars at least."

Daphne interrupted: "He can get the money."

Saied shifted his gaze to her. Considering Daphne—her fine features, brown-blond hair with sunglasses balanced on top, the stylish blue trench coat—he raised an eyebrow.

"Suppose he can," said Saied, "why should I help?"

Before Haris could answer, Daphne did: "Did you notice the steel door at the far end of this corridor? Likely not. There's a level below this one. That's the morgue. In this hospital it's used not only for the dead but also for the dying. I've worked here for nearly a year, and someone sick as you, well, a few words from me and I think you'd find yourself down there."

Saied uncurled a wry, incredulous grin.

Daphne opened the door and reached outside to where his chart hung from the wall. She planted herself next to Saied's bed, just far enough away so he couldn't reach her. Then, with the mechanical pencil that hung from a string at its top, she began tampering with the information on his chart.

"What are you doing?" Saied asked.

Daphne continued to shuffle through the forms, erasing bits of data, furiously entering other bits. She pressed hard as she wrote, breaking the tip of the pencil several times. Whatever doubt Saied showed in Daphne's abilities seemed cause enough for her anger.

She held the modified form up to Saied's face. "What can you understand on this?" she asked. "Maybe your birthday, that's about it. The rest is in Turkish. When your doctor comes, how will you tell him you're receiving the wrong treatment? How will you even know? It will just be a matter of time before your condition worsens. They'll wheel you through the steel door, then down the ramp and into the morgue, to die alone. And do you think you'll be the first person left to die in a dark, closed place?"

She threw his chart across the room. It skidded along the floor. Haris and Saied both watched Daphne with uncertain eyes. Without another word, she pivoted on her heels and headed outside.

"Wait," Saied called after her.

Daphne stopped, her hand on the doorknob. She glanced over her shoulder. Saied didn't speak to her, though. He reached for his cellphone. From it, he slowly read something to Haris: *"All our pain is in the time we wait. We're like your friend Jim. If he'd died quickly, his end would not be so difficult to remember. I've seen many who've died quickly. They feel nothing, knowing nothing of their end. Time is what allows pain. Time is the greatest enemy."*

Perched on the stool, Haris clutched its side, his knuckles turning white.

"What does that mean?" asked Daphne from across the room.

"Saladin1984?" whispered Haris.

Saied nodded.

"You're him."

He nodded again.

"He's who?" asked Daphne.

Before she could be answered, Haris sprung from the stool. His panicked gaze volleyed once toward Daphne by the door, then back to Saied in his bed. He lunged down, grasping one of Saied's tennis shoes from the floor. He held it by the heel, high above his head, and smacked its sole across Saied's cheek. He brought the shoe up again and again, striking Saied with all the futility of an ax chopping a stump. Saied held his palms over his face, protecting himself. Aside from this, he did nothing. He didn't cry out. He didn't ask Haris to stop. He took his pummeling. Then, between strikes, Haris considered Saied's hands—the index fingers, their missing tips.

He stopped.

Panting, Haris collapsed back onto the stool, dropping the tennis shoe to the floor. Daphne stayed by the door. "Saladin1984 was my fixer in the Free Army," Haris told her. "Saied is Saladin. He was supposed to take me across the border, to fight. But this whole thing has been a scam."

Haris's hateful stare rested on Saied, pleading for him to explain away what he'd done.

Slowly, Saied brought his palms from his face. His eyes found the stubby, puckered ends of his fingers just as Haris's had. "What could I do?" he said. "You see my hands. Athid did this to me. The Daesh control everything now."

"Athid is with the Daesh?" asked Haris.

Saied nodded.

"And you helped him?"

"How could I not!" Saied answered.

"You lied to me."

"They were only lies at the end," said Saied. "I was with the Free Army. I managed a refrigeration warehouse for them in Azaz, but I handled other logistics—recruitment, weapons, ammunition. This is why you and I met. When the Daesh took over the warehouse, they killed everyone. I was only spared because the refrigerators took some skill to maintain. I was a grocer before the war."

"You never even fought?" asked Haris.

"I was married. My wife lived with me in the warehouse, though she hated it."

"And Athid?"

"She hated Athid, too."

"No, how did you meet Athid?"

"He lived in the warehouse with his fighters until the regime bombed it. That's when I was injured." Saied glanced at his stomach.

"How do I know you're not lying to me again?"

Saied pointed to his Nokia on the floor. Haris handed it to him. He brought up a photo of his wife. "Do you see her with me now? Living in that warehouse, every day seemed worse than the last, so every night she and I would mourn the day that had just passed. She died in the same bombing. Were it all a lie—" Color rushed into Saied's cheeks, and Haris saw the truth of that. "Athid rescued me from the rubble and brought me to a field hospital. He kept me alive only so he might punish me. Since I had been with the Free Army, he believed I'd betrayed him, giving away his position in the warehouse to the regime. That's when he took the knife to my fingers. He did this instead of killing me because I had something to offer him."

Saied paused, resting his stare on Haris.

"You offered him me."

Saied nodded. "The field hospital was filthy, in shambles with few doctors. I would've died there. At first, after I lost my wife, that's what I wanted, to leave this world and find peace with God. But after this"—again he held up his fingers—"I felt my spirit to be dead. No part of me remained for the next life, so I decided to survive in this one, striking a deal with Athid. I knew you'd arrive soon, and I told him if he brought me to the border, we could pay off the gendarmes, get them to help us, and then I'd deliver you and the rest of your money."

"I came to fight for your cause," said Haris. "You betrayed me. You betrayed it."

"I did no such thing!" Saied jerked onto his elbows, trying to sit and square up with Haris. He then winced against the pain in his stomach and collapsed onto his back, speaking in a rasp: "Who are you? You come here for reasons you don't even understand. In Aleppo, Damascus, Azaz, the Daesh hold back the regime. Athid commands nearly one hundred men. If the money I took from you helps those men, then I've helped the cause." Saied then spoke over Haris's shoulder, to Daphne, who had stood this whole time listening by the door. "And you, let these doctors kill me if you want!"

Haris rose from the stool, ready to leave the room.

Before he could go, Daphne spoke: "Live only for yourself, fine. We'll help you if you help us across the border. You'll be paid and have money to start over."

"Five thousand dollars," he said.

"If that's your price," answered Daphne.

"You are going with him?" asked Saied.

"Yes."

Haris flashed his eyes at Daphne, not understanding the extent of her plans. She crossed the room, picking up Saied's chart from the floor, fixing the alterations she had made. Haris felt control once again slip from him. But he also felt grateful for Daphne. He had never believed for certain that he possessed the courage to cross the border, to sacrifice himself for his cause. Daphne seemed to have that courage.

Saied too gazed at Daphne. "You are Syrian?"

She nodded.

"Not Muslim?"

"My mother was Christian, my father Muslim," she explained. "It didn't used to matter."

"Much of what mattered before now doesn't, and much of

what didn't matter before now does," said Saied. "If you were purely Muslim, it'd be better." He rested his hands on his exposed stomach. He drummed his clipped fingers on the skirt of unbroken skin surrounding his scars. He looked into his mangled flesh as if consulting an oracle. "All right," said Saied. "Come back in two days. I'll make the arrangements, you bring the money."

As a reflex Haris nearly said thank you, but he stopped himself. He followed Daphne to the door. Before stepping into the corridor, he paused, turning again toward Saied. "When you wrote me as Saladin, did you mean what you said?"

Laid out on his back, Saied raised his head. "About what?" he asked.

"About time, and pain."

Saied tucked his chin to his chest, considering his body. He exhaled a single, heavy breath, like a man sighing out his life. "What do you think?"

Haris shut the door behind him.

They stood in the corridor.

"You are coming?" asked Haris.

Daphne nodded and then looked off toward the elevator bank. Haris could see her calculating what he knew about Kifa and how he knew it. "We'll go see Marty," she said. "We can get the money from him."

Haris pressed the button. He watched the numbers counting down from the hospital's upper floors. Daphne turned toward him. "Why are you here?" The elevator's hollow chime interrupted her. Its doors opened and they stepped inside. As the doors collapsed shut she asked: "And who's Jim?"

Amir had left the BBC going. The unfolded sofa bed filled the cramped living room. It was evening. Daphne shut off the television and switched on the lights. She took off her heels, and Haris stood by the door while she ducked into her bedroom. She came back out wearing a thick pair of wool hiking socks. The apartment was cold. She turned the knob on the coiled steel heater by the window. It creaked, expanding with warmth.

Daphne sat, legs tucked under her, on the edge of the sofa bed. Haris held a plastic bag with their dinner, two kebabs and two Cokes they'd picked up on the way back from the hospital. After taking his boots off, Haris sat across from Daphne. He ripped open the plastic bag, spreading it like a tablecloth between them. Silently, in their stocking feet, they ate.

Haris wondered how long she had waited for a chance to cross the border. The recklessness of her choice frightened him. He didn't want a travel companion with such a capacity for impulse. But if she had been looking for an opportunity to cross these many months, and if he was that opportunity, it hinted at her grief. He doubted his capacity to manage anyone's grief but his own. The more he thought about it, Haris wasn't sure he wanted to understand why Daphne had decided to come with him.

She lit a cigarette and offered one to Haris, who refused. "So who was Jim?" she asked, picking köfte from the kebab with her manicured fingers while she smoked.

Haris's mouth was full. He chewed slowly, formulating a response. "A friend of mine."

"A friend?"

"From the war," he added.

"And he's the reason you're here?"

Haris fell silent.

Daphne set her kebab on the plastic bag, resting her eyes on him. "I deserve more of an answer than that."

"You do?"

"I'm going to help you, you're going to help me. We should know each other's reasons."

Haris said nothing.

Daphne stubbed out her cigarette and brought her feet to the floor. Planting her hands on her knees, she leaned forward on the sofa bed, toward Haris. He dropped his stare into his food, intent on finishing his dinner. She then stood and disappeared into the bedroom.

Before Haris could swallow his next bite, Daphne barged back through the door. Under both her arms, she held spiral binders, composition notebooks, Moleskine pads. She dumped them on the sofa bed in a worthless heap. Some of the journals leafed open. Scrawled across their pages in blue ink, her handwriting was pressed hard into each one.

Daphne bent over and tidied up the mess, as if realizing she'd been careless with something of great value. Placing the journals in two neat stacks between her and Haris, she again sat with her legs tucked under her on the sofa bed. Then, more carefully, she folded back the journals' spines one by one, handing the open pages to Haris.

"They're lesson plans," she said, as Haris looked over the indecipherable French.

"From your kindergarten?" he asked.

"No," she said. "They're from after."

"After?"

"When the revolution began I was studying for my degree, but I wasn't really interested in my subject. I'd just invested so much time at the university—exams, papers, research. My life had a momentum to it, one I didn't care for. Then, as the war destroyed everything, we all learned to rebuild amid the destruction. The first thing I built was the kindergarten—for my daughter, Kifa. I didn't draw up any lesson plans then. I just began to teach with a few other mothers. To my surprise, I found more satisfaction in this modest pursuit than any other I'd taken on. War can be a blessing in this way. If you're trapped, its destruction can free you. It freed me to become my daughter's teacher."

"Then what are these lesson plans for?" asked Haris.

Daphne flipped through the notebooks, tracing her fingers over the pages as if they were covered in braille. "They are for Kifa," she said, as if it was obvious. "Every day I keep track of the school she's missed and what I'll need to teach her."

"I saw the photo of her grave," Haris blurted.

Daphne's eyes wandered back toward him.

"I came across it when I was changing my clothes in your room," he said. "I'm sorry." As he apologized, he wasn't certain if he meant he was sorry for snooping through her things, or for her loss. He allowed her to take his apology for either of its meanings, or for the two combined.

Slowly, Daphne began to shake her head. "No, my daughter is alive." She closed the one journal and opened another. Pressed between its pages was the Polaroid. She held it by the tab on its bottom. "I don't know whose grave this is," she said, looking at the photo and the journals stacked about her. "You didn't believe that nonsense about Latia staying in Aleppo for her cats, did you?

She stayed because she couldn't afford to leave. Amir paid for her to bring me this photo. This wasn't the first time. Two months ago one of our old neighbors came to Antep claiming the same about Kifa but with no proof except rumors. Amir had paid for his journey, too. My husband does this because he loves me, but he's lost hope for our daughter. What type of marriage can we have when he's abandoned her? He wants me to do the same, so that I will leave with him. Whether you help me or not, I will never abandon my daughter."

"You said nothing to Latia?" asked Haris.

"She's suffered enough. Why make her feel guilty about a photograph?"

"The journey across the border is dangerous."

"It's more dangerous to stay," replied Daphne. She spoke with clarity. Possessing one option unburdened her of choice. Haris recognized the freedom she found in this.

Daphne gathered up her journals and returned them to her bedroom. Haris stood by the window, looking out toward Antep City Park. He thought of the sleeping bundles around the elms, the boy Daoud, Saied. With such little control over their circumstances, their lives also contained but one option—they couldn't simplify themselves further. Haris wondered if he had reached that point of reduction.

Daphne padded back to the living room in her socks. She tidied up the sofa bed, throwing away the rest of their dinner. She stepped into the kitchen, taking out a saucepan, some milk from the fridge, and plugging in the hot plate. From the back of a high cabinet, she pulled down a brick of chocolate. She banged it once loudly on the counter, knocking off a fist-size chunk.

Daphne seemed to feel Haris watching her and turned around. "I'm making you a treat," she said. "I used to do this for Kifa." She poured a splash of milk into the saucepan, heating it. With a dull table knife, she hacked off shavings of the chocolate, mixing them with the now-steaming milk. Bit by bit, she added more milk and more chocolate. Haris stayed by the window, his eyes fixed outside. The room filled with the warm, sweet smell.

"I killed my friend Jim," said Haris. "That's why I'm here."

He turned to gauge Daphne's reaction. She offered none, continuing her work in silence. His confession seemed unremarkable to her. Perhaps Daphne felt she'd lost Kifa by remaining in Aleppo with Amir, just as Saied felt he'd lost his wife by working with the rebels. They could all explain themselves in this way.

Haris began his story from the beginning. He told Daphne about his home in Nasiriya, and his sister, Samia, and Shoshana Johnson, and the Allman Brothers and "Jessica." Daphne laughed about "Jessica." "I know that tune," she said, humming a few bars over the steaming chocolate. This embarrassed Haris, but then, as she hit a certain riff played by dueling guitars, she kept repeating the melody, over and over, stirring the chocolate. Haris smiled, the first time he'd ever smiled hearing that song.

He told her about being an interpreter for the Americans, about the bomber, the baby monitor triggers, and the raid on Kareem Hamad's house. By now they had returned to the sofa bed, where they sat drinking from their mugs. "Jim would've broken the boy's arm, and I would've done nothing but watch," he confessed to Daphne. "If the boy still hadn't talked, I would've watched while Jim broke his other arm."

"How do you like it?" she asked.

"Fine," said Haris, wondering if she'd heard him, wondering why she cared so much about the hot chocolate.

He continued, describing the night when Jim came to his room with the bottle of rum. "He wanted us to be friends," explained Haris, "but more than that, I think he wanted me to understand that I was like him."

"And are you?"

"I worry I've become like him," answered Haris.

"In what way?"

"He believed in the war but not as a cause. He believed in it as an impulse, the way a painter paints, or a musician plays, a necessary impulse."

Daphne glanced at Haris's mug of hot chocolate. "Some more?" she asked.

He looked down, noticing he'd just about finished. He handed over his mug.

Daphne crossed the room and poured more hot chocolate from the saucepan. As she did, Haris spoke to her back and described Kareem Tamad's interrogation. "I hadn't planned on striking a bargain with him," said Haris. "I did it on impulse."

He held his eyes on Daphne, waiting for her to deliver some judgment. Instead, she sipped from her mug, listening patiently.

"Two nights after the interrogation, Jim came by my room. When I opened the door, he stood in his board shorts, flip-flops and tank top. Tucked under his arm was the bottle of rum. It was nearly empty. 'Must be your birthday again,' I said. He laughed and, without asking, came inside. Just as before, he sat on my chair and I sat on the bed. He offered me the rum. I took a sip. Then he did. We quietly passed the bottle between us. By the time we started talking, I was already a little drunk. He told me we'd go after Kareem's uncle the next night. 'I'm sorry,' he said. 'You're probably right—his uncle probably isn't the guy. After a while, though, the wrong guy or right guy matters less.' He stopped talking and handed me the rum. He didn't want me to say anything. He just wanted me to drink with him. Once we'd almost emptied the bottle, he told me: 'Everyone has their purpose, Abadi. A hammer's made for nails, a screwdriver for screws, cars for the road. You can't fight it. You just sorta wind up there. This is my purpose, bud. I know you don't like it, but it's where I've wound up.'

"Jim looked at the tattoo on his stomach, the growing rim of fat around it. He grabbed the bottle's neck and took another pull. 'You haven't seemed to find your purpose yet,' he said, leaning close enough so I could smell his warm, stale breath.

'That makes you interesting. That's why the rest of these booger-eating terps don't like you. They only want to get to the States. You already been. Found there ain't much there, huh? It's why I like drinking with you—even more than the rest of the guys on the team. They're boring, destined to do this forever, like me.'

"Back then, I didn't understand him: nails, screwdrivers, purpose. I thought I'd done plenty to map out my life—I'd decided to leave Iraq once I earned enough to support Samia, and I'd decided to help Kareem's uncle avoid our raid. But these were all things I'd chosen not to be a part of. I'd yet to set my mind on something I would be a part of.

"Eventually we finished talking and a single sip was left in the bottle. Jim stood, heading toward the door. Before he left, he handed me the last splash of rum as a sort of toast. 'Abadi,' he said. 'I don't know what you're gonna do, but someday this war is gonna end. I want to know how you wind up. Deal?' I didn't say anything, or nod, but I looked at him and he looked at me. And I drank."

Both Daphne and Haris had finished their hot chocolate. "There's more in the pan," she said. Without asking if he wanted a third cup, she went to the kitchen and refilled their mugs. With her back to Haris, she called over her shoulder, carefully pouring out the last of the saucepan. "You were a good friend to sit with him like that."

"He just wanted to drink," said Haris.

"You know that's not true," said Daphne. She handed him the mug she'd prepared. Together they drank, and her gesture brought meaning to Jim's.

"The following afternoon," said Haris, "I snuck off to the far corner of the terp ghetto, out where we kept the Dumpsters. I called Kareem Tamad. I told him his uncle should get out of town for the week. I expected him to thank me, but he just said, 'Okay,' and hung up. Didn't he realize the risk I ran telling him this? I wanted some acknowledgment—I'd chosen the right course. But then, like a twisting in my guts, I knew I hadn't made the call for Kareem's sake. I could care less about him or his uncle. As I stood there by the Dumpsters, it became about Jim. I felt certain my friend was about to do something immoral, something he'd regret. He couldn't stop himself, so I'd stop him.

"Just before midnight, we strapped on our body armor and climbed into our five Humvees. Up and down our convoy the guys in Triple Nickel checked their radios and guns. I sat peacefully in my seat behind Jim. By warning Kareem, I'd prevented my friend from making a great mistake. Confident in my decision, and knowing we drove to an empty house, I fell asleep."

Haris's voice trailed off. Daphne's eyes rested on him, her expression poised with pity, as if she knew what came next. Before she could take his palm or touch his shoulder, Haris stood from the sofa bed. He took her empty mug and his and stepped into the kitchen. He removed the saucepan from the hot plate. He turned on the faucet, which spat warm, then scalding, water. Scrubbing their few dishes, Haris spoke, his hands nearly burning in the full basin:

"It wasn't the blast that woke me. It was Jim. From the front seat, he reached back, shaking my leg. 'Rise and shine, Abadi.' Beneath his helmet and night-vision goggles, I could see the white flash of his smile. 'Two minutes out,' he said. 'You seem nice and relaxed, bud.' He didn't turn around. As I remember it, the flash of his smile just expanded, growing and growing, until it swallowed him like darkness."

Haris grew silent. The sink's basin steamed. His forehead sweated, a few drips mixing with the dishwater. "Jim lost both his legs above the knee. I spent about six weeks convalescing with a broken arm and concussion. A few months later, once I'd settled in Michigan, Jim began to email me, asking if I'd come see him in the hospital. He told me to remember our deal—he'd wanted to know how I wound up. I never mustered the nerve to visit. Then his condition deteriorated quickly. When he lost his legs in the blast, soil mixed with his wounds. Fungus from the soil bred infection. When the doctors made their amputations, they couldn't see this fungus. The infected tissue looked healthy, but slowly it spread. They cut more and more of him until it spread to places that couldn't be cut. In the end the blast didn't kill him, the soil did."

Daphne bolted the front door and moved toward Haris. Standing alongside him, she leaned her back against the sink and propped her arms on the basin's edge, bent at the elbows, pinched at her broken shoulders. Just as Haris turned toward her, she clumsily reached for him. Her hand pressed against his lowest rib. He glanced at her delicate fingers. He pulled his own from the sink. They'd turned red and a bit numb in the scalding water. For a moment neither moved, each held by the inches of stillness between them. Then they kissed, pressing their tongues into each other's mouths. They pulled away together, neither having a taste for it. Instead, they went for each other's belts, tugging and unfastening, no thought given to anything except speed.

His numb hands fell on her breasts, hips, between her legs. He felt so little, he was pretty sure she felt the same. She turned around, just as he spun behind her. He pushed against her, just as she pressed against him. She guided him as he found his way. They gasped, she clutching back, hooking her arm behind his head, he easing his weight on top of her. It was only moments, but their movements matched. Then his movements became fierce, outpacing hers as he neared the end. He knocked her grip from the basin's edge, plunging her hands up to the elbows in the scalding water. Unable to straighten herself beneath his weight, she cursed. He heard her but didn't stop.

He stumbled off of her, turning away, tucking his shirt in. She leaned her elbows on the sink, lifting her wet hands. They stood in the small kitchen, facing each other, weighing the impulse they had just fulfilled. Haris reached into the sink, pulling the drain plug. "I'm sorry," he muttered while grasping for a towel to dry the remaining dishes.

Daphne stepped toward him, taking him by the wrists. She held his red, numb hands in hers, which were now the same. She ran cold water from the faucet, squeezed a bit of soap in his palms, and made him wash them. "It will help," she said. And washing his hands in the cold water, she washed her own. "It was the boy," she added. "Kareem Tamad—the baby monitor as a calling card, showing you his uncle's house so he'd know you were coming—he was the bomber."

"And I paid for being so blind," answered Haris. "My solution and my problem were the same. Kareem disappeared after that night. Who knows, he might be fighting across the border now. I doubt he's found much peace at home. As for me, living in the States, supporting my sister, it all proved empty. Jim was right—I needed a purpose. So I came here."

Daphne unlocked the door's dead bolt and returned to the living room, flicking off the apartment's few lights. Haris stepped to the dresser, to where Amir had given him a blanket the night before. He spread it across the sofa bed.

"You don't need to do that," said Daphne. "Amir will make up the bed for himself."

Haris looked back at her, confused.

"He's out working, or at Marty's," she continued. "I don't expect him until late. The light in my room bothers him. You won't mind, will you?" As if fearful of Haris's answer, she disappeared through the bedroom door, leaving it open just a crack.

Haris remained balanced on the side of the sofa bed, staring at his stocking feet. He wiggled his toes, wanting to feel some physical control over himself. What they had done in the kitchen, the painful, hasty lovemaking, it felt insignificant. Their impulses had intersected. It meant nothing more. What Daphne now offered required deliberation. To join her in the light of her room was to do something for her. Anxiety stirred in Haris, settling into his body. A familiar feeling. It reminded him of the morning he'd left for Detroit Metro Airport, the note he'd placed for Samia on the accent table, the last line he'd written.

Could still be true, he thought.

He stopped moving his toes.

He stepped in profile through the cracked-open door. Daphne lay on her side, eyes shut, forehead slightly knotted—still awake. A heavy duvet ensconced her shoulders. Her clothes rested in a folded pile on the floor, surrounded by her journals. Haris took his sweater and T-shirt off. He folded them, making a pile next to hers, and climbed into the bed. Beneath the duvet, Daphne's naked body radiated nervous heat. Haris placed his palm between her pinched shoulders. Her skin felt like warm stone. He spread his fingers to the scars on her back, the ones he had glanced before. He traced them between his thumb and index finger, smoothing them like seams. Her body tensed as she pressed her face into the pillow. With all her pain, and without the room's darkness to hide it, Haris felt defeated. He could have her impulses but nothing deliberate. He turned away, find ing his space on the opposite side of the bed. Facing him on the end table was Amir's book: *Responsible Conduct of Research* by Dr. Adil E. Shamoo. Amir was lucky, thought Haris. With his revolution hijacked, his home destroyed, his daughter gone, he had managed to contain himself with just one book, as opposed to Daphne's explosion of journals. Jim would've understood Amir, thought Haris. They both could reduce their lives to a single thing. That he couldn't manage the same embittered him. As Haris lay in the bed, Kareem's and Saied's betrayals of him, and his own betrayal of Jim, twisted in his guts, right where his friend once told him his soul resided.

Daphne inched toward him. He didn't move, but waited for her. Her chin found its perch on his shoulder. The warm rhythm of her breaths fell by his ear. Beneath the duvet, she placed her hand on the small of his back. Tentatively it summited his side, descending onto his stomach. Her open palm rested there. Its fingers slowly expanded and contracted, as if probing for something within. Her fingers then came together, pressing gently. Haris breathed out deeply against them, feeling a part of him release to her. She seemed to feel it too, and her shoulders relaxed. They lay together like this in the light. Their eyes closed.

Just as Haris thought he might fall asleep, Daphne left the bed. Naked, she crossed the room. She stood by the door, her skin pale except where the single bulb overhead cast shadows against it. She turned off the light, returning to bed. They faced each other now. Through the silence, Haris heard the first raindrops pelting against the window as a storm blew in. And as Haris fell asleep to the sound, the last things he saw were the whites of Daphne's eyes watching him through the dark.

IV

The rain passed through in the night, and the bedroom was warm with late morning sun. An argument in the living room woke Haris. Bare-chested, he sprung up. His mind raced around itself. His eyes ricocheted among the walls, landing on the shut door. His clothes had been picked up from the floor and set on the foot of the bed. Daphne's clothes were gone. He heard her clenched, whispered voice outside. He also heard Amir's. Quickly he put on his shirt and pants. Gripping the doorknob, he now felt a fool. Where Amir had lost hope, Daphne had continued to believe their daughter was alive, and Haris had assumed this gulf allowed certain tolerances in their marriage. The cable-knit sweater he wore, the khakis—he would have to admit his infidelity with Amir's wife while wearing Amir's clothes.

Bracing himself for this task, he stepped into the living room.

"Five thousand is absurd!" said Amir. He stood in front of the television in his powder-blue pajamas, watching the news on mute. Daphne sat behind him on the sofa bed, which had been folded up from the night before. Amir turned briefly toward his wife, who glanced back at Haris.

"Good morning," said Amir.

"Good morning," replied Haris, shakily.

"Daph's told me about your friend in the hospital," Amir said. Then he rested his eyes on his wife. "Well, I guess we wouldn't call him that, would we? Anyway, he's asking for too much."

Daphne interrupted: "You can get it from Marty."

"That's not the point," said Amir. "This fellow conned you once before. He's ripping you off again." Haris hadn't made it much past the door. Granting him a moment to catch up with the morning's events, Amir stepped toward Daphne. "Would you mind running out to get us some . . ." He glanced around the kitchen. "Some milk."

"Milk?" said Daphne.

"Yes, milk," replied Amir, gesturing for Haris to join him on the sofa.

Daphne didn't move.

"Please," Amir insisted.

She put on her coat and left.

Haris and Amir sat next to each other. Neither spoke. Haris didn't know what needed to be said, and Amir didn't seem to know quite how to say it. They both gazed out the window into Antep City Park, Daphne's place.

"I walked back through the park last night," said Amir. He pointed to a wet heap of clothes crumpled at the bottom of the dresser.

"Where from?" asked Haris, grateful they'd begun with small talk.

"The mall. I had dinner there, did some work. When I was done I just felt like walking. With the rain, I wanted to see how everyone was making out."

"How were they making out?"

"They slept in the mud, a few had tarps, but everyone was wet."

Haris stood from the sofa, stepping to the window. Taking

a closer look at the park, he could see clothes hanging from the elm branches. The leaves still cupped last night's rain and, with each gust of wind, that rain fell in shimmers and landed among tarps spread in the grass, all of them drying in the sun, bright and wide as an SOS signal on a deserted island.

"The people in that park love Daphne," said Amir. "I walk through there to check on them, in the rain no less, and all I get is dirty stares. Daphne walks through there dressed beautifully, barely looking Syrian, and they fall all over themselves with their *as-salaam alaikums*."

"They know the work she does at the hospital," said Haris.

"They know me, too. They know about my research, the work I do for aid organizations and even some governments. It's all on their behalf." Amir turned away from the window as he said this. His words trailed off, becoming hollow. "If you think I don't love her, you're wrong," he added, interrupting himself.

"I don't think that," answered Haris. He felt an impulse to say he loved her too, as if this might ennoble his actions, but to confess it kindled a shame similar to that of his declarations that he'd come to fight with the Free Army. Loving Daphne felt just as misguided, ephemeral, doomed. Also, he wasn't certain he did love her.

"When I returned last night and her door was closed with the light off, do you know what I did?"

Haris shook his head no.

"I collapsed on this sofa, held my face in my hands, and thanked God for you. She is my wife. Although it tortures me, I need her happiness." Amir glanced at Haris's empty ring finger. "Do you understand?"

He thought of Samia, and nodded.

The Polaroid sat on the kitchen counter. Haris picked it up by its tab. "She told me you paid Latia to deliver this photo."

"Latia is an old friend," said Amir. "That's why I helped her to leave."

"You didn't ask her to bring the photo?"

"I asked her to bring news of Kifa, for Daphne. That's why she brought the photo. Since we left Aleppo, I've helped a number of our friends out of the country. They bring news of Kifa as a favor, and the news is always the same. Daphne then accuses me of paying them to tell her lies."

"So that is Kifa's grave?" asked Haris.

"It's the grave of a small child buried near our old neighborhood. What does it matter if it's Kifa's or another's? My daughter is dead. Our home is gone."

"But Daphne believes she's alive."

"And that delusion is destroying her." Amir snatched the photo from Haris. "I've tried to help my wife in the wrong way. A picture isn't enough. She has to see what I've seen—that nothing is left. Our home, our family, the revolution—nothing. Then perhaps she will move on." Amir took a final glance at the photo and let it hang limply at his side. "After a time, loyalty surpasses love in a marriage. If you'll help her go back, to understand, my loyalty is greater than my claim to her."

Amir rose, leaving Haris on the sofa. He opened the refrigerator, sticking his head inside as if looking for something. Haris followed Amir and stood mutely beside him. Then he spoke in a near whisper: "Will you help us get the five thousand together?"

"What did I just tell you?" Amir snapped. With his head hidden in the refrigerator, Amir's expression remained concealed, yet his words sounded too large to escape his throat, as if he were struggling not to cry. "You might think I'm a bastard, making money here, the ways I've failed Daphne, but I'm a good husband. For her peace of mind, I will let her go." He closed the refrigerator and straightened himself, staring at Haris through puffy, red-rimmed eyes. "But I won't travel back with you. Don't ask me to."

"I won't," Haris said softly.

Amir wiped his face with the sleeve of his pajamas and drank a glass of water. "If you're taking her on this journey," he said, "you should understand what happened between us."

Haris said nothing.

"I suppose it began with the revolution. Back then we named all the protests—the Friday of Martyrs, the Friday of Rage, the Friday of Steadfastness. Many times since, I've wished I could grab my old self by the shirt collar and shout in my own face: 'Idiot! Do you know what it means to be a martyr? You march for the honor of having your life destroyed.' Even if I'd told myself, it wouldn't have mattered. When you start marching, you stop listening. I never listened when Daphne came to me with her fears. I answered her with slogans such as 'History will remember those who chose change in the moment of change.' I asked her how I could call myself a man if I abandoned my country's cause. At night, in the darkness of our bedroom, we argued. I told her she could leave and I'd stay. I never once thought of her decisions. How could she call herself a wife if she abandoned her husband? And of course there was Kifa.

"Soon soldiers replaced students and operations replaced protests. As violence spread, most democratic activists took up arms with the Free Army. I'm no soldier, so I involved myself with the Syrian National Council, but this political wing of the Free Army didn't matter. Generals matter in a war, not activists. When the government closed the schools in rebel territory, Daphne and a few other mothers started their informal kindergarten, rotating their classes from one apartment to the next. On the days we hosted, I would stay home and help Daphne. She'd usually ask me to run an errand or two, but she didn't need much. She just wanted a man in the house with so many children there.

"When the war entered its second year, a Free Army brigade needed some space for its headquarters. Eager to support the cause, I volunteered the bottom floor of our apartment building. Daphne was furious. She didn't want soldiers so near the children, and at all hours these men came and went, taking messages to and from the front, loading trucks with ammunition and food. Whenever the soldiers saw the kindergarten parade inside, some soft part of them came alive, and they found smiles or even sweets to hand out. But a few were beyond such kindnesses. I remember one in particular. He was young, barely a man. He'd lost a leg below the knee, and it pained him to walk. I only saw him when he stood outside to smoke. For some reason, courtesy, I assumed, the soldiers never smoked inside our apartment building.

"When Daphne sent me on errands, I dreaded seeing the legless soldier. He'd sit on our building's front step, his wooden prosthetic extended in front of him. He'd always taunt me, a cigarette dangling from his lips. If I carried milk for the children, he'd say: 'Where is your cow, milkmaid?' If I carried juice, he'd ask: 'Is your orchard far from here?' No matter what he said, he'd always end the same way: 'You'll walk to the front soon enough.' Then he'd point at his missing leg. 'Just remember the walk there is easier than the walk back.'

"Educated, idealistic men began our revolution, but every time I looked into this boy soldier's face and he spoke his clipped Arabic, with his cigarette yellowing his teeth, I knew the uneducated would have the final say in my country's future."

Amir became silent.

"It's all right," said Haris. "You don't have to tell me the rest."

"You're right, I don't," Amir answered sharply. "But you want to fight, you want to be like that legless boy sitting in front of my building. You're not taking Daphne to search for our daughter, you're taking her to search for a grave, and perhaps to lie down in one of your own. You should listen to how this ends."

Amir continued: "One morning when Daphne was hosting the kindergarten, she gave me a list of groceries a half an hour before Kifa's classmates arrived. As I walked down the stairwell, I smelled smoke. The boy soldier jostled a locked door on the ground floor, with a lit cigarette dangling from his lips. He blew smoke in my face and said: 'You want me to stand in the cold for your safety, milkmaid?' At the time, I didn't know what he meant. The padlock's shackle popped open, and he stepped inside as I went on my errand.

"I was at the market a few blocks away when an explosion came from the direction of my apartment. I ran outside, and what I saw stopped me—a gap in the cityscape. Blue sky replaced where our building had been. I stared into it. If regime planes had bombed our apartment, there would likely be a second pass. Another explosion split the quiet. Frantically, I searched for a plane but found none. The blast occurred in the same place as the first. This was too accurate. The air filled with a few weak, choked screams. Before I could run home, another blast erupted from the earth, then another right after it. Something within the building kept exploding. No plane had done this.

"What I saw finally made sense—the men smoking outside even in the cold, the padlocks on the ground floor, the one-legged soldier sneaking cigarettes inside. Without telling us, the Free Army had used our apartment building as an explosives depot. Now there'd been an accident, and I was the one who'd invited them in.

"Other soldiers soon arrived. I went to help dig through the rubble, but they kept me at a distance. At first, I thought this was for my protection. But as nearly thirty of them searched through the wreckage, I noticed they spent more time recovering jugs of gasoline, nitrate, and ammonium than scouring the rubble for the muffled voices which soon faded to silence.

"By the early afternoon, as I sat along the roadside, it seemed certain my Kifa and Daphne were dead. The soldiers had recovered most of the undamaged explosives and trucked them away.

They hadn't recovered a single survivor. Family members of the dead and a few sympathetic soldiers continued the search.

"Memory protects me from what happened next. I can barely piece the moments together. I am standing over a black tunnel in the rubble. I can hear Daphne weeping at its bottom, calling Kifa's name. I can hear others calling Daphne's name. I remember everyone's arms tearing at the debris. I don't remember digging, but I know I must have."

Amir held his right hand up to Haris's face. "Do you see there?" he asked, running Haris's fingers over his own.

Haris felt the smooth ends of Amir's thumb and pinkie.

"I don't remember tearing my fingernails out," said Amir, "but I must've done it digging for Daphne. They won't grow back." He pulled his hand away, clasping it with the other. "Her shoulders were pinned beneath two concrete slabs. As we tugged her free by the waist she screamed. At first I thought it was the pain of her crushed limbs, but in all her agony she called only for Kifa. It was a miracle Daphne had survived, but she had little time. I needed to get her out of Aleppo, to a good hospital. I had no choice. Kifa was dead. Daphne was alive. So I left my daughter in the wreckage of our home."

Haris said nothing. All he could do was listen.

"I have one final memory," continued Amir. "As I left, something caught my eye. Split in half and littered on the roadside was the prosthesis of the legless soldier who had called me milkmaid. I'm ashamed to say it, but when I saw his shattered wooden leg—I kicked it into the rubble."

Amir glanced down at the Polaroid, which he still held in his hand. He reached beneath the sink and tossed it into the trash. "Though I've wandered in my marriage," he said, "my heart has only been unfaithful to Daphne once. You see, I fell in love with the revolution: its ideals, its excitement, all that I would sacrifice for it, too much, twisting myself into someone I wasn't, abandoning my family so I wouldn't abandon the cause. My great infidelity is that I couldn't extract myself. I couldn't break my own heart. Then the revolution did that for me, taking Kifa. I don't tell you this to change your mind about fighting. I'm telling you so you understand, and because I want you to make me a promise."

"What's that?" asked Haris.

"Bring Daphne to Aleppo and back. The whole way. Afterward you'll be able to run off with the Free Army, the Daesh, or anyone else you choose. Don't abandon her."

Haris promised.

"Good," said Amir. "Let's gather that five thousand."

While they waited for Daphne to return, Amir changed into a sweater and khakis, then he called Marty. "Haris is the friend I mentioned to you," Amir said into the phone. A long pause followed. "Just trust me, you'll like him." Another long pause. "Yes, two o'clock at the mall, by the ice rink." Amir hung up and offered Haris a weak smile. "That's settled," he said.

Haris showered and dressed. Just as he stepped from the bedroom, Daphne returned. Cuffed around her wrists, two plastic bags hung heavy with groceries. She rested the bags on the floor, unpacking them into the small fridge.

"That's quite a bit more than milk," said Amir, digging for a cheerful voice.

"I thought I'd make you both breakfast."

She turned on the hot plate, mixing batter for pancakes in a deep steel bowl. She laid eggs and orange juice across the counter. She knocked another hunk off her brick of chocolate. Haris and Amir again sat next to each other on the sofa. Amir switched on the BBC.

"Can't we sit together without watching that thing?" said Daphne from the kitchen.

Her back was to Amir as she cooked, but he smiled at her anyway. "Of course," he said and turned off the television.

She served up the food, not making any for herself. With a

plate in each hand, she stood facing Amir and Haris. "Any more thoughts on how to get this money together?" she asked, holding out their breakfast as if it were contingent upon their answer.

"We're meeting Marty this afternoon," said Amir.

Daphne handed them both their plates.

"What time are we meeting him?" she asked.

Amir, who'd just cut his first bite of pancake, paused, holding his fork level with his face. "You should go to the hospital to check up on your friend Saied. Also, it'd be better if just Haris and I went."

"Why would that be better?" asked Daphne, narrowing her eyes on Amir.

"You know why," he said and then turned to Haris. "Marty has a thing for Daphne."

"I don't see what that has to do with anything," she said.

"He's smitten with you and you hate him," said Amir. "You think he's a pariah, a disgusting human being. You've said all this. I don't want any distractions."

Daphne dropped the matter.

Haris finished his plate, and she took it to the kitchen, serving seconds. "I don't see our car parked out front," she remarked over her shoulder.

"I left it at the mall last night," said Amir. "We're meeting Marty there."

Daphne brought Haris's plate, piled with more food than his first helping. As she passed it to Haris, her hand brushed his shoulder. Amir stared into his breakfast, finishing his last forkful of pancake, refusing to look at them.

"Last night's rain has left a beautiful day," said Daphne. "You two should walk to the mall. Everyone is out—Turks, Syrians, everyone. They're all in the park enjoying the weather."

Amir sat, unmoving, his plate empty. "No thanks," he said. "I'd rather take a cab."

Haris didn't need to ask which one was Marty. The American man-child towered in the center of Sanko Park's ice rink. He wore jeans over his skates, their bottoms frayed. His outsize hockey jersey—UMass Minutemen—added to his outsize shoulders. The few other players on the ice sported a smattered assortment of equipment: a skateboard helmet, a boxer's red Everlast groin protector, a pair of padded gloves. They stood in a line, facing an empty goal. Amir and Haris stood just behind the rink boards. Marty tossed a puck in the air, catching it in his left hand as he passed on some last instruction in Turkish.

"Tamam?" he asked the first player in line, a university-age boy.

"Okay," he replied through a thick accent.

Marty dropped the puck in front of him.

"Go!"

His shout broke sharp as a bullwhip. The boy sprawled into his skating stance, chopping down the ice. His hockey stick was too small, causing him to hunch deeply over it. He was outfitted with a single elbow pad, and his only other piece of protective equipment was a pair of thick oven mitts that served as hockey gloves. He wore jeans over his skates, just like Marty, but his weren't the wide, thick-bladed hockey skates Marty wore. They were delicate, made of cream-colored vinyl, the type used by figure skaters.

"Quick-stick! Quick-stick!" shouted Marty. He skated backward, weaving his body along the ice, paralleling the first player, who bore down on the goal and, through his cumbersome, thick oven mitts, batted at the puck. As the first player adjusted his grip, he forgot to skate, drifting across the rink.

"Line it up! Line it up!"

Marty winced, burying his head into his shoulders as if he were watching the last play in a desperately fought game, or a car crash.

The boy continued to hack his skates into the ice, nearly plowing head over shoulders, but using his stick as a crutch he kept upright.

"Shot! Shot! Shot!" squealed Marty, pumping his fist.

The boy startled. With his stick barely in his hands, he swung at the puck, looking not at the goal but at Marty. Puck met stick. Then a bone-snapping crack. The skater followed through with his shot, so far through that his bicycling legs came up over his head as he flopped to his back. The puck sailed upward, ricocheting off the top of a rink board, arcing high into the air. Then it shuttled down, right toward Amir and Haris.

Amir dove out of the way, falling to his knees, but Haris stood, gazing up, arms outstretched. He almost made the catch, but the puck struck his hands with force, slipping through his grip and knocking against his head. He picked the puck up from the ground and rubbed his fingers through his hair, where a welt already spread.

Marty sidled up to the boards. "Nice catch, almost," he said to Haris.

As Amir stood from his knees, Marty caught a glimpse of him on the floor. "Didn't see you there," he said.

Amir brushed the legs of his trousers. "This is my friend Haris. The one I mentioned to you."

Haris handed back the puck.

"Thanks, bud," said Marty. He glanced over his shoulder, to where the first player had joined his teammates. "Murat!"

From the back of the group, a big Turkish kid with a thick mat of stubble and a Gretzky jersey confidently skated forward. "Let's finish up with high-knee-crouch drills," said Marty, "ten reps down and back." Murat barked some orders at the team. Nobody did anything. Marty demonstrated, running on his toes, pumping his knees toward his chest, then springing into a crouched-attack position. Slowly, and with some grumbling, the group did the same, making their way across the rink. Marty turned to Haris and Amir. "They need some more work before we give shoot-out drills another try."

Marty glided off the ice. Haris and Amir followed him to a bench, where he changed out of his skates and slid a beat-up pair of Docksides onto his bare feet.

"Team's looking better," said Amir as the three sat next to each other.

"A little more practice, a few more players, we'll be getting some games going soon," said Marty. "You skate?" he asked Haris.

"Afraid not."

"Too bad," he replied, cramming a pair of thick striped hockey socks into his bag, tugging its zipper shut.

"Marty is the founder of Antep's first intramural ice hockey league," said Amir.

A laugh escaped Haris.

Marty stopped working at his bag. His eyes fixed on Haris.

"He's serious?" Haris asked Amir in Arabic.

"Damn serious," replied Marty in flawless Arabic. He pulled a brush from his bag's side pocket, running it through his longish blond hair. He turned to admire his reflection in a shop-window for just a moment before putting the brush away. "Most of those kids are from the university," he explained. "I teach English there on a Fulbright. Any retard can teach English. The Syria Analysis Group takes up most of my time."

"Amir told me," said Haris.

"About what," asked Marty, "the Syria Analysis Group or retards teaching English?"

Haris laughed again. "The Syria Analysis Group."

Marty took off his Minutemen jersey and put on a hoodie. He offered Haris a self-satisfied smile. The hoodie and smile reminded Haris of those determined Silicon Valley wunderkinds he'd seen in the movies or on the news, the ones who'd pledged to make their first billion before they turned thirty.

"The Fulbright gets me the visa over here," said Marty. He cocked his head at Haris but spoke to Amir: "You didn't mention he was Iraqi."

"I'm American," said Haris. "But yes, born in Iraq."

"As I told you," Amir interrupted, "Haris came here to fight."

"I wanted to hear him tell me," said Marty.

"I came here to fight," said Haris, hoping the words might shut him up.

"Then why aren't you fighting?"

Haris said nothing. Out on the rink, Marty's hockey team finished the last of their drills. The players gasped for air, leaning heavily over their sticks. One by one they stumbled off the ice, their practice finished.

"My older brother fought in Iraq," said Marty. "He was a cavalry officer."

Haris nodded. "First Cavalry?"

"Yeah, you know them?"

"Of course." said Haris. "Was he West Point?"

"No, Yale."

"That's impressive. Is he still in the Army?"

"Naw, got out," said Marty. "He wants back in, but they won't take him. He's become sort of a screwup—fights in bars, speeding tickets, stuff like that. Damn Army's a screwup factory. They take guys who aren't screwed up, screw 'em up, then tell 'em they're too screwed up to be part of the screwup factory."

"Looks like you're doing a bit better," said Haris.

Marty laughed. "Yale wouldn't even take me—in four generations, a first for my family—so I became a Minuteman. Three years out of college and I'm running a research organization, which I founded, and that has nearly two hundred thousand dollars of business under contract, and"—he popped his index finger in the air—"I am starting the first intramural ice hockey league in the history of the Ottoman Empire. So yeah, I'm doing a bit better. But you haven't answered my question: If you came here to fight, why aren't you fighting?"

Getting robbed at the border now seemed incidental to Haris, a matter of logistics. He didn't want to explain it to Marty. His reasons for fighting continued to be reduced, one subsuming another. What had begun as guilt over Jim, a desire to redeem himself through Syria's democratic struggle, an irrefutable cause, had distilled into a desire to help topple the regime, to return to the war because, like Jim, it'd become all he knew, his home. But words like the Free Army, the revolution, and places like Aleppo, Damascus, Azaz, had all become too large. A true cause, meaning an honest cause, must be personal, specific. Faced with Marty's question, he knew he'd found one in what *she* asked of him.

"Before I leave to fight, I've promised to help Daphne with something," said Haris.

Marty didn't reply. Instead, he turned to Amir, to see his reaction to another man helping his wife. And it was Amir who explained everything—the robbery at the border, Daphne's determination to search for Kifa, Saied's offer to help them cross, the five thousand dollars they would need, and the reason why Marty should give it to them: "It's been months since the

Syria Analysis Group has had a credible report on conditions in Aleppo," said Amir.

"What about that kid you get interviews from—Jamil?" asked Marty. "You saying he and his little buddies aren't credible?"

"They are, but Jamil's stuck at the border. His information is secondhand."

"Five thousand dollars is a lot of money," said Marty.

"Firsthand reporting out of Aleppo is worth more than five thousand dollars." Amir froze his eyes on Marty's. "You know that."

"Why don't you take her?" asked Marty.

Amir stood to walk away. Before Haris could grab him, Marty did, pulling him back down onto the bench by the wrist. And Haris realized that Amir and Marty relied on each other for the research they did, and for their livelihoods.

"You've known him for what, two days?" asked Marty.

"Three."

"Three," Marty repeated.

He appraised Haris as if he were a valuable painting of questionable authenticity. Whatever connection they'd formed through their discussion of ice hockey, Iraq, and Marty's brother dissolved with the discussion of money. "How do you know he's trustworthy?" Marty asked Amir, speaking as if Haris no longer sat between them on the bench.

"Daphne thinks he is."

"Daphne," answered Marty, rolling her name in his mouth like a peppermint. "How come you never bring her by?" Before Amir could answer, Marty turned toward Haris. "Your friend has the loveliest wife I've ever seen, but whenever he comes by the office he's always with someone else. Amir, what was the girl's name from the other night?"

"Latia."

"Yes, Latia," said Marty. "He could be at home with Daphne, but he stays at the office with Latia."

"Are you interested in helping or not!"

As he watched Amir's frustration, a grin curled up one corner of Marty's mouth. "I'm interested," he said in a flat, measured tone. "I'm writing proposals for two new pieces of business, one with the Norwegian government, one with the Swedish. The proposals are due in three weeks." He now spoke directly to Haris: "If you get to Aleppo and back by then, I could reference your report in the proposals. That has value. Whatever Daphne does, and if you choose to fight afterward, it's not my business."

"So you'll give us the five thousand?" asked Haris.

Marty stood, indicating their meeting was over. He shouldered his hockey bag. "I'll front you the money," he said, "but if you don't bring back my report, Amir's on the hook for it."

Haris glanced at Amir, unsure how he'd accept his indenture as collateral.

Amir immediately shook on the deal with Marty. Seeing this resolve, Haris realized Amir was already indentured, to Daphne—he was her husband. This deal seemed to offer Amir hope. Perhaps she would return from Aleppo changed, her pain eased.

Marty offered his hand to Haris. As they shook, he pulled Haris close, so only their shaking palms divided their chests: "I want that report, but that's not why I'm helping you." Marty's oafish grip clamped hard on Haris's. Amir wandered toward the ice rink, giving them enough space to speak privately. "You remind me of my brother," whispered Marty. "That's why, so don't screw up."

Marty let go of Haris's hand. He called after Amir: "I'm having a get-together at the office tonight. Bring Daphne by, won't you?"

With little conviction, Amir thanked Marty for the invitation. He said he might stop in, but Daphne probably wasn't up for it.

"All right, fair enough," said Marty, "but I really want you to think about one other thing. And I'm serious on this point."

The three of them walked along Sanko Park's marble promenade, toward the revolving doors at its exit. "What's that?" asked Amir.

"I need to train a goalie for the team. I think you'd be perfect."

Amir leaned back, laughing at Marty, who didn't laugh at all.

"I'm serious," said Marty. "The goalie needs to have a vision of everything going on in the game. You never get to score, but you're probably the most important player on the team. You're part and apart, a player, but not really. You'd be perfect." Marty glanced over at Haris. "Don't you think he'd be perfect?"

"He would be," said Haris. "He's a perfect goalie."

They drove out of the mall's underground parking lot and into the thick workday traffic. For nearly half an hour, Amir cranked through the Peugeot's low gears while they crawled along Yusuf Bulvari. Haris rested his head against the window, falling into a deep, dreamless sleep. In front of him, the low afternoon sun shone through the elms of Antep City Park. Light mixed with spots of shadow from the leaves, pulsing bright then dark on Haris's lidded eyes. It was warm. A few blocks from the apartment, Amir's cellphone rang. He was steering with one hand and working the gearshift with the other, so he asked Haris to check the number. It was Daphne.

"Will you see what she needs?" said Amir.

She told Haris to come meet her at Elit Baklava, a café.

He described how Marty had agreed to the five thousand.

"Just come meet me," she repeated. Haris noticed a hollow, defeated tone in her voice.

He drew the phone from his ear and explained to Amir.

"That's across town, on Paşa Bulvari," he said. "Tell her to head over to the apartment."

Haris went to tell her, but she'd hung up. He called her back. She didn't answer.

"How did she sound?" asked Amir.

"Upset."

"Shit," he said, pressing the brakes. He spun the steering wheel and, in the middle of inching traffic, nosed his way into the oncoming lane. "Something's the matter."

For the next half hour, Amir and Haris sat in the Peugeot, just as they'd done before, crawling in the opposite direction along Yusuf Bulvari. While Amir tried Daphne's cellphone a few more times, Haris rested his head against the window again. He shut his eyes. The sun was behind him now and he couldn't feel any of it on his face.

Daphne sat at a corner table, tucked in the back. Haris and Amir didn't see her at first. The glare off the café's white tiled floor and the sharp, sterile smell of bleach overwhelmed their senses after the time they'd spent traveling the dust-choked streets. Just by the door, shielded behind a panel of glass, stuffed aluminum platters held row upon row of blond, glazed phyllo dough, dusted with ground pistachio. Behind the platters, a squirrel-faced man with a swooping mustache stood with a boy of nine, maybe ten years, whose equally unfortunate appearance wasn't concealed by a mustache. They both wore white lab coats, the same as the doctors from Delvet Hospital, only newer. The man grabbed a square of wax paper, twirled it between his fingers, and picked two samples of baklava from a platter.

He handed a piece to Haris and one to Amir. They both ate. Between bites, Amir asked: "Did a woman with a blue coat come in here?"

Haris tapped Amir's shoulder, nodding to where Daphne sat. Before they could walk over to her, the man behind the counter frowned. "Bir şey satın," he said, pointing to the baklava. Haris and Amir picked out another selection. The boy handed them a pay slip, to be settled when they left. Without asking, he added some tea to their order, which he loaded onto a pair of trays.

Haris and Amir took their trays to Daphne's small, round table. She straddled a stool beside it. Four empty cups of tea and a large uneaten piece of baklava were spread in front of her. The stubbed-out ends of her many cigarettes sprouted from a filthy ashtray. Between her fingers, a fresh cigarette burned, its worm of ash growing long.

Haris sat next to her. He noticed a cheap Nokia smartphone, which wasn't Daphne's, resting on the table.

"What's the matter?" asked Amir.

Daphne gazed past him. She had the faraway look of someone who'd become locked within her sadness.

Haris glanced at the table. "Whose phone is that, Daphne?"

When she heard him, the wide, blank expression on her face narrowed, resting solely on the Nokia. "It's Saied's."

"Why do you have Saied's phone?" asked Haris.

Daphne took a drag on her cigarette. As she exhaled, the long cylinder of ash toppled onto her plate. "Saied's dead," she muttered, glancing down at her untouched baklava. Dusted with ash, it was ruined. She pushed the plate away.

"What do you mean he's dead?" asked Haris.

Daphne said nothing.

Amir reached across the table. Gently, he grasped Daphne's arm, tethering her back to him. He touched her with the authority of a husband who believed it within his rights to demand certain concessions in mood from his wife.

Daphne slitted her eyes at them, as if Saied's death were their fault. She seemed determined to retreat into herself, to find refuge, or at least control of a world within.

Haris picked up the Nokia. Its screen was locked. He began tapping in codes, trying to unlock it. Then it powered down, running out of batteries. Something in his meddling set Daphne off. "Leave it!" she snapped, swatting the phone from his hands, knocking it against his full cup of tea. The man at the counter held his finger to his lips, shushing them from behind his mustache. Haris waved back apologetically. He picked up the phone and wiped it dry with some napkins.

"I'm sorry," said Daphne.

"It's fine," replied Amir. As her husband, he seemed to feel it was important that he forgive Daphne's outburst before Haris did.

"So what happened?" asked Haris.

"I feel like a damn fool," Daphne confessed. "As if I'll find anything by returning to Aleppo. What's done can't be undone." But she spoke the words without conviction. She seemed to want Haris to refute the idea. The alternative, that she continue living on the border, between her old life and a new one, was unbearable.

Again Haris asked what had happened.

"When I arrived at the hospital," said Daphne, "I went to check on Saied. I got to his room, but he wasn't there. His litter had been wheeled away. A nurse who I didn't recognize was gathering his personal items—the black parka, red T-shirt, and phone. They must've just taken him to the morgue. I became upset. Not because of Saied, though I wouldn't wish him dead, but because of our plans to cross the border. The nurse took me for a friend or relative of his. She asked if I wanted to claim any of his things. That's when I took the phone. I explained that I'd seen Saied the day before, and he seemed to be recovering. She told me the operation he'd had was a liver transplant. He'd been doing fine but had suddenly become violently ill, convulsing and vomiting bile. The doctors administered a transfusion of fresh blood, but it made things worse. They typed his blood again, finding something strange. His new liver, the one he'd been given, had changed his blood from O-negative to O-positive, and the rapid switch was killing him. They administered another transfusion, but it was too late. He was too full of the old blood."

“That makes no sense,” said Haris. “Your blood can’t simply change.” He picked up the Nokia again, examining its bottom. It looked as if it might use the same charger as his phone.

Amir didn’t disagree, and Haris said nothing else. Neither of them knew, and there seemed little point to the debate—Saied was dead.

“Can we go home?” Amir asked Daphne.

She turned to him, closing the heavy lids of her eyes. “Yes,” she said, “I want to go home, but not to that apartment. If I can’t return to our old home, to where we lost Kifa, I just want to sit here.”

“Daph, we can’t sit forever,” said Amir. “I’m parked out front, come on.”

Amir slowly stood, but Daphne remained perched on her stool.

“Why do you think I wanted to meet here?” she said. “I can’t be stuck in that apartment right now.”

“Be practical,” pleaded Amir.

“If I come, I’ll walk.”

“It’s halfway across the city.”

“I can walk with her,” Haris interrupted.

“Just go!” Daphne snapped at them. “I’ll walk alone.”

Amir fixed his eyes on Daphne for a moment longer and then headed out the door, to their Peugeot parked by the curb. Turning away from her, Haris followed Amir, taking Saied’s Nokia with him.

As they drove along Paşa Bulvari, the streetlights were poised against the incoming night. The traffic had thinned since the afternoon, but was still crawling. Then, without warning, a single gust formed a heavy, dirty sky above them. A downpour slashed against their car, forcing the traffic around them to a standstill. Both Haris and Amir sat, blinded by the storm.

The Peugeot's wipers stammered across the windshield. The rain emptied the sidewalks, and discarded umbrellas littered the overflowing gutters. Shopkeepers shuttered their stores, cutting their losses with the storm. Taillights shone red, snaking the way home. Headlights shone white, catching the rain like television static. Shadows filled the inside of the Peugeot, falling against Haris's and Amir's drawn expressions, and the sound of idling traffic blended with the weather into a single hum.

For most of the journey neither spoke. It required too much effort to raise their voices above the storm. Amir hunched over the steering wheel, a cigarette burning between his fingers. Haris searched the glove box for a charger or battery for Saied's phone but found nothing. After nearly an hour, they remained in the gridlock. Up the road, at the turn onto Yusuf Bulvari, taillights and headlights mixed in a directionless mess.

Haris and Amir both came forward in their seats, craning their necks toward the scene ahead. Merging with the flashing traffic, a pair of lights strobed—a police car. They each leaned back, imagining an accident and further imagining how much longer it would take them to get to the apartment. Before either could complain, a slow clopping broke through the rain. They looked behind them, but the streaked rear windshield blocked their view. The clopping came closer and closer, becoming louder than the storm. Amir rolled down his window, holding his face to the rain to catch a glimpse.

An old man on a donkey plodded past. Sandwiched between the inbound and outbound traffic, the animal's flank pressed against the Peugeot's side. With the window down, a wet barnyard smell wafted into the car. Straddling the donkey's bare back, the old man clutched a loop of hemp reins. He wore trash bags over his clothes. In the seams of the bags rain pooled, so that when he moved his body, even a little, water spilled off him. Quickly, the old man and donkey made their way through the traffic. The Peugeot's headlights shone against them. Haris noticed the donkey's tail. It was so wet and heavy that it didn't swing from side to side but seemed to drag almost on the ground.

"If he'd stopped," said Amir, his voice raised against the storm, "I would've traded him the Peugeot for the donkey."

"Seems fair," answered Haris. "Where would you keep it?"

"In the kitchen," said Amir, laughing a bit. "I think we could fit a donkey in there."

"Is Daphne an animal lover?"

Amir gazed intently into the rain. "How is she going to get home in this?"

Amir's concern gave voice to Haris's. If either thought there was a chance Daphne would come with them, they would've turned the car around and fought through traffic in both directions to get her. There wasn't a chance. They both knew it. Bound by that rejection, they traveled together.

Up ahead, they watched as the donkey and old man took the turn onto Yusuf Bulvari, ambling past the accident and the police car with its flashing lights. "Look," said Amir. "They're even heading our way." Behind them, someone honked a horn. Several others followed. Up and down the line of traffic, everyone honked in unison. Then the noise of the rain and the idling engines returned. "Do you know the story of Cause the donkey?" asked Amir, lighting a cigarette.

"A donkey named Cause?" said Haris. "No, never heard that one."

"I used to tell it to Daphne. The donkey, you see, belonged to an old political activist—hence its name—an elderly farmer with a pistachio crop outside Shamer, near my grandfather's farm. The man's grandson lived with him, his parents having been killed during the French Mandate. One summer, the marketplace in Shamer began selling a new type of tractor that was far cheaper to maintain than a donkey, so the farmer and the boy journeyed there to sell Cause. With the boy mounted on Cause's back, the three had traveled about a mile down a dirt road—their total journey to the marketplace being about four miles—when one of the wealthy landowners pulled alongside them in an elegant black Mercedes. He stopped next to Cause and cracked his window, shouting at the boy: 'For shame! Get off that donkey! Let the man who's given you all he has ride for a change.' Then, before the boy could answer, the landowner rolled up his window and sped off. The three stood in the road, choking on dust from the Mercedes.

"Worried they might see this great landowner again, the boy dismounted and the old man rode. They continued the next mile down the road until they came upon another farmer, a bitter man whose crops had failed the last three seasons. He snatched Cause's reins by the halter. 'Despicable old man,' he snapped. 'The boy's parents died fighting injustice and you force him to walk as if you were al-Assad, the president himself.' Not wanting any trouble, the old man dismounted. He and his grandson stood with their donkey, perplexed, unsure how they should proceed. Suddenly, the boy became inspired: 'Grandfather, Grandfather,' he said, 'we can both ride Cause.' The boy's grandfather appreciated the quickness of his grandson's mind. It reminded him of the boy's parents, who had been killed by the French. The grandfather's chest swelled with pride as he placed the boy on Cause's back, mounting behind him.

"Less than a mile from the market, they passed an old woman, and the grandfather called out: 'Good morning!' The old woman turned, leaning heavily on the cane she needed to walk. At first she smiled widely, like a sweet grandmother, but before she could offer a greeting, her feeble eyes brought Cause and the two riders into focus. 'Cruel, heartless men!' she cried. 'Both of you riding a weak, aged donkey. Dismount before you kill him or I'll report you to the authorities once I arrive in Shamer!' Both grandfather and grandson clumsily dismounted, nearly falling over themselves, their disgrace was so great. 'Always there is something wrong,' grumbled the old man as they continued, overtaking the woman.

"'Grandfather,' said the boy, 'no reason to be upset. We've found the way now. We'll walk beside Cause and everyone will be content.' No sooner had he said this than a policeman galloped past on a black, thick-chested mare. 'What's wrong with you fools?' said the policeman. 'What is a donkey for except for riding? Have you walked this whole time?' Before they could tell him of the difficulties they'd had riding Cause, the policeman galloped off. Heartbroken that no one could understand his simple desire to do right, the grandfather turned to the boy and said: 'Only one choice is left. We alone must carry Cause, then no one can speak ill of us.' The boy told his grandfather: 'Cause may not accept being carried by us.' The old man disregarded the boy's warning. 'He is only a donkey. I can be cruel, too. If he objects, we'll whip him to silence.' And they lifted Cause on their backs, although it was a difficult and clumsy way to go."

Haris had listened to Amir's version of the story quietly, thinking it a bit ridiculous. But unable to contain himself any longer, he now laughed openly. "How can two people carry a donkey?"

"It's really not that difficult," explained Amir. "His hindquarters would rest here." He placed his hands on Haris's shoulders. "Then I would drape his front over my shoulders, grasping his forehoofs. Quite simple." He lit another cigarette and offered one to Haris, who waved it away as they proceeded toward Yusuf Bulvari. "Now let me finish."

"Please."

"After trudging along in this way, they managed to reach Shamer. Admittedly, when they arrived, carrying Cause on their backs, they looked very strange. When the villagers who relaxed in the many cafés around the market saw the donkey riding two people, they began to laugh, and their laughter increased until it was louder than this storm. The kindhearted old man became unhinged. 'What do you shirkers find so amusing!' he screamed. With raised fists, he kicked over a few café tables. All the while, the boy hid behind Cause, for shame. Then a fat man with the loudest laugh of all stepped forward. 'Why, you old fool! Whoever heard of something as absurd as carrying a donkey? A donkey is supposed to carry you!' At this, everyone's laughter rose even higher. They pointed and jeered at the old man, the boy, and even Cause.

"Now, the old man, if you hadn't realized it already, had a great deal of pride. Such ridicule was an unbearable disgrace. At this moment, he reached into his waistband. Ever since the boy's parents had been killed resisting the French years before, the old man had carried a revolver. He pulled it like a rabbit from a hat and waved it exultantly at the crowd, which immediately fell silent, and—*bang! bang! bang!*—the old man shot Cause, shot the boy and, wiping the sweat from his face and straightening his disheveled shirt, shot himself."

Haris fixed his eyes on Amir, whose cigarette had burned

out, its long ash crumbling onto his trousers. "That's a terrible story," he said.

"That's not the worst part," explained Amir. "It turned out Cause was worth more as donkey meat. The fat man with the loud laugh claimed it was his life that had been threatened and that this made Cause his to sell, which he did, and bought himself one of the new tractors."

The traffic had begun to move a bit, but the rain continued. Looking out his window, Haris asked: "What did Daphne think of your story?"

"She never believed that the old man would kill himself over Cause."

Amir and Haris approached the turn onto Yusuf Bulvari. They peered into Antep City Park and the rows of elm trees. Neither spoke, and Amir stopped smoking. Up ahead, a tow truck had parked next to the police car. The siren lights made orbits against the darkness, giving the turn a manic, celebratory feel, like a nightclub. A pair of workers from the tow truck held what looked like an enormous set of mechanical scissors—the Jaws of Life. These crunched and chewed at the wrecked car, a black Mercedes, just like the one in Amir's story.

Amir and Haris took the left, their turn signal ticking loudly inside the Peugeot. As they drove past the accident, they saw a man still trapped in the Mercedes, pinned behind its steering wheel. He wore a suit. Blood stained his white shirt and trickled out the door, mixing with the rainwater. His face was a sick, ghostly yellow. It reminded Haris of Saied's translucent and cavernous rib cage. A few Turks, family members maybe, gathered beneath umbrellas in their house slippers. They crouched on the wet cement, grieving in wails, their mouths nothing but dark, wet holes in their faces and their voices lost in the storm. Haris thought the man must have lived on Yusuf Bulvari, a neighbor perhaps.

Just off to the side, on the edge of Antep City Park, Haris caught a glimpse of something else. A few Syrians—two boys and a little girl—all bedraggled in the rain. They allowed the water to rinse through their hair, down their faces, legs, and arms, soaking them clean. They crouched on the curbside by a stack of damp newspapers left from that morning. From the stack, they folded paper boats. They placed the boats in the overflowing gutters, racing them by pairs and chasing them as they navigated the currents along Yusuf Bulvari. When their boats hit the intersection, the place of the crash, they declared a winner. As Haris and Amir made their turn home, they watched these children rush down the road, toward the finish line, where they cheered among the wreckage.

Amir didn't stay in the apartment long. He waited for the traffic to clear and then left for Marty's get-together, not wanting to be around when Daphne returned. Haris didn't want to face Daphne's grief either, but an entire night spent in Marty's company seemed much worse.

Alone in the apartment, Haris took a shower. After his shower, he sat on the edge of Daphne's bed. He thumbed through her journals, looking sadly at the lesson plans in French. Then he took the framed portrait of Kifa in his hands. As individuals, Amir was handsome and Daphne beautiful, but the mixture of them, in a daughter, had produced a plain little girl. One always assumed progress in children, thought Haris. Kifa seemed like a regression. Had she lived, Haris wondered how many generations it would've taken before Kifa's children, or grandchildren, were as handsome as Amir or as beautiful as Daphne.

Haris set the portrait down. It felt unfair to think of an innocent, dead little girl in those terms. He stepped into the living room, where he made up the sofa bed with blankets and pillows from the dresser by the window. Lying down to rest, he noticed the rain had let up and the stars peeked against the black sky. The clear weather made him anxious—Daphne's progress home would be quicker now. Haris shut his eyes, willing himself to sleep, but Kifa's face was projected on the backs of his eyelids. He wanted to see lost promise in the girl's youthful face, but instead her square jaw, black curls, and wayward gaze left Haris hollow. It became impossible to rest. He left his eyes open instead and, when sleep overtook him, it seemed as if they'd never closed.

His dream came on quickly, taking him to the terp ghetto:

He lies in his narrow single bed, Daphne and Kifa piled next to him. They rest in the crook of his arm, nestled against him like cats. Haris reaches beneath Daphne. He notices the skin on her back, by her shoulders. It is smooth, without scars. And the girl, Kifa, her face is the same as in the portrait, but now Haris perceives it differently. The girl is not plain. She is not beautiful either. He doesn't sense regression as he did before. He feels a visceral, protective urge. His bond to her is not subject to her beauty, charms, or lack of either. It is a father's bond to his daughter. Haris notices his arms, which enfold his family. He's wearing powder-blue pajamas, the same as Amir's. Carefully, he props himself up on the bed and climbs over its end so as not to disturb Kifa and Daphne. With his bare feet on the cold floor, he gazes back at them a second time, wondering if he'll feel differently now that he's left the warm bed.

He doesn't.

Wearing Amir's pajamas, he feels like an impostor to another's happiness. He stands in front of his mirror, wiping sleep from his eyes. But now his face isn't his own. The reflection staring back is Amir's. Haris feels the muscles in his mouth contort with shock, but the reflection smiles. An impulse to wake Daphne, to try to explain what he's seeing, rushes over him. Before he can do anything, the door to his room swings open.

Light floods inside, waking both Daphne and Kifa. Standing

shoulder to shoulder in the threshold are Jim and Saied. Each is dressed as Haris last saw them: Jim in his body armor, his helmet cinched down tight with night-vision goggles clasped to its brim, and Saied in his hospital gown, his naked backside exposed to the sun and dust past the door.

They step inside.

Kifa, sensing the danger these two pose, climbs into her mother's arms. Daphne, sensing the same, pushes herself into a corner of the bed, pulling the blanket up around her and Kifa.

"Who are these men?" she asks.

Before he can answer, Jim says: "They aren't yours, Haris."

"Who's Haris?" asks Daphne.

And Haris, understanding that Daphne thinks he's Amir, knows the men at his door see him differently than do the woman and girl in his bed.

"They can't stay with you," says Saied, as both he and Jim step into the small room.

Haris places his body in front of Kifa and Daphne, his arms spread wide.

Jim and Saied continue toward them, refusing to stop. They move to the bed, slowly, but with relentless force. Like water on stone, or a tree root through the sidewalk, or time. There's nothing Haris can do.

"Amir!" shouts Daphne.

Kifa cries into her mother's shoulder.

Haris glances at his reflection—he remains Amir. He glances at Jim and Saied—he remains Haris. Blood rushes to his head, and a great clarity envelops him. He lunges at Jim, grasping his pistol from where it dangles in a holster on his leg. Drawing the pistol, Haris raises it high in the air, wielding it like a torch to darkness. Before he can do anything, Jim and Saied both begin to laugh at him. Louder and louder they laugh. Haris turns toward Kifa and Daphne. They're both trying to tell him something, but he can't make out their words above the roaring laughter.

Then, regaining himself, Jim says to Haris: "You can't make a home for this family, bud."

"You took away my home," Haris answers.

He levels the pistol at Jim and Saied.

Jim returns to his laughing. Before Haris can do anything, he's again overtaken by his urge to protect, but within him that urge mutates with a perverse twisting in his guts. He glances at himself in the mirror one last time and, knowing what he must do, he no longer views Amir's reflection, but sees his own staring back, bringing unity to what everyone in the room now understands. There is silence, and—*bang! bang!*—Haris shoots Kifa, shoots Daphne and, fixing his blue pajamas and smoothing down the hair on his balding crown, presses the gun to his head.

And with the gun to his head he awoke.

Daphne had returned to the apartment and flicked on the light in her room.

Lying on the sofa bed, Haris groped through the darkness. He found his pants folded in a pile on the floor. In his pocket was the Nokia. He plugged it into his charger and waited as it slowly powered on.

The screen was locked, but the code immediately occurred to him—Saladin1984. He tapped in the four digits. The interface shone brightly, causing him to squint. Set as a background screen was a photo of Aleppo's skyline before the war—the square minaret of the Umayyad Mosque, the Citadel's ramparts, hundreds of balconied apartments. In the lower-left corner was the small envelope icon: Saied's email. Haris's first instinct was to sift through the account. Just as he went to do so, anxiety overcame him. Saied had cheated him before. Haris feared other deceptions awaited him in the emails. Instead of looking at them right away, he wandered around the rest of the phone's interface.

He opened the notes feature first—a scroll of bulleted annotations. They looked like grocery lists. Then, mixing with the groceries, came other items: apricots—4 kilos, milk—10 gallons, 7.62 x 39—10,000 rounds, oranges—6 kilos, RPG-7—10 rockets, salt—half kilo, rice—30 kilos. Each page was a week's worth of supplies, and the weeks ran in pages and pages.

Haris opened the photos next. The most recent were of crated vegetables mixed with ammunition and military hardware—carrots, belted machine-gun rounds, cans of condensed milk, radio batteries. Haris scrolled through them, traveling backward in time. At first the images mirrored the lists, food mixing with weapons and supplies, as if nothing else in Saied's life merited a photograph. Then a woman appeared in one of the photos. She crouched over some bedding in a cavernous cement building, which was likely Saied's warehouse. Halogen lights cast shadows across the empty space. The woman raised her hazel eyes up toward the camera. From beneath a cheap linen hijab, her lips pushed forward as if to ask a question. Haris continued to scroll backward, flicking through the images of Azaz faster and faster. As if through a zoetrope, the city seemed to rebuild itself. The woman lost her hijab. Mascara appeared around her questioning eyes, and these eyes lost their question. The rubbled streets cleaned themselves and filled with people. Then, slowly, Saied appeared in the photos, standing with his wife instead of behind the camera.

Haris stopped looking.

Satisfied that Saied had told him the truth about his life before and during the war, Haris decided to sort through the emails, beginning when he'd been in Michigan. Interspersed with this correspondence was that of other would-be fighters, some who'd crossed the border, others whom Saied had unsuccessfully urged to come. Then, this past week, just as Haris had found himself at the border, Saied had stopped replying to emails. A long string of unopened messages crammed his temporarily disabled inbox until two days ago, when a single query resumed the activity on Saladin1984's account. What followed was a negotiation between Saied and Athid.

The exchange lacked any ideological pretext, no reference to the mosaic of groups entrenched in the war. Saied simply offered Athid three thousand dollars to take a pious—albeit unnamed—fighter across the border with a woman from Aleppo. Athid agreed, but countered with a price of five thousand dollars. A frantic round of emails ensued, the last one containing Athid's final offer: four thousand dollars.

Saied never replied.

Coming to the end of the thread, Haris wanted to believe Saied had negotiated in order to get him the best deal. But he knew Saied would've kept the whole five thousand, regardless of what he arranged with Athid. Strangely, the idea of crossing the border with an Islamist hard-liner like Athid didn't make Haris nervous. He took solace in the emails' pragmatic haggling. Free Army democrats, regime loyalists, Daesh Islamists—an ideology needed funding, and this necessity made funding the greatest ideology.

Palming the Nokia, Haris lay on his back, uncertain what to do. He wasn't sure how Athid would react to seeing him again. Since coming to the border, he hadn't lost his desire to fight. What he had lost was clarity—the Free Army's revolution, the Daesh's jihad, their causes had muddled, leading nowhere. His eyes wandered the apartment, eventually resting on the mirrored wall. He'd come to define his cause in more narrow terms. He gazed at the cracked-open door to Daphne's room. Nothing had been solved for her. She still slept alone in the light. Amir would return from Marty's in the morning, and the familiar pattern of her life, Amir's, and now his own would resume in Antep.

With this on his mind, Haris composed a reply:

Athid,

My apologies for not answering sooner. I needed to confirm details. The pair I told you of are ready to depart. Please send instructions on when and where you would like to meet them.

Peace be upon you,
Saladin

Haris hit send and placed the Nokia on his chest, lacing his fingers over it. He shut his eyes, but couldn't sleep. He had taken the first step and wondered if there would be a second. He felt a measure of guilt that he hadn't waited to consult Daphne and Amir. They would have strong reservations about casting their lot with Athid—Amir in particular, for it was Athid and those like him who had hijacked his revolution, miring its democratic ideals in Islamism. Holding the Nokia, Haris stared at his hands, imagining them without fingertips.

He checked the phone. Not even five minutes had passed, but he had a response. He felt his stomach twist with anxiety, fearing the message that awaited him and what acting on that message meant:

Saladin,

Bring them to regional headquarters in Kilis the morning after next. Ensure they have the entire four thousand.

Peace be upon you,
Athid

Haris felt obliged to write back immediately, Athid's message having arrived as promptly as it did. He knew this final response would set him on an uncertain course with a purpose no larger than returning Daphne to the point where she'd lost her daughter. Had he permitted his mind to linger too long on any of this, he wouldn't have been able to go further. He wrote the reply, thanking Athid, explaining he was glad to provide him with another fighter. Then, and thinking only to curry favor with this brutal man, Haris mentioned that the new recruit's enthusiasm for the cause compelled him to pay the full five thousand, understanding such support was needed at this crucial time.

He sent the message.

Again Haris lay on his back, unable to sleep, his fingers laced over the phone. He didn't want to check for Athid's answer. He would wait until morning. Instead, he wondered why he had so rashly offered the extra thousand. What irrational urge did he harbor to ingratiate himself to everyone, even someone as pitiless as Athid? As Haris struggled to understand himself and this impulse, a single thought came clearly to him: I am an American.

V

"Where in the hell is Kilis regional headquarters?" said Amir. He tossed the Nokia across the sofa bed like a dirty shirt.

Haris stood by the window in silence.

Amir walked over to the refrigerator and stuck his head inside. "We don't have anything to eat!" he called toward Daphne.

Ignoring Amir, she came through the bedroom door, clutching an empty book bag beneath her arm and a suitcase in her hand. From the dresser in the living room, she packed an extra shirt and blanket. She took an appraising look at Haris. After a moment of digging through the bottom drawer, she removed one of Amir's sweaters. She held it up to Haris's frame, checking it for size. She packed it too.

"What are you doing?" asked Amir, standing from the refrigerator, his face flushed.

"Gathering what we'll need," answered Daphne.

Amir stormed across the apartment. He snatched the Nokia from the sofa bed. He tapped at its screen a few times, trying to unlock it. "Remind me of the password?" he asked.

Haris didn't answer right away. He gazed down into the

street, where the black Peugeot was parked. Washed from the storm, it glistened in the rising sun. Amir had returned from Marty's just before morning. After Haris had sent his response to Athid, he had waited up for Amir, secretly hoping a breakdown or some other minor disaster had delayed him, subverting their trip to the border. But now, looking at the glossy black Peugeot, Haris felt luckless. If he wanted something destroyed, that seemed enough to preserve it, and what he wanted preserved—Saied, Kareem, his own sister—well, he thought, it's dangerous to want anything. Wanting seemed enough to turn chance against him.

Amir asked again for the Nokia's password.

"Nineteen eighty-four," said Haris.

"Like *Brave New World,*" said Amir with disgust. "The Daesh's brave new world is the backward old world—public stonings, women veiled head to toe in the niqāb, the rejection of any idea not in the Qur'an. The Daesh are delusional." A fresh charge of red colored Amir's cheeks. "Daphne, please don't cross with them."

"That's Huxley," she said.

"What's Huxley?"

"*Brave New World*. Aldous Huxley. *1984* is Orwell."

"What difference does it make?"

Daphne set the book bag and suitcase by the door. "You don't know what you're talking about. That's what difference it makes." She looked at Haris as if she wanted him to take sides.

"Saied was born in 1984," said Haris.

Amir took two steps from the foot of the sofa bed, toward the window. He planted himself in front of Haris, his hands balling into fists. That his wife and Haris would side against him seemed a greater indignity than what had happened the day before, when Haris had spent the night with her. Haris now anticipated the tense exchange he had managed to avoid when exiting Daphne's bedroom on that morning. Though he knew

Amir needed him, Haris also felt an urge to raise his hands to his face, to protect himself.

But Amir said and did nothing. He just stood there making fists.

Daphne crossed the room, taking Amir's hands in her own. "Don't you see?" she said. "Who we go with makes no difference. The Islamists hijacked the revolution from the Free Army. If it weren't for the Free Army, Kifa might still be with us. They're all the same, and none are good."

As Daphne made this last point, her gaze quickly, almost imperceptibly, fell onto Haris. For him, her words were a question: Are you the same? Or are you good?

Before Haris could answer, Amir did. "I am your husband. I won't stop you from going. And I am not the same as them, I just wish I—" He swallowed to steady his voice.

He went to the dresser and began laying out more clothes for Haris.

The morning traffic was light, and for several blocks they drove alone. At the turn off Yusuf Bulvari, they passed the site of the accident. No trace of the wreckage remained. Haris sat in the backseat, his head resting against the window, his eyes wandering out to the gutters, which had dried, leaving banks of grime ribboned with silt. Spreading for block after block, washed up on these banks, were the paper boats from before—remnants of the children's game. Haris counted the stranded boats and, slowly, drifted to sleep.

When he woke they were parked on Paşa Bulvari, just in front of Elit Baklava. The Peugeot idled at the curb. Amir sat in the driver's seat, thumbing through the emails on Saied's Nokia. When Haris stirred, Amir slid the phone into his pants pocket.

"Where's Daphne?" Haris asked.

"She wanted to get a gift."

"For who?"

"The man you're meeting, Athid."

Daphne stepped from the café's glass front. The shopkeeper from before, the one with the swooping mustache, came to the door. His squirrel face strained, a smile spreading across it, as he waved goodbye to Daphne. She turned to glance over her shoulder, flitted her fingers back and left the shop. With her coat girded at the waist and her sunglasses over her eyes, Haris thought she looked glamorous, like a transplant from the thick fashion magazines his sister read. Daphne swung an expensive canvas bag of baklava by its toggled handles.

She climbed into the front seat.

"I don't think a gift is necessary," said Haris while Amir steered the Peugeot toward their next stop.

"Manners are always necessary," replied Daphne, glancing toward the backseat from in front of her headrest. "And good morning," she added with a smile. "I think the gesture will be appreciated. Don't you, Amir?"

Daphne fixed her gaze on Amir, who concentrated on the road, saying nothing. They made the turn onto Emek Cadessi, just a few blocks from Marty's office. As if from across an empty room, Amir called out: "I know how to find the Daesh's regional headquarters."

"How's that?" asked Haris, sitting up from the backseat, leaning over the parking brake.

"Remember the boy, Jamil? He'll know. It'll be for a price, but he'll know."

Haris eased back into his seat, saying nothing.

When they pulled up to the office, the air was rich with the smell of fresh baked simit and açma from the corner pastanesi. Amir idled the Peugeot in front of the garage door—a shutter on a steel roller built into the villa's outer wall.

Nailed into the wall was a sign for the Syria Analysis Group. The paint on the organization's logo—the oblong border of Syria with a lamp illuminating it from the side—was weather-beaten, scaled and flaking at the corners, long overdue for a touch-up. Tethered to the sign frame, bundles of spent glow sticks hung on small bits of twine, marking the location of last night's, and of other nights', parties.

With his cellphone, Amir dialed Marty. Nothing. Amir tried again. From the receiver, Haris heard a startled voice answer, as if irritated at being woken. Amir asked to be let inside. A moment passed and the garage door rolled open. They pulled into the villa's courtyard, where they drove past a small, untended garden, crosshatched with weeds and seeded with cigarette butts, as if sprouts might root from their filters.

They waited.

"Let's be quick about this," said Daphne.

"We'll just get the five thousand and leave," answered Amir.

"I don't want to go inside."

"We won't," said Amir, "but I think you're being a bit hard on him."

"Money or no money, it's exploitative the way he's made a business from researching the war."

Daphne gazed out of the window. A few empty lawn chairs were scattered across the yard. In the corner of the outer wall, an oleander grew. Its bare branches were thin. A blanketed heap slept in a chaise beneath the tree. A single, lazy arm hung toward the ground as if reaching for an inflated kiddie pool a couple of steps away. Buoyed by the pool water, melting chunks of ice floated alongside some bottles of Efes pilsner.

Marty opened the villa's heavy oak door. He shut it behind him by the brass knocker and stood in the threshold, atop a few marble steps. He made a visor of his hand, squinting against the sun. He wore his Docksides like a pair of slippers. A tattered terry-cloth bathrobe hung down to his calves. Its knot was tied loosely, draping open at the front and exposing his boxer shorts and navel. In the bathrobe's right pocket was something heavy.

Haris's eyes instinctively noticed the heavy pocket—the five thousand.

As Marty's senses adjusted to the midmorning light, his stare fell into the Peugeot. His eyes widened upon seeing Daphne. He jogged down the marble steps, his Docksides thwacking against his heels.

It was barely perceptible, but Haris noticed Daphne sink in her seat as Marty sauntered up to her window. She fixed her gaze straight ahead, boring into some invisible distance.

Marty knocked on the glass and quickly checked his appearance in the side mirror.

Daphne rolled down the window, finding the switch as though her hand were disconnected from the rest of her body. Seeing Marty tested the limits of her manners.

Marty, his wide grin growing ever wider, noticed none of this. "I'm so glad you're here," he said to Daphne, the weariness lifting from his voice and his words brimming with hollow charm, as if he said them only to charm himself. He leaned his head deep into the cab. "Why didn't you bring her last night, Amir?" he asked. "Fiesta's wrapped up now." He didn't give Amir a chance to answer. He turned toward Daphne. "He's always trying to keep us apart." Marty again leaned deeper into the cab, his shoulders coming through the window. "You're always trying to keep Daphne from me," he repeated, lightly scolding Amir.

"I'm here now," said Daphne, her eyes remaining straight ahead.

"Yes, and just in time to leave," he said, taking the five thousand from his pocket. "Who's helping you across the border, the Northern Storm?"

"Haris has a contact in the Daesh," Amir answered quietly. His words were forlorn and his stare hung at his hands, which limply gripped the bottom of the steering wheel.

Marty pulled his head from the window. He regarded Haris in the backseat, giving him an examining look. Haris couldn't bring himself to match Marty's gaze. Self-consciously, he ran his palm over his face, which bristled with a few days' growth of beard.

"You're an Islamist?"

"I'm not," said Haris.

Marty patted the five thousand, a banded stack of bills, against his hand like a thug with a baseball bat. "I don't know how I feel about giving this over to the Daesh. Even if I was okay with it, I mean, Jesus, Daphne, you can't cross with the Islamists."

Daphne swung her eyes away from the distant spot where they'd been focused. She pushed her sunglasses up on her head. Hatefully, she stared at Marty. "And why not?"

"Why not? Because they're savage."

"And all this isn't?" said Daphne, surveying his opulent home rented at an inflated price, the detritus of last evening's party strewn across the front yard. "You'll still get your report. And more than an update on events in Aleppo, you'll get information on the Daesh. What do you really know about them? Very little, I suppose."

Marty didn't argue this point. Instead, he reached toward Daphne, cupping the blond tips of her hair, which curtained her slender neck. "You may be half-Muslim, but you're half-Christian also. Have you looked at yourself? They'll never let you cross as you are, head uncovered, with a nose ring, dressed like a western woman."

Everything Marty said was true, but his obsession with Daphne seemed less about his feelings for her, or any real attraction. She was, Haris realized, the one person who refused all Marty had to offer. The villa, the parties, the easy research job, which paid well if you were a Syrian stranded in Antep—Daphne resisted all of it, and this made her irresistible to him.

"Goddammit," said Marty. "Hold on a second." He jogged back inside, his bathrobe flapping behind him.

Amir's gaze remained on his hands. "He's right, you know."

"About what!" Daphne shot back. She clutched the bag of baklava in her lap, nervously folding and unfolding its top with her manicured fingers.

Amir said nothing. Turning on the radio instead, he surfed through the stations for programming in English or Arabic. Before he found any, Marty reappeared at the front door and rushed down the marble steps. He clutched a white linen scarf with floral embroidery. Haris thought it'd probably been a small tablecloth.

Marty leaned in a crouch against Daphne's window. She turned down the radio. "Your five thousand is contingent on one more thing," he said, his face becoming stern, like a father setting curfew for a beloved daughter. Marty held up the scarf.

Daphne laughed on reflex as he held the scarf by its ends like a garrote.

Nothing in Marty's dour expression changed.

Daphne stopped laughing.

"Fine," she said, "but I still think it's ridiculous."

Marty ignored her. He folded the scarf into a triangle, which Daphne spread flat against her lap. Grasping both its ends, she flung the scarf over her head, looping it in a knot beneath her chin. Her shoulders sank, and she lowered her sunglasses. Their large red frames rested on her cheeks, and she stared straight ahead.

Now Marty laughed, so did Amir.

"What?" she snapped.

Neither said anything.

"What!"

From the backseat, Haris replied: "You look more glamorous than before."

Amir and Marty laughed even harder now.

"Yeah," said Marty. "You look like Audrey al-Hepburn."

Daphne, trying to remain upset, fought against a smile. She took out her nose ring, tucking the quartz stud into her pocket.

A black hole dimpled her nostril. Without saying anything, Marty took the five thousand from the pocket of his bathrobe, offering it to her instead of to Haris or Amir. He placed it in her palm. Amir reached toward Daphne as if she should give the money to him. But she didn't. She tucked the cash into the bag of baklava on her lap.

Amir depressed the clutch and jabbed the gearshift into reverse. He hooked his arm behind Daphne's headrest, watching through the rear windshield as he steered. Just before he added some gas, Marty called out:

"Wait!"

"What?" asked Amir.

Marty's gaze flitted around the cab, as if looking inside for what he wanted to say. "How are you going to talk to Haris and Daphne once they cross?"

Amir paused for a moment. He took the Nokia from his pocket. "They can use Saied's old phone." He handed it to Daphne, who tucked it into her coat. Amir again hooked his arm behind her coat, beginning to reverse.

"Daphne," pleaded Marty.

She turned toward him, but he struggled to put words to whatever he felt. From behind her sunglasses and beneath her hijab, she possessed the distance of miles. "Unless you have something to say, we're leaving, Marty."

He was silent.

They reversed down the driveway.

Marty remained in the garden doing nothing, his broad shoulders framed against his enormous house.

They left Antep, driving until the early winter sun hovered near the horizon. It cast afternoon shadows along the gentle sloping hills of Kilis Province. Where the hills spilled into farmland, herded bales of cotton spread across fields, which would remain barren until the next year. Laboring in the fields, farmers cleared and burned the harvest's stalks. Here and there flames caught wisps of cotton, and the wisps flashed like fireflies in the day. Up ahead, dangling above the smoothly laid macadam, a single traffic light was strung across the D850. It shuffled its colors to an empty road. A wind blew from the north, canting it to the side, so like a weather vane the traffic light indexed south, toward the border.

The road widened. A grass-planted median striped its center. Along its shoulder the yellow-and-white-checkered curb pointed the way toward Kilis, which lifted from the horizon in a mix of stucco Anatolian ramshackle and concrete high-rise. On the near horizon, the tarp hovels of the child refugees hung between the saplings along the D850's median. As the Peugeot sped toward this intersection, Haris could make out napping, shadowed heaps beneath the tarps. In the front seat, Daphne tightened the knot of her hijab and pressed her sunglasses up her face. Amir downshifted, easing the Peugeot into a low gear. A single boy sat on the curb underneath the traffic light. Hearing the Peugeot's approach, he stood, gripping the plastic bag of knickknacks Haris had seen before, its bottom bulging in a distorted mass.

The rest of the boys piled from beneath their hovels, fanning out along the shoulder of the road. Haris's gaze rebounded from face to face, searching for Jamil's. Amir searched as well. Daphne took off her sunglasses, and Haris noticed she looked at the boys differently, with barely concealed pity, as if they were her boys and that pity was as much for herself as for them.

From a small and isolated lean-to, built behind the rest of the tarps, Jamil strode out among the boys. He stood a head taller than most of them. His hair remained slicked back and reflected the low sun with a signal mirror's strength. He walked down from the median and onto the road just as Amir parked the Peugeot curbside, below the wavering traffic light.

As Jamil approached, most of the boys kept their distance. But Haris recognized something different from before—a few boys stood in his path, immobile, forcing Jamil to weave his way around them. Their deference was gone. Seeded within the group, a mutiny seemed to have grown.

Amir and Haris stepped from the Peugeot while Daphne remained seated inside. The boys circled around them but maintained a buffer. Just out of earshot, Haris could see them whispering to one another. As he strained to overhear their conversations, he got a better look at Jamil. His left cheek was swollen to a midnight blue, spreading to a raccoon eye, its white stained red. Haris also noticed his hands, a weave of cuts blanketing both knuckles. Jamil had been fighting. Despite his years spent in and around war, Haris couldn't recall ever being in a fistfight.

Jamil welcomed them back. "I wouldn't have recognized you,"

he said, offering his sly grin and a glimpse of his wide-spaced teeth. He ran his gaze from Haris's boots to the knit sweater he wore. "You've cleaned up well. Taking another try at the border?"

"I wouldn't have recognized you either," said Haris, pointing to Jamil's swollen face, the skin hard and cracked as risen dough.

Both Jamil's red-stained eye and his untouched white eye bulged wide. He turned to the circle of boys with a hateful look. "Since I saw you last," he said, lowering his voice, "there's been some trouble here."

"What kind of trouble?" asked Amir, his voice a bit too loud.

"If you've come for one of your research projects," said Jamil, "I've told you, I don't offer interviews for free."

"That's not why we're here," Amir replied.

"Then you *are* taking another try at the border."

Jamil looked at Haris, as if he could be counted on to volunteer the truth.

"What kind of trouble?" asked Haris, repeating Amir's question. He felt the stares of the other boys boring into his back. Slowly, by inches, they constricted their circle around the Peugeot. Haris glanced out into the crowd, searching for a friendly face. He found none and noticed several more boys with blackened eyes and busted knuckles. He remembered Jamil's gentle companion from before, the one with the glasses missing a lens. Haris struggled for his name, as if speaking it might diffuse the gathering tension.

"Where's Hamza?" he blurted.

The constricting he felt in the crowd eased, as if awaiting Jamil's response.

Jamil gazed out toward the other boys. They looked back at him, both wild with the mentality of the pack and contained within it.

Haris realized the threat he felt wasn't toward him but toward Jamil.

"Hamza left us three nights ago."

"Is he all right?" asked Amir, seemingly oblivious to the shifting dynamic among the boys.

"He's fine," said Jamil. "He's just not with us anymore."

"Where is he?" Amir began to pry.

Once again, Jamil cast his eyes over the other, mutinous boys. Giving voice to their divide seemed enough to ensure it could never be bridged. Jamil hesitated a moment, and Haris again felt the pack constrict around them. Jamil must have felt this too, because he began to speak quickly. He explained how three nights before, a group of European relief workers had come to their makeshift encampment offering to take some of the boys north, to a place where the Turkish authorities provided permanent resettlement for Syrians. "Of course they found Hamza of interest," Jamil said, his voice wavering between contempt and tears. "His glasses and quiet way, anyone would pity him. The van they came in had ten spaces for us. Hamza, who'd always been so frightened I'd leave him, left me at the first chance. When the rest of these boys"—and Jamil spat the word *boys* into the crowd—"tried to climb inside the van, I told them they couldn't go and we came to blows. They think we're waiting at the border for a new home. But that's not why. We wait here so we might return to our real home."

As Jamil said this, Haris glanced at the other boys to gauge their response. If home was less a place than an emotion, etched into their faces was forgetfulness. They couldn't remember what they couldn't feel. Still, Jamil argued with the crowd as if passing good breath into a blue-lipped corpse.

Making his way forward, the boy who had sat underneath the traffic light pushed through the others and interrupted Jamil. He thrust the plastic bag of knickknacks upward by its handle, holding it toward Haris and Amir like an unpaid bill of sale. The boy stood with mute purpose and an expectant look.

"Are you going to buy something?" Jamil asked.

Haris glanced at the Peugeot. The boys had assembled in

front of it, blocking the road, just as they'd done on his first trip in the taxi. Daphne sat in the passenger seat. One by one, she made eye contact with the boys, disarming their threatening posture with her gaze.

"No, we're not going to buy anything," announced Amir. Then, and in a softer voice, he spoke only to Jamil: "I have something to ask you." Jamil flinched as Amir rested an arm around his shoulder. Amir turned toward the Peugeot, so did Haris. The three formed a huddle. "We are crossing the border," said Amir. "Or, more accurately, Haris and my wife, Daphne, are." Upon hearing her name, Daphne glanced up from the passenger seat. Her eyes met Jamil's and flashed him a warm yet tired smile. He returned one, wincing against the pain in his swollen cheek.

"Who are you crossing with?" asked Jamil.

"The Daesh," Haris replied.

Jamil tucked his chin to his chest, nodding respectfully. "That's good," he said. "They're the best fighters." And Haris noted that, unlike Marty, Amir, and even Saied, Jamil said nothing about their ideology. The Daesh could fight. This was all that mattered.

"We're meeting our contact tomorrow morning at their regional headquarters in Kilis," said Amir.

Again Jamil nodded. He stared at his feet, as if awaiting a further explanation, but Amir said nothing more. The three of them shared a silent moment. Then, looking confused, Jamil asked: "What do you need me for?"

Haris could feel Amir's hesitation. He remembered how he'd felt when he first met Jamil, how he hadn't wanted to ask anything of a boy who lived by the side of the road. Amir's pride prevented him from requesting this final favor from Jamil, so it was left to Haris: "We don't know where the regional headquarters is."

Jamil tilted his head. "But they've agreed to take you across the border?"

Haris nodded.

"And you've agreed to fight alongside them?"

Again Haris nodded.

"Why don't you know where to meet them?"

"Can you help?" asked Haris.

Jamil allowed his eyes to wander into the Peugeot. He glanced at Daphne, but as she listened to their negotiation, the kindness left her expression. To cross the border she needed Jamil. He continued to gaze at her, but his attempts to earn a sympathetic look in return were as futile as gazing into a portrait so it might return the same.

"What do I get?"

"We can pay you," said Amir.

Jamil turned to look over his shoulder, toward the pack of boys who milled around the Peugeot, particularly the one who held the plastic bag of knickknacks. "I'll help," he said, "but I don't want your money. I want you to take me across the border, to fight."

"You're too young," Haris snapped back.

"I'm not too young," said Jamil, his tone more even and controlled than Haris's.

"How old are you?" asked Amir.

"Fourteen."

"Fourteen," said Haris.

"He's not too young." Daphne had rolled down her window. Her eyes fell on Jamil's battered knuckles and swollen face. She glanced up at Haris and Amir. Before either of them could question her, she said it again forcefully: "He's not too young."

Jamil's breath quickened, his chest rising and falling as if he were about to begin a race. He flung open the door behind Daphne's seat, tumbling into the Peugeot. Wide-eyed, he stared back at Haris and Amir. Immediately, Haris felt the crowd collapsing on them. Starting with the boy who held the plastic bag, they rushed the car. Haris ran around to the other door, and

Amir slid behind the steering wheel, turning the engine over. A few of the boys whacked at the doors with open palms. Haris couldn't tell if they wanted to come or if they wanted to drag Jamil away for abandoning them. At first Amir drove slowly, not wishing to injure anyone. Then a rock hit the window by Daphne's head, exploding a web of cracks across the glass. Amir accelerated as quickly as he could cycle through the gears. With hollow thuds, the Peugeot's side mirrors swiped a few of the boys.

Both Jamil and Haris sat in the backseat, their faces pressed to the rear windshield. Left empty-handed, the pack of boys ran to the lean-to where Jamil had slept. They tore it down and threw its tarp and stakes beneath the traffic light. As the road narrowed into the distance, the pack blurred into a singularity, and Haris watched as in a last defiant act they took turns stamping on what had been Jamil's home. Seeing how quickly these boys had turned on Jamil, someone who'd cared for them like an older brother, Haris felt empty. That emptiness twisted in his stomach—helping anyone so desperate seemed likely to end in a similar futility.

Haris looked toward Jamil, checking to see whether he was all right. Jamil sprung around, facing front. Flushed with excitement, he smoothed back his hair, which had tumbled over his forehead in their escape. A cheek-stretching grin brimmed up the swollen side of his face. He clapped his hands together once and laughed, crumpling over his legs. In a voice that could barely contain his thrill, Jamil said: "What a getaway! Just like out of a movie."

Daphne turned around in her seat.

Her eyes glimmered with fear and regret, meeting Haris's. If she didn't feel it before, she surely felt it now: Jamil was too young.

In the old city, the streets ran thick with minarets. Buried here, in the catacomb of broken roads, was the Daesh's regional headquarters. From the backseat, Jamil leaned over the gearshift. His head bobbed between Daphne and Amir as he spotted the way. From the bellied domes of the grand Canpolat, Akcurun and Ulu mosques, and from the corrugated steel roofs of back-door shanties, the faithful had built spires, clutching their way upward. Where the D850 fed into Kilis's smaller roads, the smooth highway came apart like a river feeding a delta, the single strip of black asphalt ceding to riven pathways of dirt and concrete. Ancient pedestrian lanes ran in all directions, their cobblestones too narrow for a car. Flitting in and out of traffic, and up through these tributary lanes, cheap Chinese motorcycles—Lifans, Zongshens, Jialings—traveled past, always carrying more than a solitary rider.

In traffic so thick they drove touching bumpers, down alleys so tight they pulled in their side mirrors, through it all, Jamil shot off directions. They would have been lost without him. With each turn this became obvious. With each turn he proved himself essential.

Night fell before Jamil finally announced their arrival. The street was just like all the rest. Haris felt certain they'd already driven down it. Allowing the other cars to pass, Amir parked halfway up on the sidewalk. The traffic's headlights cast a deathly glow inside the Peugeot. Haris gazed at their destination: a kebab house—Halil Usta—with a flashing hotel sign and arrow to the top floor. Turning on a vertical spit in the front window, a thick column of döner dripped grease. A man with a white apron and long knife sat on a stool by the browning meat. From time to time, he stood, shaving curled strips into a full pan. But the restaurant was empty. No one had ordered food. He seemed to do this from habit alone.

They gathered their bags and piled out of the car, all except Jamil, who stayed in the back. "Aren't you coming inside?" asked Amir.

Jamil's eyes darted toward their destination. "It's not safe to leave the car out here all night," he said. "One of us should really sleep in it."

Amir looked at Daphne, deferring to her about the sense of this. "You're not sleeping in the car," she said.

"Someone might steal it," Jamil replied, reluctantly stepping into the street.

"Haris will sleep in the car," added Amir.

"I'd rather not."

"Then who will?" asked Amir.

"No one's sleeping in the car," said Daphne. She turned toward Jamil, grasping both his shoulders and looking him in the eye. They were the same height—he still had more growing to do. "You're nervous about leaving tomorrow, right?"

Slowly Jamil nodded. His black hair fell over his forehead. He did nothing to fix it, and his aspect wilted to a boy's. Watching this, Haris knew it had been wrong to bring him.

"Are you afraid of going back home?" asked Daphne.

"I'm afraid nothing's left," said Jamil.

"Your family?"

"I have none."

"What happened?"

"Does it matter?"

"No, it doesn't. You don't have to come."

"I have to come."

"Then don't be afraid."

"Why?"

Listening to their exchange, Haris thought Daphne's words were meant for herself as much as for Jamil. She took his hand in hers and led him toward the door. As they entered the restaurant, the man who tended the döner barely looked up, as if not expecting customers. Plastic tables and chairs littered the empty dining room. Framed prints of snowy alpine scenes hung from the walls. In the back was a desk, and next to it a carpeted stairway, the steps threadbare and worn into troughs at the centers from years of footsteps. A heavyset woman sat behind the desk, leaning over a magazine. When she finished reading her page, she glanced up, her chair and the desk creaking against her weight. Looking at the four of them, she held Daphne in a particularly disapproving stare.

Daphne removed her sunglasses from where they rested on top of her hijab.

At first, Haris couldn't believe this was the regional headquarters. None of it made sense. It looked like any number of inns with a restaurant on the bottom and rooms up top. But when he glanced at the stairway running to the second floor, he noticed the scattered portraits of bearded young men, each one taken in front of a black flag with the Shahadah scrawled in lashes of white calligraphy. Seeing their faces, Haris stroked his own. Beneath his hand, he felt the beginnings of the beard he'd grown over the last few days. The expressions in the photos were all the same—eagerness mixed with fear, the two emotions canceling each other out, blending into a blank, hollow look. For years, in many American newspapers, the official portraits of dead soldiers had run weekly. He remembered when he'd seen Jim's. They'd used his boot camp photo from about a decade before. Jim's look matched those on the stairs.

Haris read the Shahadah on the black flag to himself, mouthing the words: *I bear witness that there is no god but God and I bear witness that Muhammad is the messenger of God.*

The men on the stairs were shaheeds, martyrs. It occurred to Haris that martyrdom was an American conception. When taken in the pure Arabic, *shaheed* meant something different. The translation wasn't "he who sacrifices himself," although that was often part of it. The literal meaning was "he who bears witness." Standing at the desk, waiting to check into their rooms, Haris considered Amir, Daphne, and even Jamil. Watching them, he no longer felt like a voyeur in their war—he was their witness.

The woman behind the desk shut her magazine. Amir explained they'd come to meet a man, but left his name unsaid. Without hesitation the woman replied: "Athid told me you'd soon arrive. He'll be here in the morning." She shuffled out from behind her desk, clutching a large key chain by its fob. She pointed to Daphne and Jamil. "You two will be in Room 206"—then she pointed to Haris and Amir—"and you two in 207." It seemed futile to argue about sleeping arrangements. To have a room here meant adherence to certain conventions. That night Jamil would be Daphne's son, and Amir and Haris brothers.

They followed the woman up the staircase. As they went, a single thought pierced Haris's mind: If I am a shaheed for these three, then who is a shaheed for me? He climbed toward his room, and with each step he felt the blank, hollow gazes of the portraits against his back.

———

In Room 207 there was one bed. Amir offered to flip Haris for it. Haris wanted to save his luck for other things, so he let Amir have the bed. Lying on the floor beneath a single, thin blanket, he dozed but didn't quite sleep. He passed the night in that liminal space between dream and thought, watching the seam of light beneath the door. Above him, on the bed, Amir's breaths fell in a shallow, tidal rhythm. Haris's half-waking mind turned to water, the Euphrates, its banks, his home:

He walks its length. Beneath his bare feet the sharp marsh grass bends in the wind, brushing at his shins. Cement-walled shanties, coarse and hastily poured, dot the river's way. The sun burns beneath the horizon. Haris searches for cooking fires behind the shanty walls, at first finding none, only clear sky, empty and blue in the morning. Then in the distance ahead, smoke twists upward from a courtyard. A woman steps out a door. To Haris she is unrecognizable, being both one of and none of the women he has known through his life. She strides with her shoulders thrown back, her chest out, toward a familiar riverbank of his youth. She wears a black tulle robe that shines translucent in the quickening light. The wind blows against her, and instead of hiding her body, the robe's folds cling to her hips, legs, stomach. Haris can see all of her. He wants to call out, to discover who she is, but can't find the courage. She bends down along the bank, resting her palms on the water, which lies broken, cracked by the wind. Her shoulders begin to tremble as she holds her hands on the surface. Then she stands and slowly walks back toward her home. It seems she has gone to the water for no purpose but to touch it, to ensure it still runs its course. As she disappears inside, a shudder rushes through Haris—he has lost sight of her. He scrambles up to the house. He wants to see her face, to help her back down to the river, to tell her how and where it runs. When Haris opens the door, the shanty is empty. He scours the dirt floors and crumbling walls for any sign of her. There is none. Standing in the kitchen, he sees a wood-burning stove. He puts his hand to its steel side—it is cold. He sits in the threshold of the front door, looking out at the river and beyond it, to the sun, which now crests the horizon, but it isn't a bright sun. It is dark like a shadow.

When Harris awoke in Room 207, a shadow fell across the door, obscuring the light from the hallway. Slowly the doorknob twisted, the latch unclutched. Haris turned his head away, shutting his eyes. He pretended to sleep. On his shoulders, he felt two hands pressing down. Tempted as he was to jerk around or flinch, he didn't. The gentle pressure was Daphne's way of waking him. He rolled his head toward her. Hanging across her face, cupping at her cheeks, were the blond tips of her hair. She nodded behind her, toward the hallway.

Together they walked out of the room. Between Rooms 207 and 206, a wooden bench leaned against the wall. Just down the corridor, Haris could see the portraits of the shaheeds. Daphne's gaze followed his. Then the two sat on the bench. Haris leaned over his knees, wiping the sleep from his eyes. She said nothing. Neither did he. In the sitting and the silence was the intimacy of all to come, the journey they'd share. Haris leaned back, his arm pressing against Daphne's. She rested her head on his shoulder. She pulled a cigarette from her pack. Lighting it, she inhaled once and passed it to Haris. He hadn't smoked since Iraq, since his days with Jim, and he hadn't wanted to start here, but he couldn't refuse Daphne. He took a drag and passed it back. In this way, and leaning on each other, they finished the cigarette.

Haris stubbed the butt out on the sole of his boot. Daphne's head came off his shoulder, facing him. "I'm not coming back to Antep," she said.

Haris's first instinct was to ask her what she meant. How would they deliver Marty's report if she didn't come back? Where would she live in Aleppo? How would she support herself, or survive? The answers to these questions, or lack of answers, had no bearing on her decision. War can be a blessing, she'd said; if you're trapped, its destruction can free you. In Antep she was trapped, and so she'd cross back over the border, free to search for all she'd lost.

It was the same for Haris.

"What if Kifa's gone?" he asked.

She said nothing.

"Or if you do find her, what then?"

Still nothing.

So he touched her. His palms found her cheekbones. The pads of his fingers strummed her hair. Her motionless eyes seemed lost to him, like stones set among stones. From her lips Haris felt a longing to seize her assurances, that Kifa lived, that even a delusional hope should not be abandoned, that freedom to rebuild lay on the other side of destruction, like a silence enclosed in her mouth he felt she could unlock all of this. He bent toward her. But it was as if he had pressed his lips to his own hand.

"Tell Amir to find me when it's over," she said, turning away from Haris. "I'll be waiting for him, but I can't wait in Antep."

Daphne exhaled, shutting her eyes. She leaned back against Haris, placing her head along his shoulder once more. He rested his cheek on her hair, noticing the dark little hole where she'd worn the nose ring. Haris felt his body going slack with sleep. Daphne's remained rigid. He glanced down. Her eyelashes flitted nervously. Her hands rested in her lap, palms upturned. He put his arm around her. He sealed her palms in his. Her flitting lashes slowed, and then shut. Suddenly and fiercely, her hands squeezed his. He was there. Her breath slowed, easing into a gentle rhythm.

Haris shut his eyes, too, and took all the warmth of her sleep against his body. Then he returned to his dream, walking the Euphrates, searching its banks. Guided by the sound of the current.

I thought it might be you," he said.

Haris jolted awake. Daphne's head came off his shoulder.

Athid stood over them. A single ceiling bulb cast a halo around the olive-green keffiyeh wrapped over his black curls. Slung across his chest was the satchel, with Bashar the dog poking his head from its flap. Beneath Athid's eyes, his full beard hung from his face, creeping dark as moss toward the collar of his field jacket, which matched the keffiyeh. From his jacket pocket, Athid fished out a cellphone. Its screen shone against his bloodshot eyes, which Haris remembered clearly from the night in the culvert. Athid read from an email: *"A pious fighter and a woman from Aleppo."* He gave Haris an examining look. "I take it you're the *pious fighter,*" he said with barely shielded contempt. His stare now fell on Daphne. "And you, you're the *woman* from Aleppo." Her uncovered hair, how she'd slept drawn up close to Haris—Athid's disdain for her and the idea of her womanhood seemed greatest of all.

"And Saied?" asked Athid.

"Dead," said Haris.

“I thought as much.” Athid kneaded his fingers through the brown-and-white fur on the pup’s head. “Peace be upon him,” he said, as if forgiving the faults of a friend only in death. “I suppose you want what I took from you.”

Haris shook his head no.

“You still wish to fight?”

Daphne flicked a quick, uncertain glance at Haris.

His eyes met hers. “Yes, I want to fight. But first I need to help her get home, to Aleppo.”

“What do I care about getting her to Aleppo?” asked Athid.

“We brought the five thousand,” he said.

Haris nodded for Daphne to retrieve the money from her room. As she stood, Athid snapped: “Not out here.” He looked at Haris. “In your room.” Daphne scuttled down the corridor. Athid followed Haris to where Amir slept. Passing through the door, Haris flipped on the light. Amir rolled over, letting out a groan and pulling his blanket over his head. Outside, the voices of morning birds slowly pricked awake and the low sun struggled against the horizon.

“There’s more than you two?” asked Athid, crossing his arms.

On hearing the unfamiliar voice, Amir sat up. Wearing only boxers and a T-shirt, he swung his bare feet to the floor.

“Amir drove us down here,” answered Haris.

A stiff, defiant look set into Amir’s face as he quickly made sense of who stood in front of him. “I am Amir Khalifa, Daphne’s husband,” he announced, then his eyes rested on the pup slung in the bag across Athid’s chest. “That’s your dog?”

Athid glanced down at Bashar, cradling his soft chin. “Yes,” he said, “that’s my dog. And she’s your wife?”

Amir nodded.

“But it’s you who are taking her across the border?” he asked Haris.

Haris’s stare fell to the ground.

Amir shifted uncomfortably on the bed. He quickly stood, crossing the room to a chair where he'd flung his khakis and sweater the night before. He changed behind it.

"Why aren't you taking her?" Athid asked.

Amir froze, crouched forward with his pants pulled over only one leg. He looked back not at Athid but at Haris, as if it were he who had asked this pointed question. Feeling Amir's gaze on him, Haris wanted his answer. He felt he deserved it. He knew Amir's story. He'd inferred Amir's reasons from it, but he'd yet to hear Amir say why he would never go back, only that he wouldn't.

Amir finished dressing and explained to Athid that he'd been an activist in the revolution's early days. He fired off a list of protests he'd been involved in, offering each as a credential. He explained his activity with the Syrian National Congress, the loss of his daughter, Daphne's determination to return. With greater and greater speed he wove together his story of the revolution as if it might untangle the irrefutable truth that it had all failed.

Athid patiently allowed Amir to continue, but he didn't seem to listen. Holding his mouth open just the slightest bit, Athid waited for the opportunity to again ask the obvious. Finally Amir grew quiet, giving him that chance. "If your wife wishes to return home, why aren't you taking her?"

Athid spoke as if the story Amir had just told him was meaningless.

Amir came from behind the chair and stepped in front of Athid. Standing toe-to-toe with him, Amir seemed small. They were nearly the same height, but Athid's hands hung heavily from his sides and his broad face seemed strong as an anvil, designed to absorb anything. "Why?" replied Amir. Emotion quivered through his narrow shoulders as he spoke. "Because I regret my revolution. Because you and other fighters have made a graveyard of my home. If we'd never created the revolution, the Daesh, the Free Army, none of you would exist." He held a long, slender finger in Athid's face. "You are my fault, everything I've lost is my fault. I won't go back to see it."

Daphne entered the room.

She now wore the hijab Marty had given her, and in one hand she clutched the bag of baklava by its wooden toggles. Athid's eyes found the bag and, seeing Daphne was now covered, he warmed to her a bit. "What's that you've got?" he asked.

"A gift," she said.

Before Daphne could offer the baklava, Jamil pushed past her, shouldering his way into the room. Standing in its center, he found himself directly in front of Athid, his head not even rising to the level of Athid's chin.

Jamil took a step backward.

"And who is this?" asked Athid.

Jamil said nothing. Instead, he reached into the bag Daphne carried and presented the box of baklava. "It's for you."

"And who are you?" asked Athid.

"He's too young to fight," Daphne blurted.

Jamil fixed his eyes on her. She turned away from him.

"Is that why you've come?" Athid asked Jamil, who glanced a last time back at Daphne. Haris took a step toward her, grabbing her elbow, steadying her. She had brought Jamil, now she couldn't let him go.

Athid spoke gently to Daphne: "He's old enough. Men younger than him are fighting."

"And dying," interrupted Amir.

"And dying," said Athid. "But at least they fight and die, instead of just die."

"I came to fight," answered Jamil.

"Good," said Athid. He reached down and set his hand against Jamil's shoulder. Bashar poked his head out of the satchel. Athid set him on the ground, and the pup jumped up on Jamil's leg. "He likes you," said Athid. "Why don't you run downstairs with

Daphne? Take the dog with you and get us some tea." Athid looked at Amir and Haris. "The three of us have some business to discuss."

Daphne clutched the bag of baklava to her chest. The five thousand was in it.

"The business you have to discuss is with her," said Haris. "It's her money."

Athid buried his hands in the pockets of his field jacket, letting out a heavy breath. He cast his stare at Haris and then sat in the chair Amir had changed behind. "Did the Americans teach you that? To give women control over your affairs?"

Perched on the foot of the bed, Haris turned away from Athid.

"You see," said Athid, "he doesn't like it when I talk about the Americans."

"It's her money," said Amir, sitting next to Haris on the bed.

Daphne crossed the room. "It's fine," she said. From the bag of baklava, she pulled out the banded stack of bills. She rested her hand on Haris's shoulder. He faced her, and she placed the money in his hand. "You take care of this."

Haris nodded up at her.

"Jamil, come," said Daphne. He scooped up the pup, and she took the boy by the arm, leading him downstairs, to where they'd get a tray of tea.

Amir shut the door behind them.

Leaning back comfortably in the chair, Athid laced his fingers across his chest. "She's quite something," he said to both Haris and Amir. The pair ignored Athid's comment, resentful of the power he held over them. He was quiet for a moment, watching Haris. Then Athid eased forward and began to speak the names of places: "Haditha, Nasiriya, al Qaim, Haqlaniyah, Ramadi—"

He became silent.

"Nasiriya and Ramadi," said Haris.

"I fought the Americans at both," answered Athid. "With

them, you were against my cause but had none of your own. Perhaps that's why you've returned here."

Haris looked back, blankly. He felt Amir staring at him, as if he awaited an answer, some alternative to Athid's logic. With elbows balanced on his knees, Haris slumped deeper into himself.

"When we first met," Athid added, "you wanted to join with the Free Army. Now you want to join with the Daesh?"

"I am against the regime," said Haris. "That hasn't changed."

Athid shook his head, holding Haris's eyes with his. "If you make this crossing, you're not against the regime but with us. We'll help you get your friend to Aleppo, but our cause will become yours. If you feel differently, I caution you to stay on this side of the border."

Haris didn't reply. He was coming.

Amir stood, stepping into a corner of the room, creating distance from Haris. "Your cause," said Amir, nearly spitting the words, "a caliphate to toss our world into the Dark Ages."

"Dark Ages?" said Athid. "Turn your eyes to the country you left. These are the Dark Ages." Retrieving the box of baklava, Athid placed it on a rug in the room's center and sat cross-legged, gesturing for Haris and Amir to join him. Slowly each did and Athid served them each a piece. For a moment they ate in silence.

"The Prophet predicted all this," began Athid, as if from a place of intimate knowledge. "He said it starts with the boys, writing and speaking of a new future in the streets." Athid stopped and looked at Amir for a moment. In that look, it seemed Amir and the democratic activists of the revolution's first spring were the boys Athid referred to. "The message spreads, breeding outrage and a war fought by the men. This is what we see now. In that war, an Islamist army rises, uniting to destroy all others. Then a tyrant is killed. This is Assad. His army will fall. Afterward, among the Islamists, there will be many pretenders. The fighting among them will go on."

Haris listened intently, but Amir's attention wandered to the baklava. Licking his fingertips one after another, he seemed unconcerned with Athid's prophecies.

"You know all this?" Athid asked him.

"It's all happening right now," said Amir, picking another piece from the box. "The infighting, the rise of the Islamists, how does that end?"

"The Syrian people thirst for an Islamic State," answered Athid. "After so much war they want justice. Once Assad falls, when there is fighting among the pretenders, a man will come. He is a common man, but he will have a vision. In that vision, God will tell him how to destroy His enemies, bringing peace to all peoples. That man is the Mahdi."

Haris stared at Athid without a word.

Along his sleeve, Amir wiped the sweet pistachio syrup from his mouth. "Where do you think they are with our tea?" he asked Haris.

"You can't imagine these events," said Athid.

"Daph's been down there quite a while," Amir continued, ignoring Athid.

"You think poorly armed as we are, we can't defeat Assad and his backers?"

With a sharp jerk of his head, Amir stared back. "It's not that."

Athid continued: "Our weapons don't matter as much as you think. Even Albert Einstein predicted what's happening now. He said that the Third War would be a nuclear war, but that the Fourth War would be fought with sticks and stones." His gaze settled on Haris. "That's how we beat you in Iraq, with sticks and stones. Whether we are helped or not, this is how we will create our Islamic State, even with the powers of the world against us."

"So the plan is to wait for the Mahdi," said Amir.

"He walks among us now, a simple man of the people, the true redeemer." Athid swallowed a piece of the baklava in a single bite. "But you don't believe me?" he asked Amir.

"I believe that you believe this."

"What will you do if all I've said comes to pass?"

"If the Mahdi comes?" asked Amir.

Athid nodded.

"That means there will be a peaceful and just Islamic State?"

Again, Athid nodded.

"Then I'll return to my home."

"And, like a prodigal son, you will be welcomed," said Athid. He grinned ear to ear, leaned forward, and laid a heavy arm across Amir's narrow shoulders.

Daphne pushed the door open, carrying a tea tray with both hands. Bashar ran figure eights around her ankles. Jamil hurried ahead of them, setting the hourglass-shaped cups onto saucers and placing one in front of each man. Daphne offered sugar. Amir took a cube, while Athid waved it away. "It is written," said Athid, "that the Prophet never took sugar in his tea."

Amir placed an extra cube in his own cup.

Jamil and Daphne finished serving and sat on the floor as well. Bashar crawled into Jamil's lap. "Has everything been settled?" Daphne asked.

Haris and Amir both glanced at Athid, uncertain about the answer.

He took a sip of his bitter tea, wincing a little as it burned his mouth. "There's a truck leaving tonight for Aleppo. It's carrying aid—medical supplies, rice, those types of things—but it's also carrying a dozen or so laborers who came to Kilis to work for wealthy Turks, bringing wages home each month. I've paid off the gendarmes, that's all settled, but the road past Azaz is contested. The regime actively patrols it. They usually don't bother civilians who smuggle themselves through, but it is a risk."

"You feel comfortable with that risk?" Daphne asked Athid.

"It's not my choice to make. You're the ones going."

"Where will you be?" interrupted Amir.

"I'm going to Azaz but no farther." Athid blew on his tea,

making small ripples against its surface. "Right now, I have no reason to be in Aleppo."

Daphne said nothing. She looked at Haris, her eyes asking for the assurance Athid seemed unable to provide. "How do we know the truck driver will take us the whole way?" asked Haris.

"You don't trust me?" answered Athid.

Amir shifted in his seat.

"Not enough to give you the five thousand up front," said Haris, "and with no assurance."

"Assurance?"

"Collateral."

Athid took another long sip of his tea. "Half now, half brought to me in Azaz once you get to Aleppo. Arrangements have been made. People must be paid." He held up his cup—only half his tea was left. "As for collateral . . . the best I have is my companion Bashar. Jamil can take him and have the driver bring him back with the money. That's my offer, otherwise I'll finish this and go."

Athid's threat to leave unhinged something in Daphne. Before Haris could even counteroffer, she stammered: "Yes, that's fair. Half now, half brought to Azaz from Aleppo." She reached into Haris's lap, where he held the thick stack of bills. She counted out what they owed Athid. Then, as she placed it in his hands, she gave him a soft, pleading look. Athid glanced back. His red, cloudy eyes seemed empty.

"For one with such a sweet appearance, your wife is quite determined," he said to Amir, shuffling the cash as he also counted it. "The blond in her hair, her blue eyes, she looks Christian, like the Virgin Mary."

Daphne offered a pursed, annoyed smile. She tightened down her hijab and put the rest of the money in the pocket of her trench coat. Then she sat up a bit, asserting herself. "If I look like the Virgin Mary," she said, "you look like the Prophet Muhammad."

Haris glanced at Athid, concerned he would take offense.

"No," said Athid, laughing softly. "I don't look like the Prophet, peace be upon him." He added up the last of his cash, mouthing the arithmetic. Once he'd finished, he shuffled the bills into a neat stack, folded them, and tucked the fold into his field jacket. As he zipped up his pocket, he leaned in close to Daphne, locking her eyes with his own. A wide grin crept up his face.

"I look like the Mahdi."

Long shadows hung from the buildings. Outside the hotel, the afternoon traffic eased in the early evening hours. The truck would pick them up past dark, and the Peugeot was parked alongside the curb, where Haris was unloading it before the sun set. He bent into the trunk, gathering his things and Daphne's—a book bag, a suitcase, a couple of extra sweaters. Then he heard a ball bouncing behind him and Jamil's shrill voice, breaking into a laugh.

He glanced down a dirty alley which ran the length of the hotel. There, standing beside Jamil, was Athid. The two were kicking a soccer ball against the hotel's side, each trying to get it past the other while Bashar chased after them. Jamil's shots were controlled and swift but lacked power. Athid's shots were powerful but imprecise, each ringing like a detonation against the wall, intimidating Jamil, who was agile enough to block them but backed away at the last moment.

Haris watched for a few minutes. Whenever Jamil hesitated to make a block, Athid scored what must have been a point in their game. He'd then take his next shot even harder than the one before. Athid was winning handily. But he took no joy in it. He glowered at Jamil, muttering instructions about how he needed to be more aggressive, to not hesitate. Jamil listened but to little effect. No matter how quick he was, he couldn't bring himself to place his body in front of the ball. Then, and by accident, one of Athid's shots hit a crooked brick in the hotel's side, causing the ball to rebound at an odd angle. The strike hit Jamil clean in the face, bloodying his nose, knocking him back.

Athid helped him up by the arm. "That's enough for now," he offered, suggesting they return inside.

Jamil kicked the ball again. It ripped through the air, but Athid blocked it, sending it straight back at Jamil and much harder. Jamil moved quickly, but he couldn't maneuver his leg in front of the ball. Instead, he managed to head it back at Athid. The shot didn't have much force, but it surprised Athid that Jamil would make the block with his head, so much so that the ball sailed past him, scoring Jamil a point.

Athid smiled.

They continued with their game. Athid took his heavy, poorly aimed shots with all the strength he had. Unafraid after being hit, Jamil now blocked each of them, his shots coming with greater speed and certainty. One by one they flew by Athid, who dove after each, incapable of blocking them. His breath became heavy with the effort. Soon Jamil had built a sizable lead. Athid refused to quit, though. He sprinted up and down the alley, his torso bent awkwardly forward, his legs unable to keep pace, until finally he tripped on a stone, toppling shoulder first into the dust. Bashar, who'd been chasing after them, sauntered to Athid's side, licking his cheek. When Athid stood, he limped a bit. Picking up the ball, he cradled it under his arm.

"All right, you win," he said, brushing off his clothes and tightening his keffiyeh.

Jamil apologized, though for what he seemed unsure.

Athid wrapped his arm over Jamil's shoulders. His face exuded a warmth Haris had believed him incapable of. The two stepped out of the alley. On seeing Haris by the Peugeot, Athid cinched his arm around Jamil's neck.

"This is a good one you've brought along," said Athid.

Jamil beamed back at Haris, his face filled with the satisfaction of a little brother pleasing an older one. Haris turned away and leaned into the trunk to shove a few extra bottles of water into his book bag and Daphne's suitcase.

Having been snubbed by Haris, Athid withdrew. His expression flattened, again becoming wide and hard as an anvil. "Let's have a break," he said to Jamil. "Before the truck comes, I'll tell you something about the portraits hanging inside. Like you, they were my friends." With his arm looped around Jamil's neck and Bashar trailing behind, Athid led them toward the martyrs.

After packing his bag, Haris struggled to open Daphne's suitcase. It was stuffed to the brim, and its zipper wouldn't budge. Haris lifted the suitcase from the trunk. Setting it on the street, he noticed how heavy it was. He stood torquing on the zipper with his whole body. Finally it opened, a spare shirt and a few pairs of socks springing out. This extra clothing wasn't the weight he'd felt. Crammed inside were nearly a dozen journals—the kindergarten lessons.

Haris glanced back at the hotel. No one was watching him. He pulled out a single volume, placing it on the fender, thumbing through the pages, each filled with Daphne's familiar scrawl. If she found Kifa, Daphne might finally use her lesson plans. If she found nothing—

Haris wondered if she could ever abandon these journals.

Quickly, he repacked her suitcase, heaving it back into the trunk. Just as he did, Daphne stepped outside the hotel with Amir. Seeing Haris fumble with her things, Daphne lunged toward him.

"It's okay. I can get that."

Before Haris could reply, and before Daphne could grab

her suitcase, Amir managed to step between them. "I'll bring it inside." He snatched the suitcase's handle, lifting it from the Peugeot. Its weight shuttled his arm toward the ground. "What've you got in here, Daph?" he asked. Then his face turned grim.

Daphne placed her hand on his arm.

He flinched away. "It's quite heavy."

"Amir."

"I don't suppose I'll be seeing you for a while."

"Amir, please."

Haris shouldered his book bag and turned to go inside, to leave them alone.

"Stay here," said Amir.

Haris stood between them.

"She's with you now."

Haris held his eyes to the ground.

"Look at me," Amir insisted.

Daphne tugged Amir toward her, but he pulled away, dropping her suitcase into the dust and gravel of the street. Turning his back, Amir barged inside, leaving her. Haris bent down to pick up her suitcase. Before he could, Daphne grasped the handle. "I've got it," she said, trudging off after Amir.

Haris locked the Peugeot and followed.

Inside the hotel, Amir was nowhere to be seen. Athid stood with Jamil on the stairs, whispering to him the histories of the long-dead martyrs. Jamil didn't study the portraits as much as he did Athid—the way he intoned their stories, wreathing each of their dead faces with glory. By the front window, where he'd been the evening before, the man with the white apron sat at a small plastic table next to his column of warming döner. The long knife he used to cut the meat rested across his legs. A deck of cards sat in front of him. He turned them over, one after another, piling them into two stacks, playing High-Low or, as it was called in

America, War. As Haris sat in the restaurant, Daphne emerged from the back and took a place at the man's table. He smiled, and instead of playing against himself, he began to play against her.

Evening listed toward night. With the darkness, sounds in the street—barking dogs, the easy laughter of children returning home—grew louder. Passing headlights mirrored off the restaurant's front window. Each one caused Haris to glance up in expectation as they waited for the truck to arrive. To clear his mind of the journey to come, he watched Daphne and the man play their game. Card after card turned. It took no skill. The odds determined the winner and loser—luck, really. Seeing Daphne lose with such consistency, Haris felt anxious. Her lucklessness defied probability.

After half an hour or so, Amir appeared in the back of the restaurant. He carried a plastic bag filled with something heavy. Setting it across his lap, he sat at a table, waiting by himself. The time passed quietly until finally the man with the apron stood and laughed. He placed his long knife on the table with a hollow clank and shuffled the deck.

"This really isn't your game," he said to Daphne, smiling broadly.

She looked away.

A pair of wide lights slowed and then stopped in the street. They shone inside. Everyone cast their eyes into the glare, blinking against the heavy beams. A coughing diesel engine mellowed into a flat, static rumble. The headlights quivered, throwing uneven shadows into the restaurant, then flicked off. Tucked along the curb, just beyond the Peugeot, the truck idled. Out on the street a door slammed. Daphne flinched at the noise, as if struck by a single jolt of electricity. Everyone watched the front of the restaurant, where a squat man with a full paunch—the driver—stepped inside. He rested his hands on his hips, the knuckles callused and wrinkled as if carved from wood. Bending backward, he stretched out some stiffness. His eyes were swollen with exhaustion, webs of veins grasping the whites as if netting them to their sockets.

The man with the apron stood, long knife in hand. He held a piece of pita as if it were a mitt. He shaved off curling ribbons of döner, catching them and, in a single motion, rolling the bread and meat into a sandwich. Without a word, he handed the driver his dinner. This ritual seemed to be a familiar one and, seeing it, Haris took solace in the idea that their border crossing was routine.

The driver wolfed off an enormous bite of his sandwich. As he chewed with his entire face, his bulging eyes found Athid, who was still speaking to Jamil on the stairs. Glancing down at his watch, the driver nodded toward the truck. Then he left.

Athid zipped up his field jacket and headed into the street to ensure his cargo was properly loaded. Jamil followed close behind, carrying Bashar in the satchel slung across his chest. Walking past Amir, he planted himself beside his table. "Safe journey," Jamil said, holding out his hand and trying to sound grown-up.

Remaining seated, Amir shook while looking away.

"And thank you," said Jamil.

Amir stood clumsily, knocking against the table's edge, his grip still clasped around Jamil's. On his feet, he towered over the boy. Amir was groping for the right thing to say, and then blurted: "Let me know once you've arrived safe."

Jamil gave Amir a confused look, as if he missed how this might be possible. Arrived safe? Safe where? At the front? His mind seemed unable to form a proper response. Instead, he replied, "Of course," and followed Athid into the night.

Across the restaurant Daphne still sat at her table, the finished card game spread in front of her, her head hung to her chest. Haris stood quietly above her. It was time to go. Daphne looked up only when Amir stepped next to Haris. Her eyes were full and wet, her jaw clenched. Enough regret rolled through her that the grief she shared with Amir could've been confused for love, or at least the love they once shared, and maybe still did.

Amir reached into the bag he'd brought. From it, he pulled a heavy volume thickly annotated with multicolored Post-its—*Responsible Conduct of Research* by Dr. Adil E. Shamoo. "You take it with you," he said. "It'll help with your report."

"Won't you need it while I'm gone?" asked Daphne.

"I can make do for a bit," answered Amir.

"Then I'll see you in a bit."

Haris watched their exchange. It seemed divorced from their argument in the street, divorced from what they both understood—Daphne wasn't coming back. What they knew about each other, about where each was going, about where each had been, they couldn't say. So they couldn't say goodbye. They were trapped, waiting on opposite sides of a divide.

Daphne walked outside. Amir watched.

Haris was the last to leave. As he shouldered his way through the door, he glanced behind him. Amir had sat down at the table where Daphne had lost at High-Low. One by one he sorted through the hands she'd played, reading each of Daphne's cards as if trying to figure out where it had all gone wrong, where her luck had failed her.

They gathered around the back of the idling truck. The air beneath Haris's knees was warm, smelling sweetly of exhaust. A tarpaulin was draped over the flat bed, its flap buttoned shut. The driver reached up, tugging the retaining pins from the tailgate. It slammed down. He stepped onto the rear tire, throwing open the flap. Traffic sped by them, barely slowing, headlights washing over the truck bed, forming an even pulse. Illuminated by the rhythmic light were the others who'd make the crossing, families heaped together in rows. The men slept, their heads tilted back, exhausted by weeks gone by in Kilis or Antep eking out a wage. The women bent forward, tending anxiously to their children, readying for a return to the war. A few sets of eyes peered at Haris, Daphne, and Jamil, but with little interest, their stares returning to where they sat, and the darkness.

"Climb in," said Athid.

Before Haris could pick up his bag, Jamil vaulted onto the tailgate.

Athid grabbed him by the shoulder. "You'll sit up front with me."

The driver pointed to Jamil's satchel and Bashar. "Not with that dog."

"It's all right," Jamil said. "I can go in back."

"No, it's better if you ride in the cab. We've much to discuss, and you should see the places where you'll be fighting. Let Daphne look after Bashar." Athid's voice was warm, fatherly. Jamil handed over the satchel. Then Athid turned toward the driver, fixing him in an insistent stare. The driver said nothing more, and walked briskly up to the truck's cab.

Standing among Haris and the others, Athid dispensed some final instructions. He explained that they'd pass through the border crossing just outside Kilis, that under no circumstances were they to open the tarpaulin. Once across, they'd take Route 214 into Azaz, but south of Azaz, past the last of the Daesh checkpoints, the regime actively patrolled the road. "So stay under the tarpaulin," he said. Haris and Daphne nodded. Athid gave them a last, appraising look. "Okay," he answered. Then, with that matter settled, he looped his arm around Jamil's neck, playfully leading him up to the front of the truck.

Daphne hoisted herself into the bed. Haris followed, and as he stepped onto the rear tire, climbing into the back, Jamil stood on the cab's running board, glancing at him from over his shoulder. Their eyes met. The truck lurched into first gear. Jamil lost his balance for a moment, as if he might stumble onto the road. Then Athid reached out and pulled him inside.

Beneath the covered flat bed, the air was thick with breath. Haris and Daphne faced each other, perched on the benches nearest the tailgate. As they drove through Kilis, Haris craned his neck toward a seam in the tarpaulin, stealing glances of the neon shopfronts and lamplit homes. Everything blended into a kaleidoscopic night scene. Watching the street slip toward the border, Haris would've traded places with any of the lumbering passersby.

Outside of Kilis, the road ran straight and even toward the border. The glowing cityscape dissolved. The darkness in the fields matched the darkness in the truck bed, and the seam Haris glanced through became an indistinguishable aperture, black as everything else.

He leaned back on the bench, brushing shoulders with the man next to him.

"Lost interest?"

Haris turned toward the voice, his eyes meeting an impenetrable night. "Not much to look at," he answered.

"You are from Aleppo?"

"No," said Haris, not wanting to offer anything more about his business.

He could feel the man nod through their touching shoulders. From deeper in the truck a baby, or maybe several, began to cry. Someone coughed violently. For the first time, Haris noticed the ascending din of so much proximate humanity—breathing, hacking, crying. This racket became louder and louder. Or, as Haris realized, it didn't become louder, he only became more aware of it.

"That's good." The voice rose above the other noises, cutting them down to a relative whisper.

"What's good?" asked Haris.

"That you're not from Aleppo, such a troubled place." The man shifted in his seat. "Neither am I," he said. His warm breath, thick and musty as broken earth, fell into Haris's face. "I live a ways outside the city."

"What do you do there?"

"I raise crops." The farmer reached into the pocket of his tattered suit jacket and pulled out a small envelope. He pressed it into Haris's hands so he could feel its modest size. "Last year was cotton," he said. "It's tough on the soil. In this packet is barley seed, next season's planting."

"Your whole crop is in that one envelope?"

"Everything I'll need for the year."

Haris felt anxious for the farmer, holding so much in so small a place. "The war must be hard on you."

The farmer said nothing. The sound of the others inside the truck became louder in the silence. Then, speaking as if he tried to draw an ugly truth back into himself, the farmer answered: "My crop grew before the war. With the war, it grows the same."

"But your family?" asked Haris.

"It's only my wife and daughter. They are safe. I'm able to provide for them."

"But to see this in your country—"

Haris and the farmer knocked against each other as the truck downshifted, rattling into a lower gear. The darkness outside slowly yielded to an orange, sulfuric light. Haris leaned forward, gazing through the tarpaulin's seam. Beneath the floodlit border crossing, he could see the café where he'd sat the week before with Saied and Athid. In the distance, past the café, was the large tent which served as a mosque. A stream of refugees came and went from it in the night. Haris strained to recognize a familiar face. At first he couldn't find one, but then, as he looked, he felt he recognized them all—eyes cast to the ground as they walked, shoulders stooped against the wind. What he recognized wasn't a single person but a single form of suffering, one he knew in himself: a home and a life taken away. Purposelessness.

"I'm supposed to care for my family," said the farmer, "not run off and fight."

"I came to fight," said Haris. The words wandered out of his mouth. He didn't know he'd spoken them until he heard what he'd said.

The farmer no longer paid attention to Haris. His focus had shifted to the woman next to him, and the little girl in her lap, sleeping against her chest. Any temptation within Haris to dismiss the farmer as a coward or shirker for not fighting dissolved at seeing how he watched over his family. He refused to fight not because he didn't believe, but because he did, in them. As he was thinking this, Haris's stare found Daphne across the truck's bed. He wondered how he looked at her, if somewhere in his eyes was the look that had passed between the farmer and his family.

The truck jerked to a stop. It idled at the shut steel gate of the border crossing. Haris peeked out at the Plexiglas booth where the gendarmes stood their post. He saw the familiar silhouette of the tall, slim gendarme from before and his short, thick colleague. The booth's door swung open, spilling its light onto the road. From a television inside, the maniacal loop of a laugh track pierced the night's silence. The short gendarme shuffled toward the truck, his unbuttoned blue tunic sustained behind him in a current of breeze. He came around to the passenger side of the cab, climbing up the running board. Athid's arm extended from the window, a thick white envelope in his hand. He passed it to the gendarme, who glanced at its contents, a wide smile loosening all the way to the bristled corners of his face. A few unintelligible words passed between him and Athid. Then the gendarme began to laugh, his voice blending with the television inside the booth. He jumped down from the running board. As he walked around the back of the truck, Haris wondered if he'd look in the bed and, if he did, what the gendarme would say, or not say, upon seeing him again.

Instead, the gendarme passed by, uninterested in whatever traveled beyond his small checkpoint. The door to the guard booth shut. The gate opened. The recorded sound of laughter receded to silence as darkness returned to the road.

The truck accelerated down Route 214, a single corridor running through the outskirts of Azaz. Rimming the city, fires burned from a recent round of shelling. Scarves of mist slipped between buildings, and everywhere else night lay thick in the streets. Then the light came up gradually, like the end of a show, and Haris squinted into the flames, finding the skyline. It was picketed with upended telephone poles tossed onto rooftops, their dark wires draping softly down the pockmarked façades, cascading to the curbsides. Over the years of fighting, the houses next to the road had been pounded to mosaic by explosives as varied as the bits of wood, cement, and glass they left behind. The houses in the heart of the city had fared no better, with entire walls lopped off clean, like shoe box dioramas. The truck slowed, a splash of water running over the hood. Up the street a burst main threatened to drown Azaz before it could burn entirely.

With his face pressed to the tarpaulin's seam, Haris watched the shivering flames reflect in the black flood and in the shattered windshield of a white Peugeot, its front crushed against a collapsed telephone pole. All four of its doors had been knocked open, and it was the same model as Amir's. They drove closer and the fires burned brighter, revealing a constellation of bullet holes running up the car's hood and the bodies of men flopping out from every door. The dead, frozen in their last actions, each of their poses different, but their final, most simple purpose shared—get out of the car.

Their truck lurched hard, taking a dogleg. Haris jostled against the others in back. A few tumbled from their seats, patches of light falling against their faces as they cursed the driver. Then, at this bend in the road, they stopped.

Those in back looked toward one another, searching for some assurance as to why they weren't moving. Concerned stares passed among them, uneven as the flickering light which crept inside through the tarpaulin's seams. Finding no assurance in each other, most everyone in the bed strained to look outside.

So did Haris.

Set up at the bend in the road was a checkpoint—three men

standing by an empty fifty-five-gallon diesel drum with a single strand of concertina wire blocking Route 214. A fire burned in the drum, its flames lapping at the rim. The men warmed their hands over the flames, rifles slung from their shoulders, their packs piled by their feet. They wore a mix of camouflage uniforms, some plain olive drab, some an oblong design of black, green and brown, and some in the American pixelated pattern. Their full beards hung from their cheeks like weights, hollowing out their eyes. And these eyes looked at the road but not the truck which had borne down on them. Up the road, just where the flames receded back into darkness, a dead dog lay by a blast crater. The speckled pattern of the explosion fanned out into the brittle macadam and across the dog's body, where it had bitten hunks of fur and flesh from its stomach. Gathered around the corpse were three cats, the same number as the men. The cats ate the dog, picking at its entrails with their nimble mouths. From time to time, when the cats fought over the most succulent portions, Haris could see the men laughing as they watched, their teeth white in the night.

The truck idled in front of the concertina wire. The passenger door opened, and Athid grabbed the large side-view mirror, swinging down to the running board, then hopping onto the road. He glanced at the dog but walked by, choosing to ignore it. He approached the three men. Instead of shaking hands, they held each other at the elbow in a half embrace, touching their temples together, as one would kiss cheeks, but instead they nuzzled like deer in the forest, this being the most intimate greeting.

Over the noise of the idling engine, Haris couldn't hear what they said. Athid seemed to ask the soldiers questions, gazing past their checkpoint and down the road. All three answered in unison, seeming to tell him what lay along this narrow ribbon of darkness, which connected Azaz to Aleppo. Haris hoped their knowledge of regime checkpoints and patrols was accurate, but beyond hope there was little else he could do. Then, as he and the men seemed to finish discussing the road, Athid called back to the cab. Jamil stepped outside and jogged over, doing his best imitation of an earnest soldier.

As Jamil stood rigidly in front of the group, Athid spoke forcefully to the three, issuing some sort of order. At first the men milled around the fire, their sidelong stares resting skeptically on Jamil. Then one of the men bent down, digging through his pack. He took an olive-green tunic from it, thick and worn as a painter's smock. He bundled it in his hand and shot it quick and hard at Jamil, who caught it. Holding up the tunic, Jamil gazed back at Athid, who nodded as if he should put it on. Watching Jamil dress in this, his first uniform, Athid smiled and tousled the boy's well-combed hair. Jamil matched Athid's smile with his own. The three men kept their eyes fixed to the fire.

The hushed complaint of morning birds came from the east, across an inky void of barren fields. Hearing the birds, the three men dug through their packs, removing prayer rugs, which they unrolled on the bare earth. Coming to their knees in the darkness, they made their prostrations, touching their foreheads toward the breaking day. Jamil took his place among them, but without a prayer rug he knelt in the dirt. Next to him, Athid did the same. Jamil glanced over at Athid and, noticing the manner in which these soldiers prayed, he mimicked them, extending his fingers toward Mecca.

Inside the bed of the truck, no one prayed. They watched each other.

"These Islamists will die with their hands pointing the way." The farmer's voice awoke his daughter. Cradled in her mother's arms, she began to cry. The girl seemed inconsolable, her breaths coming in tiny, hyperventilated huffs. Her mother swayed her from side to side, clutching her to her breast. The tighter she held her, the more she cried.

Sitting across the bed, among the ten or so other travelers, Daphne leaned forward. She reached into the satchel draped across her shoulder, setting Bashar in the girl's lap. At first the girl writhed away from the pup, frightened by it, clutching her mother even tighter. Then Bashar leapt up, licking her face.

The truck bed filled with the girl's laughter.

"I used to teach children her age," Daphne explained to the farmer's wife.

As the girl laughed, the three men on the checkpoint rolled up their prayer rugs. They went back to standing beside the fire burning in the fifty-five-gallon drum. Athid joined them, having ordered Jamil to return to the truck. One of the men pulled back the single strand of concertina, clearing the route toward Aleppo, a half hour's drive farther.

As Jamil wandered back without Athid, his stare fixed on the dead dog just up the road. He jogged over to where it lay, kicking off the cats, which still hunched over the rotting carcass, scavenging. Then Haris noticed the men on the checkpoint, including Athid. They all shot Jamil resentful looks for disrupting this, their only entertainment.

Jamil took his seat up front. Then the truck lurched into first gear, making its way south. And the driver veered slightly toward the road's shoulder, crushing the dog beneath its wheels.

The checkpoint slipped behind the rear horizon and Aleppo had yet to form ahead. The farmer's daughter calmed. She sat on her father's knee, facing him, holding the pup in her lap. To occupy her, he'd taken the packet of seeds from his pocket, allowing her to run her fingers through the coarse grains inside. As she did, he explained how precious the seeds were. She seemed to understand, continuing to stare into the packet with calm fascination.

"You're a big girl, yes?" said the farmer.

She nodded.

"Then you hold these seeds until we return."

The farmer's wife protested, but he ignored her. Being

trusted with something important would teach the girl a valuable lesson. He slid the envelope into the pocket of the homespun dress his daughter wore, buttoning its top. The little girl rested her hand there, not moving it.

The farmer gazed back at Haris, who watched. "It's a great responsibility."

Haris couldn't tell if he meant the packet of seeds or raising a child.

"Do you have any children?" he asked.

Haris shook his head, and the farmer frowned.

"And you?" he called across the bed to Daphne.

She had clamped her eyes shut, pretending to sleep.

The farmer leaned forward, tapping her knee. "Do you have any children?" he asked again.

Slowly, Daphne opened her eyes. Haris looked away, not wanting to hear her answer, but he could feel her gaze on them both. "A daughter," she said.

"And what do you think of him going to fight?"

She sat up a little straighter. "It's his decision."

"An easy one for him to make with no children," said the farmer. "It's only when you have children that you understand such a decision."

"People with children usually aren't the ones doing the fighting," muttered Haris, unable to keep quiet even though he didn't want to argue with the farmer in front of his family.

"Sometimes those with a family fight." The farmer glanced back at his daughter, who still held her hand over the pocket with the envelope of seeds. "Before I was a father, I saw angry, idealistic young men take up jihad in Chechnya, Iraq, the Balkans. I thought they were driven by a cause. But the fighting doesn't go on because of ideas. It goes on because of loss. If I was robbed of my daughter, I would be lost from this world. I'd take up arms and fight like a dead man alive, killing until I was killed."

Dead man alive, thought Haris. He noticed Daphne had again closed her eyes.

Approaching Aleppo, Route 214 became a series of raised roads, which fanned out across parched fields, their furrows hardened and untended. Submerged beneath the horizon, a low, throbbing sun slit a seam of red light across the eastern countryside. Layers of cirrus clouds glowed pink in the altitudes, and the outskirts of Aleppo sprawled to the south, coming into view. White minarets dotted the skyline, some snapped in half, some surviving the years-long battle. As the first morning light fell across them, they became a milky red phalanx, against which countless fighters had thrown themselves.

"There, do you see?" The farmer grabbed Daphne's arm, pointing up ahead. A hollow cinder-block house stood where several dirt roads intersected. A large pad of poured concrete spread in front of the house, and its doorway and windows were empty and black like the sockets of a skull. "That's a school."

"Looks like a gas station," said Daphne.

The man shrugged. "Maybe once, but now it's a school. I thought you'd like to know, having been a teacher."

"What grades do they offer?"

"None."

"Then how is it a school?" asked Daphne.

Haris gazed out the side of the tarpaulin to the city's outskirts. More squat cinder-block homes peppered the distance. Cooking fires burned beneath their chimneys, the smoke and early light blending into tangerine clouds. Here and there, Haris caught a darkened silhouette peeking from a door or from behind a crooked window, only to immediately tuck away. Then Haris noticed two beams cast against the road.

Headlights.

He couldn't make out what type of vehicle it was, but it seemed determined to intercept them. He felt their truck lurch into a higher gear. Up ahead, Haris saw the school's faint, grubby outline. If they could get past it, the car, which now kicked up a wide tail of dust, would pull behind them and then, maybe, they'd be able to outrun it.

No one in the back of the truck spoke. Each set of eyes calculated time and distance, figuring if and when they'd be stopped. At a few bends in the dirt road the chasing car fishtailed in the loose earth, kicking up more massive dust clouds. The school was close now. The car was close, too. Haris could make out the brand—some type of Toyota sedan. Then, just as Haris thought that with a little more speed they might outrun their pursuers, the truck loosed a salvo of backfires while its engine groaned, reaching its highest gear. To Haris, it seemed that groan came from the back of the bed, where he and all the others felt helpless as cargo. The little girl climbed from her father's knee into her mother's lap.

The Toyota pulled in front of them, coming to a halt near the intersection of the dirt road and the school. The truck's brakes whined as it pulled onto the shoulder. Haris and the others froze where they sat. The Toyota's doors swung open and then slammed shut. The sound of boots crunched down the asphalt, drawing closer, then stopped. A voice called up to the cab, demanding that Jamil and the driver step onto the road. Haris heard the truck's heavy doors open and close. He strained to hear Jamil or even the driver speak. There was only silence. Just as Haris felt tempted to press his face to the tarpaulin's seam, chancing a look, he heard a set of steps approach the tailgate. He leaned against his seat, trying to become small in it. He glanced next to him, at the farmer, whose attention was fixed on his family. Then he glanced at Daphne, whose attention was fixed on him. They held each other with their stares.

The back of the tarpaulin flung open. A blue half-light rushed into the bed. A soldier stood at the tailgate, the barrel of his rifle leveled on them. He wore a floppy red beret and freshly pressed camouflage utilities. He was clean-shaven, his cheeks paler than the rest of his face, as if only the night before he'd removed a thicker beard.

Haris sucked in a quick breath.

The soldier noticed, looking in his direction. Haris turned away, but not before he spotted the patch on the soldier's uniform, crossed sabers within a laurel—Assad's Third Corps.

"There's more back here," the soldier shouted toward the cab, where the other one stood. In the instant he looked away, Daphne removed her head scarf. Something about this upset Haris. At this moment of peril, she'd decided to fly a false flag, appearing secular to save herself. Then again, the head scarf had been a false flag in the first place. Even if Daphne was Muslim, she was half-Christian also, and no part of her was religious.

As Daphne spread her hair flat, the other soldier came around to the back of the truck. He had the same fresh-shaven appearance as the first, but he wore a black beret, its felt creased with deep wrinkles. Haris also noticed his shoulder patch, one from an unrelated unit—Assad's First Corps in Damascus.

"Everybody out," ordered the soldier with the black beret.

Haris sat unmoving on the end of the bench, blocking the exit. Daphne tugged his arm. They stepped down from the truck, Haris helping Daphne with her heavy suitcase filled with journals. The sun had yet to break the horizon but it soon would, and Haris felt physical relief as he left the tarpaulin's dank confines. On the road, the air was cool in the morning.

With rifles leveled, the two soldiers herded everyone into the fields. Jamil walked just ahead of Haris with his head down, continuing to peek toward Aleppo. His face was filled with a raw fear, eyes spread wide as if taking in the last of the world. To escape his captors, Haris thought Jamil might sprint down the road at any moment. If he did, Haris promised himself he would do what he could to save the boy, even though he didn't know quite what that would be.

The farther from the road they traveled, the more certain Haris felt they'd never return to it. Glancing behind him, he saw the farmer, who followed with his family, his daughter scooped up in his arms as she still cradled Bashar, his wife holding his free hand. When an old, infirm couple from their group stumbled among the dry, brittle furrows, the two soldiers offered some help, making sure everyone kept together.

They didn't march far, maybe a hundred meters or so. Just outside the school was an elm. Its wide, leafy branches caught the first of the breaking day, shimmering in the wind and clean early light. The two soldiers stopped them beneath the tree, forming everyone into a row and asking to see their papers. Only a few in the group had papers, and the soldiers seemed unconcerned by this. Then they asked everyone to remove their valuables, the explanation being some type of customs declaration. Haris and Daphne opened their bags, and Daphne tossed the second half of their payment, the twenty-five hundred, into the dirt. Her thousands were added to the thousands of everyone else, their many months of wages and toil strewn across the earth. Then Haris noticed the little girl, standing next to her father, the farmer. Bashar lay at her feet, and she held her hand against the pocket on her dress, hiding the envelope of seeds.

"No one has any other valuables?" asked the soldier with the red beret.

The little girl didn't move.

Haris glanced toward Jamil, who stood with his head hanging to the ground, lost in some thought. He hadn't emptied his pockets. He hadn't moved. The soldier with the red beret butted him in the kidney with the stock of his rifle. Jamil stooped, his leg crooking at the knee. Then he straightened and dropped some pocket change and a comb into the dirt.

The soldier with the red beret paced behind them. "You are all loyal supporters of the regime, yes?"

Haris felt his heart accelerate in his chest. He glanced to the side, trying to observe the soldier, but instead he caught a glimpse of Jamil, who now gazed across the road and into an otherworldly distance, perhaps the place they were all headed.

While the soldier with the black beret sorted through everyone's possessions, the one with the red beret ambled in front of Haris, examining his beard, which wasn't quite long enough for an Islamist but wasn't nearly a clean shave. "If anyone is against the regime, this is the time to step forward."

A broken sort of hate spread through Haris. He had come all this way to do what seemed a simple thing—to fight for a cause he believed in. Now, before he'd even had a chance to fight, he would stand motionless, claiming to support the regime, renouncing the rebels to save his own life. He remembered how he'd betrayed Jim for what he thought was a greater good and, forced to commit another betrayal so he might live, Haris didn't want to live anymore. I'd rather they kill me, he thought.

He shifted on his feet to step forward.

Before he could, Jamil did.

"You're against the regime?" asked the soldier with the red beret.

Jamil said nothing, no grand denunciation, he just stood there shaking, as if he'd stepped naked from a cold bath and waited for someone to hand him a towel.

The man with the wrinkled black beret took Jamil by the arm. He looked at the other soldier and nodded, as if Jamil's obvious fear were proof enough of his conviction against the regime. "Come with me," he said, leading Jamil toward the Toyota.

Haris shifted on his feet again, as if he might step forward.

But Daphne pinned him next to her. She wouldn't let him move. Her hand clamped his elbow so tight he could feel his pulse. Her weight pressed against him. To join Jamil, to let himself die, was also to betray her.

"The choice you make is your own," said the soldier with the red beret.

Daphne held Haris even tighter.

Haris watched as the soldier with the black beret sat Jamil down on the Toyota's far side, by its front tire. Haris stared toward the road, where he imagined he might never return. He anticipated a shot, Jamil's execution at the hands of these regime thugs. Watching Jamil so intently, Haris didn't notice when the soldier with the red beret took a few steps back. Haris also didn't notice when he leveled his rifle on their group.

Haris heard the first shot as he watched Jamil.

What he heard didn't correspond with what he saw.

Where was the execution? Why was Jamil still sitting upright?

Only when Daphne's grip moved from Haris's arm to his hand, and when she squeezed it once, hard, did Haris look away from Jamil. Right then, Haris smelled the cordite. Now he saw the shots coming down the row toward him, and the soldier with the red beret firing. The bullets seemed to explode out of each person's body. One by one they fell to the earth, stacking in neat piles around him. Haris didn't sprint away. Instead, he chose to take a last snapshot of his senses. I am holding Daphne's hand, he thought. Jamil is running for me across the fields. The men in the Toyota aren't regime soldiers. They must be Daesh. This must be a test to separate those who doubt from the true believers. But it's also just another con, a highway shakedown, the way the Islamists finance their war. Jamil understands, but it's too late. He'll live. He may yet fight alongside the rebels. But it's too late.

Then Haris's legs were taken out from under him. Lying flat on his back, he lost sight of the blue horizon. Haris faced what was left of the night directly overhead. He breathed once and felt his ribs cracking against each other. Look how cold the light of the stars is, he thought, and his breaths came like air blown into a torn plastic bag. My lungs, was his next thought. He patted his hand against the dirt, which was wet and newly warm, turning to mud around him. Then he found what he'd briefly lost, Daphne's hand. He squeezed it again, but his strength wasn't what it had been a moment before.

And her strength was gone.

He turned on his shoulder, gazing across the fields to where the soldier in the black beret had caught Jamil from behind, holding him beneath the ribs. Jamil bicycle-kicked, trying to free himself before the soldier flung him into the dirt. Haris hoped Jamil didn't protest too much. Nothing could be undone. The boy should take his place within the war, not waste himself on Haris's behalf. What a fool I've been, he thought. I've died for nothing, a misunderstanding. I came to fight against the regime, even if that meant fighting alongside the Daesh. If I'd believed enough to die for that cause, as Jamil believed, I'd be alive. But as this idea formed in his clouded mind, he turned and felt Daphne's broken shoulders next to his. They were pinned back, even in death. He remembered how she used to walk through Antep City Park, her confident stride, and the one night in her bed, running his fingers over her scars.

With him, she'd managed to sleep in the darkness.

The two soldiers took off their berets, using them like sacks to collect everyone's valuables from the now soaked earth. Haris could hear the cracked, fading breaths of others mixing with his own. One by one the soldiers kicked each of the bodies on the soles of their feet, looking for a reflex. Here and there, Haris heard extra, finishing shots. A dim presence crept at the side of his vision. He saw the soldiers continue, body to body, until they came to the little girl, who had fallen beside her father and mother. Bashar licked her face, cleaning it. None of the three moved when the soldiers kicked the soles of their feet. This is a good thing, thought Haris. He remembered what Saied had told him: *Time is what allows pain. Time is the greatest enemy.* This family had never been apart. They'd avoided the pain known by

Daphne and Amir. Even in death, the war had been gentle with them.

Keep watching, thought Haris as the soldier patted down the girl's dress. Then, as he moved past her, a great satisfaction coursed through Haris. They hadn't found her envelope of seeds. Though he could still feel his broken ribs grinding against each other, the pain in his chest eased.

They'd all be buried together, and Haris imagined the seeds in the girl's pocket growing shoots that would swaddle them beneath the earth, the barley sprouting upward, an unexpected crop reaching toward the sun.

Haris stared at the horizon. Any second, day would break. Any second, the soldiers would kick the soles of his desert-suede combat boots. His shallow breaths came quicker and quicker. He wasn't sure if he'd flinch when they kicked him. He knew he didn't have much time, but still, he swore to himself that he'd hold on just a bit more. He wanted to see the sun.

VI

They kept sprinting toward him across the ice. With less than a minute left in the last period, the championship came down to Amir's ability to tend goal. The Bruins, a team sponsored by Levant Research Associates, were down 0–1 against the Minutemen, Marty's team from the Syria Analysis Group. The Bruins had pulled their goalie. They now had more players on the ice. All through the winter, Marty had drilled the Minutemen for this eventuality, but now, as the forwards descended on Amir, there was little he could do. The championship cup, a silver Anatolian goblet of enormous size, yet to be engraved with the name of the first season's victor, sat on a bench at rink-side. Marty had bought the cup. He'd organized the league. And he'd be goddamned if the Bruins would take it from him. But it all came down to Amir.

Stealing glances at the analog game clock, a thrift store piece of junk, Amir watched its second hand sweep toward victory if he could only hold on. The three forwards charged, passing the puck quickly between their sticks. Each time the puck moved, Amir adjusted himself on his skates, wobbling a little. It had been nearly six months since Daphne and Haris had disappeared, not nearly enough time to become a proficient goalie. Still, he'd managed to do a good enough job so the Minutemen made the finals, beating out four other teams. And since Amir had agreed to play in the league, and since they'd begun to win, Marty no longer asked about the five thousand he owed for the report Daphne never delivered.

The forward who advanced down the right wing cut to center, heading directly at the goal. Amir bit his skates into the ice, planting himself in a crouch so he could spring toward the shot. Then, at the final moment, the forward passed the puck to his teammate on the left wing. Amir saw that he'd been duped, but his body couldn't react fast enough. The shot came from the opposite direction. It sailed toward the open left side of the net while Amir collapsed toward the right, blocking in the wrong direction. He anticipated the cheers from the opposing team, but instead of cheers he heard the hollow metallic tang of the puck striking the goal's crossbar.

Amir sprung back to his feet. Searching for the puck, his gaze met Marty's wide, panicked eyes farther up the ice. The three forwards emerged again, sweeping from behind the goal and passing the puck quickly among them. Less than ten seconds of play remained. This would be their last chance. And with the desperation of a last chance they came at Amir, shoulders down, in a line. Amir struggled to keep sight of the puck. Then he lost track of it altogether. The three forwards converged on him at once. Unable to see where they might shoot from, Amir had to protect the whole goal. He spread his body wide, throwing it in front of the forwards, who fell upon him with hacking sticks. The last play of the game now devolved into a scrum over Amir's body. Marty and the rest of the Minutemen joined the fray, also chopping away at Amir, trying to get the puck. Of all the players on the ice, Amir was the only one who didn't care about the puck. All he cared about was protecting the goal. He lay on his side, flailing his legs and arms up at any empty space. At last, a whistle blew.

End of game.

One by one the forwards and defensemen of both teams peeled away from the goal. Each side was uncertain about the outcome. They glanced into the net, but couldn't tell if anyone had scored. Then, slowly, Amir stood, checking himself. As he came to his feet, the puck dropped from where it'd been buried in the pads around his ribs.

0–1, Minutemen.

Marty leapt down the ice, pumping his knees and fists in the air. He came to rink-side and picked up the silver goblet, holding it triumphantly above his head, kissing it. The rest of the team joined him, except for Amir.

A knot of spectators had formed around the rink boards. Amir pressed through them, slowly skating from the ice. He sat on a bench just to the side, peeling off his pads, a jumble of secondhand and thirdhand equipment Marty had scrounged. While all attention was paid to the Minutemen's victory, a boy with a missing leg and mismeasured prosthesis hobbled over with the help of a cane. In one hand he carried a plastic bag, which seemed too heavy for him.

"You are Amir Khalifa?" he asked.

"Who wants to know?" Amir barely glanced back. He'd just managed to slide his thick padded blocker off his left hand, and he worked to unbuckle the catcher from his right.

"My friend Jamil asked that I deliver something to you."

Amir jerked his head up. A wispy beard grew from the boy's cheeks in patches, and it would still be some years until he could grow a full one. His eyes were sallow, as if stained by a long sickness. Jamil's friend looked like a tired, worn-out version of Jamil.

The boy offered the plastic bag he carried.

"Where's Jamil?"

"I last saw him along Aleppo's southern front," said the boy. "When they took me to the hospital here, he gave me this for you." He held the bag out again.

As soon as Amir felt its weight, he knew what it was.

He pulled out Saied's old Nokia and a thick volume, bound in blue leather. Quickly he opened the journal, its spine creaking. Page after page of Daphne's scrawling handwriting stared back. Amir began to check each one, looking for some clue of what had happened to her and Haris.

Before he could finish, the boy turned his back to Amir, staggering through the spectators, who still celebrated Marty's triumph. "Where are you going?" Amir called out. The boy ignored him and continued to walk down the marble corridors of Sanko Park, headed for the exit. Amir quickly took off his leg pads and skates. He slid on his shoes, but within moments he'd lost the boy among the crowded shopfronts.

By the time Amir returned to the rink, the celebration had ended. Marty was packing up the last of his equipment. "I've invited everyone over to the office in about an hour," he said.

Amir nodded.

"You are coming?"

Amir shouldered his heavy sports bag and clutched the plastic bag he'd been given. He wanted to find a quiet place to sort through the journal and Nokia.

"C'mon," said Marty. "It won't be a party without you."

Amir shrugged and walked out the mall's front, toward the parking garage.

"I'll see you soon!" Marty called after him.

Belowground in the garage, Amir loaded all of his things except for the plastic bag into the trunk of the black Peugeot. He wedged himself behind the driver's seat and, turning on the overhead light, he spread the bag's contents on his lap. Carefully, he thumbed through the journal. Each page had been filled, except for a final few, which had been left blank. Scribbled in an uneducated hand along the top margin of the last one was a note:

Daphne and Haris. N of Aleppo.
Rte 214. By school. Under elm.

Amir reached for the Nokia, powering it on. Saved to its background was a photograph. The squat cinder-block house with its empty windows and door sat in a dry, rutted field. The sky was very blue. Framed against it, in the center of the photo, was the elm, its branches bare and gray, yet to green. At the base of the tree, where its roots clutched at the earth, a single thick tuft of barley grew. Its long feathered stalks bent heavily in the wind, a strange and stubborn crop it seemed.

Amir powered down the Nokia, placing it on the seat next to him.

He couldn't just leave them there, but he didn't know what he should do.

He wandered out of the parking garage and into the day. It was warm. Spring had arrived early this year, and in front of him the trees in Antep City Park had begun to leaf. He had nowhere to be. So he decided to take a long walk home beneath their shade.

Acknowledgments

My gratitude to Matt Trevithick and Daniel Seckman for making their duo in Gaziantep a trio, to my mother who is my first and most generous reader, to Lea Carpenter for her inexhaustible belief, to PJ Mark for being the finest champion and the finest friend, to Marya Spence for her keen insights, and to my pal Diana Tejerina Miller, whose energies and talent made this book better. I am also indebted to my children, Coco and Ethan, who with fearless hearts took this journey with me.

A NOTE ABOUT THE AUTHOR

Elliot Ackerman, author of the critically acclaimed novel *Green on Blue,* is based out of Istanbul, where he has covered the Syrian Civil War since 2013. His writings have appeared in *The New Yorker, The Atlantic, The New Republic* and *The New York Times Magazine,* among other publications, and his stories have been included in *The Best American Short Stories.* He is both a former White House Fellow and a Marine, and has served five tours of duty in Iraq and Afghanistan, where he received the Silver Star, the Bronze Star for Valor and the Purple Heart.

A NOTE ON THE TYPE

This book was set in Scala, a typeface designed by the Dutch designer Martin Majoor (b. 1960) in 1988 and released by the FontFont foundry in 1990. While designed as a fully modern family of fonts containing both a serif and a sans serif alphabet, Scala retains many refinements normally associated with traditional fonts.

Typeset by Scribe,
Philadelphia, Pennsylvania

Printed and bound by Berryville Graphics,
Berryville, Virginia

Designed by Cassandra J. Pappas